3

STAYING POWER

Also by Judith Cutler

POWER ON HER OWN

STAYING POWER

Judith Cutler

 St. Martin's Minotaur ♏ New York

www.minotaurbooks.com

Library of Congress Cataloging-in-Publication Data

Cutler, Judith.
    Staying power / Judith Cutler.—1st St. Martin's Minotaur ed.
        p. cm.
    ISBN 0-312-31194-X
    EAN 978-0312-31194-0
    1. Power, Kate (Fictitious character)—Fiction. 2. Police—England—
Birmingham—Fiction. 3. Businessmen—Crimes against—Fiction.
4. Birmingham (England)—Fiction. 5. Policewomen—Fiction. I. Title.

PR6053.U864S73 2004
823'.92—dc22   2004042824

First published in Great Britain by Hodder and Stoughton, a division of Hodder Headline

First St. Martin's Minotaur Edition: June 2004

10 9 8 7 6 5 4 3 2 1

For Robert,
remembering Florence:
the Duomo, the piazzas, the food
– and the snow and the flu and the en suite bathroom down
the hotel corridor

ACKNOWLEDGEMENTS

This book could not have been written without the help and co-operation of West Midlands Police, especially Dave Churchill, Rona Gorton, Terry Street and Yvonne Williams. Angie King and Jayne Coyne shared with me their invaluable experience. Edwina Van Boolen and Frances Lally have been constant sources of support and criticism. Thank you all.

STAYING POWER

PROLOGUE

'Go on, take one. You have to keep swallowing or those tubes in your ears'll get bunged up.'

Kate dragged her eyes from the Italian coastline, still just visible beyond the edge of the wing, and put down her sodden tissue. 'Sorry?'

'You have got a snorter, haven't you?' It was the youngish man in the next seat. 'Here, I said have one of these: you must keep swallowing or your ears'll give you hell when you land.' He was offering her a paper bag.

She took one of the sweets – old-fashioned barley sugars – and smiled her thanks. She was afraid that more would encourage him to chat, and there was nothing she could do to escape if she wanted to.

'I'm sure I saw you somewhere back there.' His head jerked at the receding shore.

'Heard me sneeze, more like. Most people get designer leather in Florence. I get a designer cold!'

'You still got something nice in leather, though.' He laughed. 'I can smell it from here. The name's Alan, by the way. Alan Grafton.'

'Kate Power. Oh, I bought a bag,' she admitted, burrowing for it. She needed another tissue anyway.

'Mind if I look at it?'

Her eyebrows shot up.

'Oh, only the outside. I wouldn't dream of asking to see the inside of a lady's bag.'

She prepared to grind her teeth.

He continued, 'No, it'd be too like looking at the bottom of my case. All that stuff you always mean to deal with one day. But your bag wouldn't have had time to silt up yet, would it?'

In spite of herself, she laughed. Her chest rattled alarmingly as the laugh became a cough.

'You're going to have to see a doctor about that,' he said.

She shook her head. She was only just off sick leave, for goodness' sake. The holiday in Florence had been to celebrate the return of her knee to normality. She'd injured it while she and her colleagues were raiding a house. It had also been something of an order from her boss: 'Make sure you come back fit,' Detective Inspector Cope had said. 'Don't want any passengers in my squad.'

His boss, Graham Harvey, had said much the same thing, though in kinder terms. 'You've had a dreadful time this year, Kate. Go and get some sun and put some good food and good wine inside you. Make sure that cousin of yours looks after you.'

She'd not bothered to pass the last instruction on to the cousin, who'd feel – as a war correspondent – that it was she who needed any cosseting going. But Kate had enjoyed her week. They'd done all the touristy things in Florence, walking everywhere, even when her cold had struck.

'The weather can't have done you any good,' the man continued. 'Fancy, snow in Florence in November!'

'Pretty well December.'

'Even so ... I don't know about you, but I only brought autumn-weight clothes. But that wind provided a wonderful excuse to buy cashmere sweaters,' he added.

He plainly wasn't going to shut up. She glanced sideways again. He'd be in his mid-thirties, lightly built. He was indeed wearing a beautiful sweater.

'Why the interest in my bag?' Perhaps she was leading with her chin.

'Because I've just ordered five thousand pounds' worth of them. And three thousand pounds' worth of sweaters, like this. I'd already bought the most beautiful shoes and briefcases on my last trip'

'Do you have a shop?'

'No, no, I'm a middle man. I have these wonderful trips abroad and buy all these lovely things, and I sell them on to distributors. Who no doubt shove a huge mark-up on to them. Not that they're cheap, anyway. Even with the pound at its present level. Now,' he said, grasping the bag, 'this is a nice bit of leather. But what's it lined with?'

She'd hardly registered. 'Fabric, I think.'

He passed it back. 'And you'd have bought it from one of the outdoor markets, not the Leather School or one of the boutiques.'

She nodded. Even a sergeant's salary didn't run to that sort of price.

'Well, mine are leather lined. As are the shoes I'm after. Did you buy any shoes?'

'Two pairs. Comfortable as gloves.'

'Lined?'

'One pair, I think.'

'Well, the others'll stretch, you mark my words. They'll be useless in three months. Gloves? Now those *are* nice. Silk-lined. Tell you what, you must have shopped for England!'

Their conversation continued intermittently all the way across the Alps. From time to time he'd press another barley sugar on her, making an opportunity to talk about his plans.

'If this deal delivers what I hope it'll deliver, I shall move into silk scarves. Then designer clothes. It's all a question of the right outlets. And quality control. I'm going to have to be meticulous about quality control ...'

She let him run on. It was nice to meet people with passions about things, even if you couldn't imagine sharing the passion. And it meant she didn't have to talk much. She wondered how he'd react when she told him about her job. Experience had taught her it was often better to wait till people asked her what she did, rather than volunteer the information officiously. At last, when they were free from plastic food trays, he got round to it.

'I'm a police officer. I work for the CID in central Birmingham.' This was usually the cue for silly quips; she was sorry she couldn't look at him full-face to watch his reaction.

Whatever his eyes might have revealed, his spoken comment was predictable enough: 'Goodness me, I must watch what I say, mustn't I?'

'Not if what you're talking about is legal,' she laughed.

'Well, it certainly is my end,' he said. 'And I've run these credit check things on my clients – I know their money is good. So I should be all right.'

Was there a tiny note of doubt in his voice? If only she could hear properly: the cold had left her deaf in one ear – the one nearer to him.

'Have you had any exciting cases lately?'

She couldn't tell him about the most recent one. Apart from anything else, investigations had still been going on when she went on leave. 'A lot of car theft,' she laughed. 'And while I was away I think they were going to do a major job rounding up stolen mobile phones.'

'No juicy murders?'

'Not a lot, thank goodness.'

'But aren't they exciting?'

She reflected on the sights and smells of a murder scene, and shook her head. 'Not for the victim, that's for sure. And for those of us trying to solve the crime there's just a hell of a lot of dogged work.'

'You've got all this scientific stuff to help you, haven't you?'

She nodded. 'In the end, it comes down to asking the right questions and making sure you listen to the answers.'

Despite his sweets, landing at Birmingham Airport closed down her hearing almost entirely.

'No, keep your fingers away! You can damage your ears that way. Keep swallowing. They'll click eventually.'

She shook her head. My God, if they stayed like this! Even after the carousel had finally trundled out her case, she was still at the bottom of an auditory ocean.

'Have you got transport?' he asked. '*Transport?* Or are you on the train? *On the train?*'

They set off for the station together.

'No point me asking you out for an intimate dinner, I can see.'

'Not this week!' Her voice was distant, echoing.

'OK. Next week. What's your phone number?'

She fumbled for her police business card. He struck her as the least dangerous of men, but she wasn't about to hand out her home number.

He flipped out one of his.

The train for the city was bulging with football-scarved passengers. It was clear they were going to be separated.

'Take care of yourself!' she shouted.

'Don't worry – I always do.'

Chapter One

'Look what the cat brought in! *Buenos noches*, DS Power. God Almighty – keep your distance, woman. I don't want the whole bleeding squad infected. It's bad enough with young Fatima, here, giving us all the willies not eating. DC Khalid doesn't let anything past her lips on account of it's Lent or whatever these people have. And then you come in here looking like a death's head on speed.'

'Morning, Gaffer,' Kate said equably. 'Always nice to have a warm welcome home.' There was nothing new about DI Cope's wet-Monday, bad-traffic mode. She dumped her bag and case and leaned over to the new woman's desk. What had the Gaffer said her name was. Ah, that was it. 'Hi, Fatima! I'm Kate Power.'

The new constable – probably, like Kate, in her late twenties – stood up, embarrassing Kate by her formality. Her handshake was firm and pleasant, and if she'd been irritated by Cope she showed no signs of it. She had to look up to Kate, who felt that even at five foot five she was towering over her. And she was so slightly built Kate wondered how her frame stood up to the month of Ramadan dawn-to-dusk fasting.

'I've put her with Selby,' Cope announced. 'Now you and Colin seem to have become partners and Sally's gone back to Wales, there's no two ways about it.'

Kate thought there might have been several ways. There'd be other new people coming into the squad. One at least. A replacement for Reg. Surely it would have been better to wait. This was the worst case scenario. Sure, she liked working with Colin, and he with her, but she was sure that either of them would have been prepared to partner Selby – temporarily at least – simply to spare Fatima. Not that Selby would have wanted to work with Kate. There were unsettled scores, weren't there?

'I'm sorry it's Ramadan,' she said to Fatima. 'I'd have asked you out for a coffee at lunchtime.'

'So long as you don't mind me watching you drinking—'

'Done.' Kate smiled and returned to the tip that hid most of her desk. She could tell which paperwork had been left by Colin – it came in files and stood in a neat stack. The rest had been apparently dumped by a mechanical digger.

She stripped off her coat and slung it on the back of the chair. She wouldn't be sitting for some time, the pile was so high. She opened the top drawers on either side of her desk to act as further filing space and picked the first item from the pile. It looked ominous. An internal mail envelope. Sealed.

Slitting the Sellotape, she found a sheet of memo paper.

> *Kate*
> *My office. Before you even think about starting on this lot.*
> *GH*

She grabbed her bag, cramming in extra tissues.

'Ah, not staying long, I see, Power. Before you go, the boss might like to see you.'

She nodded to Cope and headed down the corridor. She stopped and looked around her. Somewhere the police authority had found enough money to fit new name plates on senior officers' doors, white lettering on apparently removable blue metal strips. Someone could have a wonderful malicious time, changing them around. Where did managers get these ideas?

At least no one had tampered with *DCI Graham Harvey* — yet. She tapped and waited.

'Come on in, Kate!'

How on earth did he know it was her?

Graham waved her to a chair — she took the comfortable one, since he was already making tea, a sign of good humour. 'I recognised your footsteps.' He smiled as he passed her the mug, sliding an empty envelope to use as a mat. He looked her up and down a moment before he continued, 'And I thought a holiday would do you good!'

'Oh, it did. I loved the place. Have you ever been, Gaffer?'

Wrong question. His face clouded. 'My wife doesn't like travelling. There's her diet, for one thing. And she gets travel sick.'

'So does my cousin. But she bought these acupuncture wrist bands.'

He grimaced. 'Her job involves travel, doesn't it? She doesn't have any choice. Where's she off to now?' He came round her side of the desk, half-perching on it.

'Central Africa again. Checking out the famine in the war zone. She says it's a good way to diet. All that Italian food — she reckons she put on half a stone last week.'

'It doesn't look as if you did. God, don't take that the wrong way, will you? I've just been on this anti-sexism course. All about not calling people 'love' and not making personal remarks about what people are wearing. So I mustn't say you look extra nice — I mean smart — this morning.'

'Present from Florence.' She smoothed the skirt. 'To celebrate the snow.'

He nodded. 'I saw. On Ceefax.'

What sort of life must the poor devil lead, to have time to watch Ceefax! Or — she fought down the suspicion — he might have wanted to know how she was getting on.

9

'Anything interesting been going on here? Apart from the arrival of Fatima?'

'Whom Cope has paired with Selby. While I was away on that course. Well within his authority, of course.'

'So it'll be difficult to unpair them.'

'But impossible to leave them paired. I'd like to think,' he added, turning his attention to his tea at last, 'that Cope hoped spending time with an intelligent, articulate woman like that would civilise the man.'

'Oh, I'm sure they'll find so much to talk about! What's her degree in again?'

He consulted a file. 'Philosophy. She got a first. And she did her doctorate at Manchester – isn't that where you did yours?'

She nodded. 'But I only did a master's.'

'No wonder you're feeling one degree under! Oh dear, I suppose you're too young to remember the adverts. Some cold cure or something. Anyway, young Fatima—'

She nodded. 'Maybe we shouldn't worry too much. She must have a hell of a lot going for her. Not just to do what I'll bet her community disapproved of, but to rise so fast in the Service. Perhaps she'll just lacerate him.'

'And if she does, how will he respond? Keep an eye on things, Kate. And remember, if there's any indication he's started on his clever games, I'll have him out of the squad before he can blink.'

'Games'? Was that what they called bullying on that course of his? She nodded again, grimly. 'Any other news?'

'None. Everything in that last case of yours progressing nicely. Here – have a read through this at your leisure.' He passed her a thick file.

She liked the way he'd put it. He was good at giving credit where it was due. It was one of the things that made him so well-respected in the squad.

'Thanks. Look, Graham,' she said, awkwardly, 'since you couldn't get to Florence, a bit of Florence has come to you.'

He took the package as if nervous of dropping it, and fingered the tissue paper, the ribbon. She was glad Italian shops made such a fuss over details like that.

'Only a few sweets,' she said. Costing about a pound each, but that wasn't for him to know.

He opened the box. 'They look too good to eat. Marzipan?' He took a miniature apple and sniffed. He nibbled. 'They're flavoured! Well, I'm blessed. Thanks.' He added, as if as an afterthought, 'You shouldn't have done.'

'That's what friends are for,' she said.

Colin was just emerging from the loo as she passed it. He gave her a hug and a friendly kiss.

'Hell, Colin – you'll be on a disciplinary if Harvey sees you!' Cope. Did he materialise at will? His grin was the Cheshire Cat's with malice aforethought.

'But it'll be worth it, Gaffer. Just for a touch of the fair Kate's lips.'

'Kiss of death, more like. Look at the colour of her nose. Got anything for us from Joe Public? It's that new local TV programme, Kate. *Grass on your Neighbour*, or something. Punters are supposed to phone in with info.'

'*Local Crime Call*,' said Colin, parenthetically. 'Or they could call it *Crank Call*. Knock and they come out of the woodwork. We've got car-ringing, unsolved murder, cruelty to hamsters, and wife-beating.'

'In that order?'

'Oh, and loads more, Gaffer. I thought I'd sift through them while Kate excavated her desk.'

'Sounds OK. We'll meet up one-ish to go through them.'

'I was taking Fatima out for a phantom coffee, Sir.'

'Well, neither of you will miss it, then. Take her out for a phantom beer tonight instead.'

Kate nodded. It might actually make more sense. Didn't fasting end at sundown? Or were there special prayers first?

'Get her outside half of mild and a bag of pork scratchings,' Cope added. 'Do her the world of good.'

Colin coughed. 'I think Muslims are like Jews, Gaffer. No pork.'

'Bugger it – so long as it's kosher, it's all right, isn't it?'

Fatima nodded: 'No problem. But I may have to take a rain check on the drink. My family – they – we always try to eat together unless there's a big rush on here. They'll be expecting me tonight. But maybe – would tomorrow night be convenient for you?'

'Better, actually. It means I can start getting some of my holiday washing done and pop into Sainsbury's. Whatever did we do when shops shut at five-thirty?'

'We did what women should do,' Fatima said, straight-faced. 'We did the shopping when we'd taken the kids to school and before we started the housework.'

'So we did.' That was presumably the life Graham Harvey's wife lived now, minus, of course, the inconvenience of children.

'And we cooked complicated meals and ironed our husbands shirts beautifully.'

Kate grinned. 'Now I know what I want. I want a wife.'

A smear of ketchup on his chin suggested that Cope had managed to find time for lunch before his session with Colin and Kate. She wondered why his wife didn't produce a packed lunch for him to keep him from the cholesterol-filled temptations of the canteen. Graham's wife did – a plastic box full of thinly cut sandwiches, their fillings neat and disciplined. One piece of fruit and a small chocolate biscuit. Every single day. And yet it would have done Graham good to pop into the canteen from time to time – a break from his endless paperwork with the bonus of a bit of company. He might have been a happier man – he might even have been a better cop – if he'd done so.

Until recently, Kate had depended on take-aways or a

friend's charity for weekend meals, but during her sick leave the long-awaited working surface had been installed in her kitchen and she was now the proud possessor of a hob and a sink. On the downside, though, the residue of her belongings had come up from London, and what would eventually become her sitting room was stacked with uniformly large cardboard boxes, full of kitchen utensils and CDs. All the appurtenances of her life with Robin. No, she mustn't even think about him and his death. Unpacking the boxes would be more than enough reminder. That was why she must get them done as soon as possible. She must keep her fingers crossed for a quiet run up to Christmas. The bonus would be that she could have the downstairs carpets laid. At last. In fact, she'd do two boxes before she went round to see Aunt Cassie tonight.

Back to the present with a bump.

'Where do you want to start, Gaffer? The likely or the unlikely ones?' Colin asked, waving two bundles of message sheets.

Cope raised his eyes skyward, and reached down for the waste-bin, which he wagged under Colin's nose. 'You can file those here,' he said. 'Not so much unlikely as off the planet.'

Kate shook her head. 'Waste not, want not. No smoke without fire. All the other clichés, too. I'll look after them all.'

'What, even the cruelty to hamsters one?'

'Especially that. OK, I know you think I'm off my head, but you never know.'

'You know you're wasting your time with the hamster. Come on!' Cope flourished the bin again.

'Tell you what, Sir – I've got this mate in the RSPCA—' Colin said.

'Ah, you let them waste their time on it. What else?'

Kate held up five or six more slips of paper. 'Allegations about vehicles with no tax discs, Sir. I'll pass these on to the DVLA, shall I? Or their local nick for uniform to deal with?

And there's a few here – no, these are dog licence ones. Do we have dog licences, these days?'

It took Cope an apoplectic second to realise she was joking.

At the end of the hour, they'd agreed that Selby and Fatima should check an allegation that a well-known pusher of cannabis had moved up a division and was dealing in Ecstasy tablets, and another that a prominent councillor was into hard-core porn.

'They'll have to be discreet, mind.'

'With respect, Gaffer, I don't think that's a word in Selby's vocabulary.'

'It's time you got your knife out of that bloke, Power. He'll be taking up a grievance against you if you're not careful. And then who'll look a right plonker, eh?'

Selby, with a bit of luck. 'OK, Sir. But I don't think he's necessarily the best person for this job.'

'Nor's Fatima, not yet. Or rather, not with Selby,' Colin said. 'She lacks experience. She's a good cop, by all accounts, but she could probably do with a bit of mentoring.'

'For which you're no doubt volunteering, her being a nice looking wench with big tits. Come off it, Colin. We're short of men and you're asking me to pussy-foot round while people learn the job! You're off your head. Take the silly bleeder away and knock some sense into him, Power.'

'It's funny, you know, Colin,' Kate said, as they walked downstairs together. 'You have this lovely break from work and expect that somehow things will have got better. And you come in and the office is even untidier and the loos even smellier and the corridors even scruffier—'

'And Harvey even more stressed and Cope – is he any worse? Or is he just the same old, evil-tempered, ignorant bastard he always was?'

✻   ✻   ✻

She'd bought a bottle of Tuscan wine for her neighbours, and popped round with it before she set off for Sainsbury's. Instead of the affable natter with Zenia and Joe she'd been hoping for, she found Zenia flu-bound, so ill that, when she chased her back to bed, she found the sheets were soaked through with sweat. And so ill she let Kate strip them off and make the bed afresh. Shopping for both households then. It was, as she told Zenia, good to be able to pay back some of the favours Zenia had done her when she had first moved in. Not to mention that team of cleaners.

Chapter Two

'Come on in, girl.'

Kate was hovering on the threshold of her great aunt's nursing home room.

'How can I hear what you say if you've got your mouth covered up?' Aunt Cassie demanded.

Kate had long suspected that the old lady actually lip-read most of what was said. Persuading her to try a hearing-aid would be interesting, to say the least.

Kate touched the mask she'd persuaded a nurse to find for her. 'I said, I've got a cold: I wanted to see you but I didn't want to give you any germs.'

Aunt Cassie turned aside petulantly. 'Are you deaf? I said take the damn thing off. That's better. When did the cold break?'

'Last week. Thursday night.'

'And today's – Tuesday? Monday? Monday. You lose all sense of time in this place. In that case, I shouldn't think you're very infectious. Well, then. Sit down where I can see you. Goodness, look at your nose. And your mouth. No cold sores?'

Kate looked around, found the arm of her chair. 'Touch wood, it's something I've avoided so far.'

'Mind you, no one would have wanted to kiss you with

your lips all cracked and skinning like that. Did you meet any gorgeous young men? I remember back in the fifties I came back from Rome with my bum all black and blue.'

'I've failed, then. Or perhaps it was because I was with Pippa – you remember, Donald and Eva's daughter.'

'My God, no one'd risk pinching *her* bottom. Does she still walk as if she's carrying a gun and wouldn't think twice about using it? Never get a man that way. They like a bit of femininity, these men.'

'Not Pippa's man, Aunt Cassie! She's sleeping with a US general – a five-star general, which means—'

'Oh, don't bother me with that. She can look after herself. Always could. Never came to see me. Not like you. Coming to see me on the train all by yourself, even when you were a child. I appreciated that. I still do,' she added, gruffly, as if embarrassed by such an admission.

Kate smiled. She had Cassie's house as evidence, curse it as she might have done when it was at its appalling worst. What she'd have liked to say was that she'd always loved Cassie, and coming to see her was an unbelievable adventure. All she dared risk was, 'I know. Tell you what, it was nice to come home, now your house – my house – is no longer a building site. Zenia from next-door – you remember? She's laid low with flu at the moment – she brought in a team of cleaners she rounded up from the hospital where she works while I was away so it's beginning to look good. All my stuff from London's arrived, by the way. Books, china, even saucepans.'

'Have you got a fridge yet?'

'Up and running. And a freezer. And a washing-machine. It feels like home.'

Cassie nodded. 'So it should. And when am I going to see some photographs?'

'Soon. I've got a few frames left on one of the films I took to Florence, so I'll shoot them off when I get a chance.' She'd even record the continuing horror of the living room and its boxes.

'Didn't you meet *any* young men while you were away? I've a mind to be a great-*great*-aunt. There's a woman in a room down the corridor never stops going on about her family. Never.'

'There were a couple of nice South Africans: we had dinner with them one night because there wasn't a vacant table and we all spoke English. I think we swapped phone numbers, but I'm not holding my breath. And there was a young man on the flight back – very solicitous. He'd been on a huge shopping spree – oh, his work, not pleasure. Which reminds me—' Kate fished in her bag, producing Punt e Mes and Vermouth. 'Just as a change from gin,' she said. 'And here are a couple of oranges to add to the Punt e Mes – thin slices, just like lemon in gin. And plenty of ice. Is what'shername still keeping your ice-bucket topped up?' Cassie had arrived at a highly unorthodox agreement with one of the nursing staff to ensure her gin was always the right temperature.

'Silly girl got herself pregnant. There's a new girl. Rosie, I think she calls herself. A care assistant. She's in some sort of trouble, too. I know she is. But she won't talk to me. I said, "My great-niece is in the police," I said. "She'd know how to help." But she just sniffed and said everything'd be all right. I gave her your phone number, just in case. So if she calls, you'll know why. Now, tell me about this young man . . .'

'If you ask me,' Cassie said, 'he's got to be careful – yes, I will have another drop of that stuff with the orange – that young man. Go on: it's not rationed! All that money – what if he can't sell the stuff on?'

'He must have some sort of contract with these firms, I suppose. And he said he'd run credit checks on them. I'm not sure how you do that – do you get a bank reference?'

'Banks! The references they give are designed to protect the bank! They're so hedged round with *to the best of our knowledge* and *without prejudice*, what they say isn't worth the paper it's written on. No, you need to ask other firms – that's what my Arthur always used to say. And he ought to know.' She spread her hands, grotesque with arthritis under those heavy rings. Arthur had done Cassie proud before he retired from his jewellery business. 'His nephew's sorted out those diamonds for me. The ones you found under my floor. Well, your floor now. Got a better price than I expected. But he's kept back the best three: two for ear-studs. And one for your engagement ring.'

The best way to divert her from this theme was to pursue another topic. Kate asked, 'So you talk to other firms who've dealt with your customers – ask if they always pay their bills.'

'And how prompt they are in paying. You people in the police get a nice pay-packet at the end of every month. You don't in business. You get what other people pay. Arthur was often owed thousands of pounds, thousands. But he kept afloat because of his reserves. And because people would give him credit. When your creditors start pressing you, you need to know when you're going to be paid. Indeed, *that* you're going to be paid. So, before you give anyone credit, you contact people who'll know whether they can be relied on for prompt payment and how much credit they can be trusted with.'

Kate nodded. 'This guy seemed to think he'd sorted every-thing out.'

'How thoroughly?'

She spread her hands. 'His problem, not mine. Maybe I'll phone him later this week – we talked about having dinner when my cold had cleared. But don't get all excited – it wasn't like in those books you've taken to reading. It wasn't love at first sight, Auntie.'

Cassie sniffed. 'When is it ever? But are you over that Robin of yours?'

Even now, when someone mentioned his name unexpectedly, it was all Kate could do not to cry out. Perhaps if she freshened her own drink she could manage. Not enough to risk her licence. Just for something to do while she put her thoughts in some sort of order.

She turned back to Cassie. 'I don't seem to be throwing up quite so much these days. Oh, I still miss him – when we climbed up the Duomo dome, I wanted . . . Oh, you know how it is.'

'Better to cry than to be sick.' Cassie thrust her bedside box of tissues at her. 'I'd say you were well on the way to recovery. Just remember there's no man who isn't replaceable.'

'Amen to that!'

Kate nearly dropped her glass. She turned to see who'd spoken. It was the care assistant with the ice.

'They've all got these quiet shoes,' Cassie complained. 'They scare you to death when they come creeping over the carpets. Mind you, I suppose I'd better enjoy the carpets: when you start having accidents they demote you to rooms with vinyl flooring – easier to mop up, I suppose. Now, how are you, Rosie? Come over here and let me have a look at you. No more cupboards walking into you?'

'You and your jokes, Cassie!'

'How else did you get your black eye and split lip? Come on, Rosie. I told you, Kate here's in the police. You can tell her.'

Kate smiled, in vain, she thought. Rosie stared at her, nodded, and went out. She was limping slightly.

She'd no idea what time it was when she got back from Cassie's, but she thought she'd better make a last check on Zenia. Zenia's washing was done: she had some of those old-fashioned, slatted, drying racks – the memory forced itself on Kate – the sort Robin had hung over the Aga in her old house. *Just hang the clothes up, that's all.*

Zenia herself did look slightly better, but coughed every time she tried to speak. In the end they flapped hands at each other and Kate slipped home.

Her house was silent. Silent enough to hear the rain tapping the uncurtained windows downstairs. Snapping on the radio she dragged her washing from the machine. No, she'd better tumble it. She could do with some racks like – like Zenia's.

What about a whisky?

What about a cocoa, more like?

Perhaps it was the cold making her feel so low. Or rather, the cold's residue of thick mucus and throbbing sinuses. And the cough, which had made an unwelcome return as soon as she came into the kitchen – all the powdery cement chipping off the floor. Roll on Friday and the new floor-covering, chosen for cheapness rather than style.

It'd be nice to curl up with the phone, and have a natter – to talk to someone on her terms, as opposed to Cassie's. Phone who? One of her London mates, of course – an old pal from the Met. Why no one in Birmingham? Because there was hardly anyone she could call a friend. Oh, inside the squad there was Colin, but his private life had a very thick veil across it, and though at work they could confide in each other, she still wasn't sure of his welcoming a call at this time. What about that young man on the plane? Alan? No, too late for a stranger to call. There was no one else. Certainly not Graham Harvey, whose wife's interest in his calls necessitated dialling one four one.

Kate squared her shoulders. Better an empty house than an unhappy one. If she got through another of her London boxes, she'd reward herself with a hot shower and a couple of those delectable Italian chocolates.

And tomorrow she'd start organising herself a social life.

Chapter Three

'It's Mr Rhyll, is it?' Kate asked doubtfully. 'I'm Detective Sergeant Kate Power and this is Detective Constable Colin Roper.'

The pharmacist, an intelligent looking man in his early fifties, stood back to let them into his inner sanctum, the dispensary. 'Hill,' he said, moving his lips, tongue and jaw with some emphasis. 'Hill.'

She rubbed at her ear. Of course: Mr Hill.

He looked at her closely; she rubbed her ear again.

'That's where they got in.' He jerked his head upwards at a small skylight. 'I've had the glass reinforced with polycarbonate sheeting, I've had that grid fitted. And still they managed to get in.'

'Must have been after growth-enhancing drugs,' Colin said.

'Or maybe it's a teenage girl, size six,' Kate said, trying to stifle a cough.

'If we can sort out your crime, you couldn't sort out Kate's attack of plague, could you?' Colin asked, stepping back a couple of paces. 'I'll swear it's become a death rattle.'

The pharmacist laughed and passed them mugs of coffee. He leaned back on his stool. 'Which shall we deal with first?'

'The crime,' she said, coughing again.

'Are you sure? OK, apart from that one vulnerable spot, the

place is like Fort Knox: all those grids, the metal pull-down blinds and the alarm. Oh, I've talked to your crime prevention people. Implemented all their suggestions. That was after Chummie got in up next-door's fire escape, into their lavatory, up into the loft and down through my ceiling.'

'After the usual, I suppose?'

Hill nodded. 'I gave a list of what had gone to your local colleagues, the uniform people. You can have another.' He turned to his computer and clicked on the Print icon.

'You're lucky,' Kate said, 'that they didn't take that.'

For answer he slipped down from the stool and peered under the bench. Kate and Colin looked too. The computer shell was attached to the bench with half-inch bolts.

'No one can say you're not doing your best!' she said. 'But they could still come back for that thing's innards – that's what they like these days. Portable and sellable.'

'Like the stuff they've taken,' Colin said, scanning the list as it peeled from the printer. 'You know, I have this fantasy I'll come out to a job like this to find they've skipped all the serious drugs and just nicked a trolley load of surgical appliances.'

Hill grinned. He was an attractive man, carrying his years well. 'Don't hold your breath. Especially you, Sergeant!'

'Kate,' she said.

'Kate.' He checked the list. 'Mind you, you'd be safe enough: they've left the chest sprays, this time.'

'*Chest sprays?* Why nick chest sprays?'

'They cost a bomb overseas. Fifteen hundred pounds for a Ventolin. A month's salary for a professional in some parts of Africa.'

'And less than six pounds on the NHS.'

Hill shook his head, his mouth tightening. 'Yes, but think what six pounds means to someone round here. Particularly if there's another couple of items on the scrip. The times I have to choose which drugs they have to have, as opposed to those they simply ought to have.'

They shook their heads, chastened. Kate tried to smother another cough. Hill relented, gesturing grandly at his shelves. 'Look at this lot here. Proprietary this, antibiotic that. What I'd recommend, however, for that chest of yours, is a lot of steam. Just steam. You can add a drop of menthol if you really insist, but believe me, steam's the best remedy. A basin with a towel over your head's cheapest, but I can sell you one of these little plastic inhaler affairs if you really want to part with your money – you put the hot water in here, put the mask over your face – and there you are.'

Kate dug in her purse. 'I couldn't have some of those really evil cough pastilles that stink the place out? If I've got to suffer, everyone else might as well too. Two packets – my neighbour's bad, too.'

Hill reached through the hatch into the shop. 'Those should fumigate a whole building,' he said, wrapping them and taking Kate's note.

The shop door pinged, and they could hear the assistant murmuring to a customer.

Hill turned to the hatch. 'OK, Helen. If that's Mrs Shaw's scrip. I'll do it now. That's another thing they didn't nick,' he said, turning back to them. 'HRT. Now, it's OK if I get this roof light fixed now, is it? So I can order more supplies.'

'Fixed?' Kate repeated.

'Bricked up. That should stop them.'

'It'll also make it very dark in here. And hot.'

'Electric light and extractor fan. And blow the electricity bills and the environment. They won't drive me out.'

She'd moved towards the door, but stopped. 'Has anyone said they want you out of here?'

Hill shook his head. 'Why force a ready supply of drugs and syringes to dry up? Mighty inconvenient for some, I'd have thought.'

'If you have any more thoughts about it, you will contact

us, won't you? You're the fourth pharmacy that's been done over this week,' Colin said. 'That's four too many.'

Hill reached through the hatch for the prescription and laid it next to the computer before answering. 'Of course,' he said. 'But this is the start of last night's surgery rush. And in half an hour it'll be this morning's surgery rush. And there's a small matter of a builder to organise. Thoughts may be hard to come by.'

Thoughts were also hard to come by in Kate's office, for the rest of the day. She'd still got the rest of her desk to clear – Forth Bridge painting – and her concentration was well below its peak, despite the steam inhaler.

What had impressed Cope most, of course, had been the vile smelling pastilles.

'If they're that nasty they must be doing you good,' he said, breathing in deeply as he stood over her desk. 'Good job you're not needed on obbo, though. They'd hear you coughing up your guts five hundred yards away.'

'And smell her,' Colin added. 'What on earth's in them?'

Kate made a show of reading the small print. 'Creosote, amongst other things. Ah well, I suppose if it's good for my fence it's good for me.'

'Depends if you're made of well-seasoned wood,' Cope said. 'Now, have you picked up anything on this chemist's shop business?'

'We're waiting for precise lists from all the pharmacists,' Kate said. 'The guy this morning was particularly efficient: the others haven't come through from uniform yet. Colin's just going to chase them.'

'Oh, it'll be the usual – uppers and downers and anything they can sell on the streets.' Cope hitched his trousers higher over his belly. 'No need to bother with that, surely. Just chase the usual dealers. Get out on the streets and pay a few visits. We're supposed to be cleaning up crimes, here. Being thorough's one thing. Pratting round with academic research is quite another.'

Kate stopped herself reacting, but out of the corner of her eye she saw Colin's eyes opening wider.

'Come to think of it, we could get Selby and young Fatima on that, couldn't we? OK, by you two?' Cope continued. 'Except, if Power went, the air would be a lot sweeter. Are you sure it's only creosote in there?'

Kate stood. 'What if there's anything unusual been nicked?'

'You mean, elastic stockings, something like that?'

'Possibly. Or at least vitamin pills. Why on earth nick vitamin pills?' She pointed to an item on Hill's list.

'Choosing the healthy option, of course,' Colin put in.

'But they're cheap and on all the vitamin supplement counters. You could shop-lift them easily enough.'

Cope looked at her sideways. 'You got some sort of hunch, Power? Hmm? Because if you have, stick with it. *That's* what makes a good cop.' He turned on his heel. The words, *Not your fancy qualifications* hung in the air as if he'd spoken them. Perhaps he had: she was still deaf enough in her right ear to miss things. Certainly Colin had jumped in as loudly as he could with some joke about Mystic Meg, but Fatima was flushing and burrowing ostentatiously amongst the papers on her desk. Selby was smirking as he tapped away with painfully slow jabbing strokes, as if attacking the keyboard.

What Kate would have liked to do was go after him. But what could she have said? He'd just paid her one of his rare compliments, backhanded though it was. He could, after all, have dismissed her theory as woman's intuition.

She coughed again.

'I think it had better be me making those calls,' Colin said. 'You sure that pharmacist was right? You're sure you shouldn't be banging on your GP's door demanding some antibiotics?'

'Sure. I really don't feel too bad – I feel a damn sight better than I did last week anyway, and I was quite happy legging round the sights of Florence. Though there weren't all that many people looking at the pictures in the Uffizi with a bag of clean tissues in one hand and a bag of wet tissues in the other.' She grinned and returned to the piles on her desk.

Out of the corner of one eye she could see Colin busy on the phone: he was tapping his pencil in clear exasperation. At the other side of the room, she could see Fatima still checking through a pile of files like hers. Except Fatima wasn't being slow and methodical; she was looking increasingly frantic. Kate could see there was something wrong well before the younger woman grabbed her waste-bin and started to burrow through it, peeling open balls she'd screwed up, then scrapping them again. It wasn't long before she repeated the whole process.

It was time for a coffee anyway. Kate grabbed her mug, and sauntered past Fatima's desk. It was a pity she couldn't offer her a drink. As it was, she settled for a matey lean on the desk. When Selby abandoned a particularly frenzied attack on the keyboard to tip back in his chair and watch, she leaned even closer, mouthing, 'What have you lost?'

Fatima flushed. 'Is it that obvious?'

Kate nodded. 'Even Selby's noticed, I'd say. What is it?'

The flush deepened. 'I feel really bad about this: it was a message for you. A phone message. I took it just before you came back in this lunchtime and wrote it down. Then I got involved with something and I can't find it anywhere. I suppose I didn't leave it on your desk?' she added, without much conviction.

'What was it written on?'

'The usual phone pad paper.'

'In that case, I don't think so. But I'll check.' She made the coffee anyway, and returned to her desk. It was a good thing she never balled paper before slinging it — it certainly made the sifting process a whole lot quicker. But no more successful. 'What's the joke, Selby?'

He was shaking with ill-suppressed laughter.

'You've no idea how funny you two look. Like a pair of squirrels looking for nuts.'

She raised an ironic eyebrow – she'd never credited him with a taste for the imaginative image. And then looked at him hard. 'If you've had anything to do with this, you'd better look after your own nuts,' she said. 'All this football coaching means I've learned to kick balls quite hard. And very accurately.'

The trouble was, it wasn't the first time notes had gone missing. In an office as full of paper as theirs it was difficult to make specific accusations, but she had a good idea that they hadn't walked without some human help. Or sub-human, come to think of it. Meanwhile, Selby looked as righteously indignant as he could.

'What was the message, anyway?' she asked at last.

'It was personal, the caller said.'

'Good job it's gone missing, then,' Selby observed. 'You know how the gaffer likes people sorting out their love life in working hours.'

She bit her tongue: it was too public a place to remind him that his working hours hadn't exactly been filled with unadulterated toil – she'd caught him playing endless games of computer patience before she went off sick, and had promised him trouble if she caught him at it again. 'Love life, was it?' she asked Fatima. 'News to me if I've got one of those.'

Fatima looked troubled. 'Well, it was a young man. He didn't – wouldn't – give a name. Just gave me a number, asked if I'd make sure you phoned him. And now—' she spread her hands despairingly.

'So what was on the note?'

'Your name. Please phone – this guy's number. My name.'

'I'll put an SOS up on the white-board – ask people to check their files to make sure it's not got caught up with them. And I'll have a quick whiz round the waste-bins.' She bent down by Selby's desk. 'No, don't put yourself out, Selby: I'll do it myself.'

But she hadn't got the bastard: his bin was as clean as anyone's.

At last, accepting the inevitable, she shrugged. 'Well,' she said, 'if it's important he'll no doubt phone again.'

Kate had taken Fatima to one of the quieter of what were almost official police watering holes. It wouldn't do either of them any harm to show they weren't averse to joining their colleagues. She suspected she'd already got a bit of a reputation for being stand-offish which wasn't a bonus for anyone and which could do Fatima, the rookie in the squad, real harm.

She bought mineral water for two and settled at the table.

'They'll try on all sorts of things,' she said without preamble, 'to test you. They did with me. It's never fun. I was too pig-headed to ask for help, but if something as important as a phone message has disappeared, sticking it out on your own isn't a course I'd recommend.'

Fatima sucked the lemon slice. 'DCI Harvey's already had a word with me. He told me – well, it was as good as an order – to tell you if there was excessive horseplay.'

Kate smiled. It was the word she'd used herself in the autumn, but Harvey had repeated it with an ironic turn – no doubt that was how he'd used it to Fatima. 'Good. And I hope you will.'

'I want to be accepted, Kate. I don't want a reputation as a grass.'

'Don't think of it as grassing: think of it as whistle-blowing. Of course it's not easy to distinguish between the two. Why do you think I kept quiet? Come on, Fatima, there's legitimate fun – they sent me all over the build-ing, hunting for non-existent files, my first day. And there's bullying. You'll know if you're being bullied. And there's the sort of stupid thing that may have happened today which is detrimental to our work. OK, *could* be detrimental, if it was an official, not a private message that got lost.' She stopped. She sounded horribly like a schoolteacher. 'Fancy some crisps?'

Fatima shook her head. 'I shall be eating with my family later.'

You could almost see the word *Sergeant* being suppressed. Swallow the rebuff or accept it? She compromised. 'You know I'm speaking just as a woman? Because I wouldn't want anyone to go through what I went through? Right?'

Fatima's nod was courteous but not enthusiastic.

Kate tried a different tack. 'You're from Bradford, aren't you? Do you know any people in Birmingham?' Foolish – the woman kept referring to her family. 'You know, in the police?'

'I'm living with some cousins at the moment and my mother's come down to stay for a bit. I've not had much time for socialising.'

Poor woman. Free but not free.

'Are you looking for your own place?'

'Oh, yes! I mean – it's lovely being with people you know – but after being away at Uni and living on my own . . .'

'They still think you're fourteen and ask you if you've cleaned your teeth!'

'So if you know anywhere—'

'House share or flat? Not that I do at the moment – I hardly know anyone either. I'd only been in the squad a few weeks when I had to go on sick leave – I hurt my knee when someone drove a van at me.'

'Didn't people visit you?'

'Some did. Even Cope. But I think I might not have been the most friendly of women – my partner had died and I think I put barriers up I didn't even know about. Not a good thing. So I'm very grateful to you for coming tonight – I need to get out more, mix more, myself. Another drink?'

'My shout.' There was a certain note in Fatima's voice which said that she was grown up and used to pushing her way to bars, despite her height and religion.

Kate nodded, accepting the rebuke. 'D'you know, I think I'll go wild and have a tomato juice.'

Chapter Four

The face drew Kate's eyes. No matter how often she'd told herself never to look at the face, always to fix the scene in her memory first, she couldn't keep her eyes off the face. The bulging eyes were reproaching her.

No. The location. Always check out the location; details that looked trivial but might not be: burn those into the brain so that even the foulest, most repulsive damage to a fellow human couldn't eradicate them. Don't look at that face again. She looked at a canal: tatty, still awaiting the restoration they'd done further out of the city. No one had prettified the ugly backs of buildings, the myriad drainpipes in a mixture of peeling paints. Many leaking. Tufts of buddleia and willow-herb, not quite dead. The towpath here was cindered, not paved in red and blue bricks: European funding had obviously run out downstream. And now to the bridge over the canal: a high parapet and metal spikes designed to stop anyone doing what this poor bugger had done. Or had had done to him. He swung – the thin blue rope could have been nylon tow-rope. Backwards and forwards, quite gently.

Don't look at his face.

There'd been nothing gentle about his death. He'd not broken his neck, but strangled slowly, painfully. There were for some reason what looked like bloodstains on his sweater.

She had to look more closely. Yes, there were deep slashes across it. Something very sharp – a Stanley knife? The arms, too. At least, the left one. The right wasn't so bad.

The last indignity: death had relaxed his sphincters, evidence of his final frailty for all to see.

Dead. Yes, the police surgeon was by him now. A middle-aged man, tall and bulky enough to be an old-fashioned cop, was perched on a ladder someone had leaned precariously between the bank and the parapet.

'Poor bastard's dead all right: get your well-oiled machine into action, Mr Harvey.' An exit line before pacing away. But for such a big man he had a very short stride, and the effect was comic.

In other circumstances.

Harvey called him back. 'You're not waiting for the patholo-gist, Dr Blake?'

Blake hunched his shoulders: 'Urgent house-call.'

He didn't even bother to infuse conviction into his voice.

Catching sight of her for the first time, Graham nodded and muttered. 'OK, Kate – lights, camera, action.'

'All three ready and waiting, Gaffer,' she replied, in the same false-perky tone. They were all professionals, after all. No time to be upset or sentimental or even angry. At least, not until the investigation was under way. 'Gaffer, this is—'

His eyes shot past her. He straightened his shoulders. 'Looks as if Neville's come down. Have you met the new Super yet, Kate?'

She shook her head. 'Gaffer!'

But Harvey was already walking towards the newcomer, a sharply dressed man a couple of years younger than he.

'Gaffer!' she said loudly enough to make him turn, in irritation.

'I'll brief Neville and wait for the pathologist. You'll handle the press,' he said.

Her eyes widened. Someone had to, but preferably someone

with vocal chords that produced more than a croak. 'Sir!' It sounded like an objection.

His eyes froze her. 'You've been trained to talk to the press, haven't you? And you're aware that it's the Service's policy for one of the officers closest to the case to do so.'

She stood her ground. 'There's one thing you ought to know, Gaffer. I can ID this bloke.'

A flashlight went off, bringing the dead face into grotesque life. The last external rite had started.

'What! Why the hell didn't you——?' He glanced at Neville, as if hoping he hadn't heard.

'I recognised the sweater. And thought his features——' she gestured – 'I can just about ... He sat next to me on the plane back from Italy. His name's Alan Grafton, and I've got his business card on my dressing-table at home.'

She couldn't read Harvey's expression, not the bit that wasn't anger.

'Not exactly quick with the information, Power. OK. Deal with the press and get someone to go and get the card.' Harvey turned towards Neville, who was talking to a woman operating a video camera. He spoke to Kate over his shoulder. 'Tell you what, take them down towards Brindley Place. It's well away from us and all the stuff we've got to do.' As he spoke, his eyes ranged over her face.

She had a terrible fear that he was getting rid of her, protecting her from the ugliness of the pathologist's initial examination – nothing to the real thing, for goodness' sake, and she'd seen enough of those. But Neville was on the move again, and it would do neither of their careers any good to be seen bickering, particularly in these circumstances.

She nodded.

'And that card – get it yourself. You won't want any-one to know your burglar alarm code. And you'd better get into dry clothes – you don't want to go down with pneumonia or something, not with the squad short-handed like this.' His voice had dropped, then became public and carrying.

She set off for Brindley Place, wondering how he knew about the alarm. She'd had the system fitted just the day before she left for Florence.

One of the uniformed lads, rain coursing down his yellow jacket, caught her eye, raised an eyebrow. 'Always as cheerful and polite as that, is he?'

Her face found a smile. 'You should see him on a bad day.' And then ashamed of her disloyalty, she said seriously, 'He's OK, Harvey is. A really good cop.'

'Guess he got out of the wrong side of bed today, then! Didn't even blink when you said you knew the guy.'

'Probably that new Super pulling the strings a bit too tight. Anyway, we've got to sort out the ladies and gentlemen of the press.' She gestured down the towpath.

'There are several places down there that serve a mean cup of coffee. Even at this hour. Or can be persuaded to.'

She nodded. 'Good idea. Thanks.'

'Tell you what, though – Kate, isn't it? I'm Cary Grant. You can tell from my typical English good looks!' Actually he was African-Caribbean, on the handsome side of good-looking. He grinned. 'Hey, you'd better find a mirror or something.' He pointed to her eyes.

'You're a star, Cary,' she managed.

As she burrowed in her pockets for a tissue, her hands too cold to make contact, he produced a large old-fashioned white linen square.

They both swore as the sound of a paparazzo's motor-drive alerted them. The bastard would have nice view of him leaning concernedly towards her as she mopped her make-up. Her kagoul hood had blown back to let the drizzle soak her hair. What little of her pride was left groaned.

'All I bloody needed,' she said. 'It'll be all over the *Evening Mail*, won't it? Hope your wife won't mind, Cary.'

'She might if I had one. Tell you what, I'll phone you —
maybe a jar after work one night?'

She probably sounded off-hand. 'Fine.'

Time to stride down the towpath and talk to cameras and
mikes. The cautious words were already framing themselves.
Hell, all anyone knew was that a man had been found hanging.
It wasn't down to her to give an ID. Someone from his family
would have to do that, anyway, poor bugger, peering at the body
on a slab if they were quick, a drawer if they weren't.

What would the press ask? Was it murder? Suicide? God
knew. All she could do was mount a holding operation, with
charm and promise of plenty of co-operation later. She gave
them words they all knew only too well: *pathologist*; *post mortem
examination*; *inquest*; *identification*; *help with inquiries* ... No hint
of an ID.

Given it was their job to prise information out of her, and
hers to withhold it, it was an amicable enough session, made
even better when another uniformed constable appeared with
cups of tea and coffee. One of the reporters produced some
more. She thought her dithering might be a result simply of
the bitter weather — others too seemed to be having trouble
guiding the cups to their lips, while they jiggled alarmingly if left
on the saucers. Everyone's, not just hers. She produced earnest
but wan smiles for the cameras, and broke up the gathering by
descending into a bout of coughing.

'Kate? Over here!' Colin emerged from the shelter of a pub
doorway. 'What the hell are you doing hanging around outside
on a day like this?'

'Acting on orders, Colin. As we all do. Tell you what,
you wouldn't like to drop me off in Summer Row? My
car's there, and the Gaffer wants me to nip off home and
get something.'

'I'll run you home. Yes! Come on. My car's had its heater
working overtime this last hour — there was this diesel spillage
out Oldbury way, and the traffic's tied up like a pervert in

bondage. I suppose the esteemed gaffer noticed my absence,' he added, unlocking his car.

'He didn't mention it.'

'Too busy sounding off at you, was he? Come on, hop in. We'll be going against the flow of traffic back to Kings Heath and it should have cleared a bit by the time you've had a hot shower and steamed your head.' He did an illicit U-turn, escaping the still solid traffic into town, and heading for the Five Ways island.

'I haven't got time to—'

'Listen to me, little sister. That stiff's going to be a long time stiff. No need for you to join him before your time. What have I said?'

She gestured wildly, holding back the vomit as long as she could. He pulled in, leaned across her to fling open the door. She made it to a gutter grating.

It had been such a long time since anyone had smoothed back her hair like that. As if holding someone's forehead would make the spewing easier. Perhaps it did. It was certainly good to have Colin there to heave her to her feet and pass her a bunch of tissues.

'Stomach still unruly,' he said, as they set off again.

'Again rather than still. I knew the bloke, you see. The stiff.'

'Jesus! And Harvey made you talk to the press!'

'Who else could he have asked?'

'He could have done it his bloody self, that's what. He could have made them wait until the path. had finished poking things in orifices.'

But that would have meant Kate watching the body being cut down; the insertion of a thermometer . . . .

'I said, how well did you know him?'

'Hardly at all. I just sat next to him on the plane last Sunday afternoon. He was full of advice about my cold. We were going to do dinner sometime.'

'Eligible bachelor, then?'

'A bit older than me. Not much. Quite presentable. In business. He'd been doing a few deals in Florence.'

'Oh, ho! Are you thinking what I'm thinking? Is this a Mafia job?'

Kate stared.

'Come on, Kate. The Italian connection! And didn't they string that guy up under Tower Bridge or London Bridge or whatever?'

'Alan Grafton wasn't an international banker and, nicely-proportioned as that little bridge is, it's scarcely your famous tourist site. I don't know, Colin. But I'd certainly like to find out.' It took longer than she'd liked to shower and dry her hair, but Colin wouldn't budge till she'd had a second breakfast. By the time they set out again, he'd even phoned the lads on the scene to stop her car being either clamped or towed away.

Harvey was waiting for them as they reached the office, and gestured Kate straight to his room. He pointed to the comfortable chair. 'Sorry to have to spring this on you, Kate. But – when they went through his pockets they found your business card.'

If she got her mind in gear, perhaps she could keep her stomach under control. 'We swapped them. We got talking on the plane – well, he did most of the talking – and ... He was a decent enough guy.'

'Attractive? Did you – like – him?'

She leant on the word slightly. '*Fancy* him, you mean? He was just a pleasant companion for a couple of hours. As I say, he did most of the talking, but I missed a lot of what he said because the changes in atmospheric pressure made me deaf. I'll write down everything I can remember – I've just gone through it with Colin, which helped me to remember odd snippets.'

He nodded.

'Here's his card, by the way.' She passed it over, pathetically small in a polythene bag. 'I wonder if he ran his business from home – look, the home telephone number and fax numbers are the same.'

'How involved d'you want to be?' he asked abruptly.

'He wasn't anything more than a casual acquaintance.'

'Odd he should have your card on him and nothing else.'

'And *nothing else?*'

'Nothing else. That makes life a bit more interesting, doesn't it?'

She welcomed the ironic glimmer in his smile.

'Very much more interesting, I'd say. Graham—' she checked the door was still shut – 'you remember a couple of months ago there were a few problems out there.' Her head jerked in the direction of the office. 'Messages going adrift, that sort of thing.'

'It hasn't bloody well started again, has it?' Graham was on his feet, thunderous.

'Might have done. Too early to tell. All I know is that Fatima was going spare trying to find a message she'd taken for me. And never found it. We put a note on the white-board asking people to check if they'd picked it up by mistake.'

'Why are you telling me now? Not that you're wrong to. I'm just interested in the context.'

'This sounds crazy. It's just I've got this awful pit-of-the-stomach feeling it could have been Alan Grafton trying to phone me. No evidence at all. Just—' she shrugged.

'We could check back through the in-coming calls. I suppose you never thought of that earlier?'

What was the matter with the man?

'I believe Fatima did,' she said, cool to match his coldness. 'Call box.'

'Predictable, I suppose. OK.' He appeared to close the conversation. Then he seemed to think better of it – he opened his mouth – before changing his mind yet again.

Kate looked him in the eye. 'The post mortem, Gaffer.'

He stiffened. 'You won't want to be involved – I—'

'I am involved, aren't I? May I accompany you to the post mortem?' she asked, correct as at an interview.

'Are you sure about – I mean, it's not the most enjoyable thing even when you don't know the guy on the slab. Why push yourself? There isn't any real need . . . .'

It seemed as if the equal opportunities course he'd been on hadn't been a hundred per cent successful. He was trying to protect her, wasn't he? Quite definitely. Some might think it was as demeaning as being harassed. And there was no gainsaying the fact that to protect someone implied you were strong and they weak.

What she ought to do was explain about equality. Now. But Graham wasn't the sort of man to take kindly to a lecture – in this morning's fluctuating moods it could be counter-productive, in fact.

And they were supposed to be friends, after all.

She smiled. 'I appreciate the thought, Graham.' Was that a mistake? His eyes flickered. 'But you know as well as I do you have to take the rough with the rough in this job. The most intimate I got with the man was sucking his barley sugars. I can – forgive the pun – cope.' She pulled an apologetic face.

He shook his head, but produced the closest thing to a genuine smile she'd seen that morning. 'OK. But there's time to change your mind. And it wouldn't be a sign of weakness if you did.'

Chapter Five

They were ready, now, the whole team, gowned, booted and mentally braced. Graham turned to her. 'There's still time to back out, Kate.'

In front of them all.

'When Robin was killed it wasn't his wife who did the formal identification,' she said. 'It was me. And you never know, having seen this man recently, I might just spot — Ah!'

Graham followed her eyes. He stepped forward. 'Morning, Duncan,' he said, shaking hands with the pathologist, a man somewhere in his forties — not being able to see his hair or even hair-line made it difficult to be precise. 'You know everyone, don't you? Except for Kate Power, Duncan — she's the new detective sergeant in the squad.'

Duncan who?

Smiling her professional, dimple-free smile, Kate offered her hand, which Duncan held on to for a moment too long. His eyes — dark brown — opened a little wider under well-shaped brows. All he said, however, was, 'Good to meet you, Kate.'

She nodded, said nothing. There was always a lot of loud banter before an autopsy, but flirting in morgue overalls was new to her. At least, she told herself sourly, he had the good taste to do it before cutting into the corpse.

'You're very quiet — not going to pass out on me, are you?'

Duncan asked, holding the door for her. The teasing intimacy in his voice matched the overlong handshake.

'In my experience it's the particularly macho men that do that,' she said. Which made her wonder: why wasn't Cope insisting on being here?

Her reward – if that was what she'd wanted – was a dazzling smile which revealed dimples to match her own, and a dip of the head, as if he were acknowledging a hit. Then everyone's smiles disappeared under masks.

Cameras busy, attendants started to undress Alan Grafton.

Kate knew how the body would look – she'd looked closely on the faces and necks of several people slowly throttled. But she braced herself to look not just at any corpse but at Alan. How might he have felt about this? His naked body being scrutinised not by the tender eyes of a lover, but by hard, professional eyes, seeking clues not to feelings but to death? There was no more intimate relationship than death, however. She and Alan would never have looked at each other as lovers as closely as she peered at him now. And yet by focusing on details, she could lose sight of the man. Which she must do: she must shut down emotion, open the intellect, however hard it was to do now the theorising was over and she was here in person. Perhaps Graham might have been right.

She dragged her eyes back to the corpse.

The bruising and marks she'd expected, the discoloration, the blood-suffused face and eyes. What she hadn't expected, but what explained the bloodstains she'd seen from the towpath, were the score-marks, much deeper than she'd guessed, across his body and arms: what the pathologist would later define variously as abrasions and lacerations. They ran diagonally across his body, top left to bottom right, like the hoops of red tape she'd worn in infant school sports teams. There were similar ones on the left arm; those on the right were much less deep.

'So why on earth would he do that to himself?' Duncan

asked. 'Oh, yes – little doubt about it. Something like a kitchen knife – but a very sharp one.'

'Maybe a Stanley knife, Sir?' Kate put in.

He glanced up at her and nodded. 'Good idea. Look, you can see the start and end of each slash.' He demonstrated against his own arm and trunk. 'And he'd have to change hands to do the other arm. The question is, of course, why?'

Which might have been the question Alan himself was asking, frowning over, as Duncan made the incisions in the scalp, pulling the facial skin forward and downward in a last grimace.

It was certainly the question on everyone's lips after all the measuring and recording, opening and probing. Why? They knew the how of strangulation, after a day neither eating nor drinking, of fixing a rope to a parapet over which he'd then clambered to let himself make the final drop. They knew that.

But not why.

'Are you quite sure it was suicide?' Graham insisted.

Duncan shrugged. 'Look, you know I didn't find any external or internal marks to indicate that anyone might have manhandled him – dead or alive – to that spot. Your SOCO people have probably got film even now in their cameras of the marks he made on the parapet when he was shinning over. There are probably fibres from his rope on his clothing. That's for the forensic science team to discover.' His shrug said he had done his part.

'But he had everything to live for,' Kate said.

'In my experience, if what you are living for fails, then you might as well die. Right, ladies and gentlemen, as a precaution I shall wait until all those samples have been checked before issuing my final report but you shall have the preliminary one in the morning.'

Dismissed, they started to troop out, Kate in their midst. But just as she was about to speak to Harvey, Duncan called her back.

'I couldn't help but be intrigued by what you were saying,' he said. 'No doubt all your colleagues know why he should have wanted to live, but it was, of course, news to me.' He looked down at his hands. 'Could you give me ten minutes to scrub and maybe we could take the smell of this business from our nostrils with a cup of coffee.'

From the corner of her eye she could see Harvey's neck stiffen. 'I've an idea we may have to take a rain check on that – there'll be a meeting back at work,' she said.

'Could I have a phone number – in case anything comes up?' he pursued, all dimples and twinkling eyes.

OK, he'd asked for it. She flashed her dimples, too. 'The same number as DCI Harvey,' she said. And then, for the hell of it, for the *irony* of it – for how often did a woman get asked by one man to join him for a coffee when he was still red with the blood of the last one – she grinned. And added her extension number.

Jesus, that she should find such a thing funny! But she did. She'd had the giggles over far less funny things after other post mortems: post anatomy-lesson hysterics, one sergeant had called them. Better than bottling it all up, he'd said. And she was sure he was right. Look at the others now, either so grim-faced it might have been their own father eviscerated there on the slab or so jolly it might have been an end-of-term treat.

Harvey looked ostentatiously at his watch as she hurried up. 'I think there's time to talk this through before we wrap it up for the inquest,' he said. 'Will you drive or shall I?'

As she picked her way through the traffic and inched into the last space, she knew she had to say something. That she couldn't trust the path's findings? That she had this instinct throbbing away? A combination of the two. When and how to tell Graham she wasn't sure. Maybe if they all sat down over a coffee, not just the two of them, it would come out naturally. In fact, the more she thought of it, the more she was convinced that it had to be in public: if he shot down her suggestion in private, there was no way she could float it again. It might be better to ask someone else to put the question, the request, whatever it could be called.

'Cup of tea?' he asked, opening his door as if assuming the answer would be yes.

'I'd like a quick wash, first, if you don't mind. The smell of the place seems to get into every pore, doesn't it?'

'Isn't there a line in some play about the perfumes of Arabia?' he smiled.

'Isn't that from the play it's bad luck to quote?'

'No such thing as bad luck,' he said. 'We make our fortunes or misfortunes.' The smile was completely gone, his face so bitter that she almost cried out.

Instead, she said slowly, 'I wonder what Alan Grafton did to bring his misfortune. He was telling me all the precautions he'd taken, all the plans he had for the future. And then—'

'We'll have to prepare a report for the coroner,' he said at last. 'And you want to be the one that does it, don't you? Don't you think it's a hell of a risk, Kate, to grub around the life of someone you knew?'

'He's dead. He was kind to me when he was alive.'

'You don't owe him that sort of interest just because he gave you a sweetie!'

'Someone's got to do it.'

'I don't like it. I really don't like it.'

'Tell you what, Gaffer: sleep on it.' She smiled the professional smile, then blazed at him with the full force of the dimples as he hesitated.

'OK. I'll think about it. We'll talk about it in the morning when we allocate tasks. And it depends on the size of everyone's in-tray, not just yours. So don't start thinking you've got to stay up half the night to clear it just so that you can persuade me.'

In the same quiet pub she'd taken Fatima to, Colin brought over a couple of halves, and tossed a film-wrapped sandwich at her. 'You look done in. Mind you, you deserve to. He'd have let you off the p.m. if you'd asked. And rightly too.'

She shook her head. 'I didn't even need to ask. He wanted me to stay away. Doesn't want me on the case at all. It's me that's driving him.'

'You're a fool, then,' he said without heat.

'Thanks. OK, you may be right. But I already know what Grafton had been up to — I'd only have to go over all the stuff he told me with whoever was investigating.'

'True. Anyway, you seem to be able to wrap him round your little finger.'

'Not today. He's in a weird mood. Foul one minute, kind the next. Marginalises me when he should be introducing me to someone. I don't know where I stand with him.' She shook her head. 'Poor bugger. Mrs H must be giving him a hard time.'

'When is she not?' Colin sipped his beer reflectively. 'Mind you, if he's like this at home, what sort of life would it be for her?'

Before she could reply, a bulky figure loomed over their table.

'Hi, Gaffer!' Colin sounded more welcoming than she felt. A dose of Cope was surely the last thing either of them wanted.

'You needn't sound so bloody cheerful. Hell, why not? End of another day, isn't it?' He perched on an inadequate stool, slopping some of his pint, and mopping with a beer mat. 'You OK, Kate? You didn't tell me you knew the guy that topped himself.'

'I don't think I actually stopped long enough to have a conversation with anyone, Gaffer. In fact, I think this is the first time my bum's touched base today.'

'Better have another sandwich, then.' He pushed away and headed for the bar.

They exchanged a raising of eyebrows.

Colin finished his half before speaking. '"Kate", eh? How did you get into his good books?'

'Worrying, isn't it?'

Before they could speculate, Cope was back, three glasses on a tray. 'They'll bring some sarnies in a minute. Knew the stiff and watched them slice him open. You've got guts, young Kate, I'll say that for you.'

'I haven't closed my eyes and tried to go to sleep yet,' she said.

He stared at her.

'Oh, it's one thing telling your head it'll be all right, isn't it? And another finding out later. No, I didn't pass out or spew or anything. I was too busy wondering how he came to have those knife cuts all over his body. The path. reckoned he'd done them himself.'

'Sounds like he was pretty angry,' Cope said.

'Angry?'

'They say suicide's the ultimate act of anger,' Colin agreed. 'What else could they be, anyway?'

Kate shook her head. 'I suppose I thought – I don't know. He was wearing a very smart jumper – it was as if he'd been trying to destroy that. Or, to fit my theory, someone else had wanted to destroy the jumper, and didn't mind if he got hurt in the process. And I'd have liked this other person to have dragged him, kicking and screaming, to his death. Except, of course, there's no evidence at all on his body of anyone's violence except his own. The whole thing's quite consistent with a not very efficient suicide.'

'So why are you hooked on the idea of murder?' Cope said. 'Ah!' He stopped as the barmaid brought a plate of sandwiches. 'Thanks, love! You'll be bringing the chips?' He pushed the plate into the middle of the table. 'Cheese and salad. You never know with you young kids: you might have been veggies.'

Kate smiled. 'Certainly not a day for rare meat.'

'My dad was one of eight,' Cope said. 'The other seven – all older – were girls. Well, my gran decided to keep a few hens – quite a tough old bird herself, my gran. Had to be, with my grandad drinking himself to death. Anyway, guess whose job it was to kill these birds when they'd stopped laying. Even though he'd be no more than seven and had raised them from chicks. "Just cut their heads off," Gran said, handing him the chopper. And of course the bloody things didn't stop running round ... No, my dad wouldn't eat chicken for years. Well into his forties, he'd be. I remember the rows about it with my mum. Still, there you go.' He plunged his teeth into a sandwich. 'Thanks, love,' he added, as the barmaid produced the chips, a huge plateful.

They smelt good. Kate decided it was an act of duty to stop him eating the lot, and helped herself, liberally. The more food in her stomach, the better she felt. But Cope was eating very sparingly.

'Funny thing, murder,' he said at last. 'There aren't many that people get away with. But there are some clever buggers around, no doubt about that.'

Kate looked at him.

'And these scientist guys don't always get it right. In fact,' he added, pausing to drink, 'sometimes they make a right balls up. If there happened to be a meeting tomorrow, and if anyone happened to ask my opinion, I'd say we should poke around a bit more before we come to any hasty decisions about what we should tell the coroner.' He nodded, and took another draught. 'Despite what those above might say.'

Kate nodded. 'Thanks, Gaffer.'

'What if it turns out to be suicide, after all?' Colin asked.

Cope shrugged. 'We have to dig up all the background anyway. And if young Power's nose is twitching, I'd say we go along with it. So long, of course, as it doesn't take much time and it doesn't cost much. Now, about this new Super, Rodney Neville. Have you heard ....'

An hour and many scurrilous tales about their new overlord later, they split up. Colin was his usual discreet self: no one would ever find out about his movements unless they asked very direct questions. Kate had to get back to the nick to collect her car, and Cope fell into step with her. She sensed he had something to say, but the conversation – if it could be called that – skipped from observations about the weather (it was still raining steadily) to squad gossip and back again. At last they were by her car. Perhaps she should take a risk.

'Well, we'll see if my brain can switch off tonight. I'm expecting the odd nightmare, I must say. It's those long cuts down the torso, isn't it?'

'And in your stiff's case, they bring a whole new meaning to hanging, drawing and quartering.' His laughter rang out brutally.

She joined in. Laughter was the best medicine, they said. Maybe they even meant this sort of laughter.

'Tell you what, Power, I've seen more post mortems on more stiffs than kids like Fatima's had hot dinners. You get used to them, right? And yet—'

'Do they ever stop getting to you?' She sensed he needed prompting.

'Well, there was one. Really turned me over. Not so long ago, as it happens. There I thought I could cope with most things and I go to this p.m. on this kid. Baby, really. And there's the pathologist, young lad he'd be, same age as you. And he's got this radio on, blaring out pop music. And this tiny baby on the slab. And he's laughing to his mate about what he's going to do to his bird, and he's got this baby there. And in he goes. I tell you, Kate, I couldn't take it. I wanted to smash that bastard's head. Poor little bugger, doesn't make its first birthday, and this bastard can't even give it a bit of tenderness, a bit of pity. I tell you what, I—'

But footsteps were approaching them, and he broke off. 'Mind how you go, then, young Kate. And remember what I said: a good hunch is worth a hell of a lot of science.'

Chapter Six

Well, she'd got through the night all right. But she'd woken up sharply, at about six, and had been afraid to drop off again. No point in tempting fate. What about a run? No: in this rain, with this cough, it would be crazy, wouldn't it? As would her football training session tonight. She'd have to phone one of the Boys' Brigade officers and make her excuses. It was a shame: she enjoyed working with the boys, and hoped they got something out of it, apart, that is, from seeing their team creep up from the bottom of the league.

One thing she could do was deal with the rest of her holiday washing. After all the months she'd had of no mod cons whatsoever, it was a pleasure to be able to load her new machine – even if to set it she had to stand on the bare concrete floor and to read incomprehensible instructions in a wide variety of languages. And she still had enough time to check on Zenia, who was now progressing visibly, and to beat the rush hour.

If she could choose a parking spot, she must be one of the first of the squad to get in, so she stopped off to pick up the post.

'After a few worms, are you?' the receptionist greeted her, looking at his watch.

She hesitated – was this a snide reference to her loathing for maggots? No, not from Harry – he'd be thinking about early birds. She hoped he hadn't noticed the missed half second. 'With a bit of luck. Hey, you look very smart, Harry – what's with this uniform then?' She scanned the crisp shirt, the shoulder tabs.

'Oh, it's all a con. It seems Joe Public doesn't feel secure if us receptionists are civilians, same as them. They prefer something a bit more official, like. So here we are.' He preened.

'Looks very good to me. Anything you want me to take up?'

He reached for a folder over-balancing a stalk of filing trays. 'This is the latest batch of reports from that *Grass on your Mates* programme.'

'Anything interesting?'

Harry pulled himself up as if on parade. 'DS Power, you know I'm only a civilian receptionist.'

She responded in kind. 'Indeed, Mr Carter. But I also know you were a highly-respected beat cop for years.' She leaned her elbows on the high counter, grinning. 'Come on, Harry – you'd nose anything out.'

'Well, funny you should ask, as it happens. I was talking to one of the lasses who works on the dedicated line. Bright kid. Seems there's a woman phones in. With a posh voice. And she stops in mid-sentence, drops the phone, like. And she's dialled one-four-one.'

Kate cocked her head. 'Did she have time to say anything?'

'Only, "Good morning – I want—". And stops. According to Mandy. But there's a bit of a whisper. Inaudible, though. Funny. Then it happens again, same time next day. And again a third day. Same time, same sort of thing. And out of all the calls Mandy's taken, all these different voices, that's the calls that stick in her mind.'

'And yours! OK. I'm hooked. You'll get Mandy to let me know if she phones back, won't you?'

'With that lot to work your way through, you won't have time for anything extra.'

'Try me. Come on, Harry, you set this one up for me to get interested in. Admit it,' she said, grinning again.

'Maybe she won't try again.'

'And maybe whoever takes the call won't be Mandy and won't be alert enough to pick it up. We'll have to wait and see. Anyway, I can hear my coffee calling me. See you, Harry! And thanks for giving me extra work.'

'Ah, you youngsters don't know you're born ... OK, Kate: our ears and eyes are pinned open!'

The reports on the pharmacy break-ins were all neatly clipped together on her desk, together with a note in Colin's writing that they should check on another couple – they'd been dealt with by uniform while she'd been watching Alan Grafton being cut up. He'd asked for complete lists of missing items.

Head down, she was in the middle of the rest of her in-tray when first Selby, then Fatima, arrived. Selby headed straight to the kettle, which no one had got round to filling. He shook it ostentatiously. Empty. And no one had had the decency to fill it! So he headed for the machine, which produced a stream of liquid. Stirring it vigorously – it smelt something like coffee, though she knew from experience that that was the nearest it got – he went and stood beside Fatima. Then he left it, on her desk, while he went and made a phone call. Fatima eyed it and him, and moved the cup.

So what was he up to? The woman was fasting, they all knew that. So he wasn't being kind, that much was certain. She looked anxiously at Fatima, but she was apparently engrossed in what she was reading.

'Bloody Nora!'

Cope.

He erupted into the room soon after his voice, waving the tabloid papers he always took. 'Bloody Nora, Power – you and that ugly bugger Grant all over the bleeding papers.' He plonked them on his desk, conveniently open at the right pages.

Everyone in the room surged round.

'Made it to Page Three, has she? No, not with them tits,' Selby yelled. ''Ere, Colin, your bleeding girlfriend's all over the papers!'

Colin grinned and produced another newspaper. 'Syndicated to the *Independent*, too. I fancy this one's composition's better. And the definition certainly is.'

All the papers had much the same headline – variations on *the caring face of our boys and girls in blue.*

'All very touching,' Kate said, irritated that she should be blushing. 'They might have let me comb my hair first!'

'I wonder if Cartier-Bresson let his subjects comb their hair.' Graham Harvey's voice was quiet but nonetheless cut across everyone else's.

There was a general shuffling to something like order, if not attention.

'Well done, Kate,' he continued, smiling. 'Nice to have a star of TV and radio right here in our midst. But not for very long, I'm afraid, ladies and gentlemen. The Super wants to see you in his office, Kate. About five minutes ago.'

'Not till she's touched up her lipstick!' Cope objected.

Kate stuck out a hand towards him. 'Lend us yours, Gaffer, will you?'

If Kate was surprised by a large TV and state-of-the-art video in Detective Superintendent Neville's office, she wouldn't show it. Nor would she allow her eyes to widen at the thousands of pounds' worth of computer technology making itself at home on his desk, or, indeed, at the general ambience, which owed little to the scuffed Victorian accommodation they all shared. Clever disposition of lighting and plasterboard had entirely changed the appearance of the room, which was newly-carpeted. The furniture was new, too. Stylish. To match his suit and haircut, no doubt.

She told herself it was natural that a new man would want

to establish himself so totally. He would no doubt wish to eradicate all evidence of his predecessor, currently occupying some other type of Her Majesty's accommodation, though no doubt considerably less gracious and shared with company even less genteel than the squad. But it was unusual that he'd eradicated all the usual macho traces: not a sporting trophy, not a photo of a police or other worthy in sight. In fact to her mind, the walls were rather bare – they could have done with some jolly prints, the sort she and Colin had put up until they'd spawned girlie posters over Selby's desk and everything had had to be removed, including little patches of paint where the Blu-Tack™ had been.

'DS Power!' He emerged from behind his desk and clasped her hand, covering with both his. Unlike hers, they were newly manicured. His aftershave was subtle enough to be expensive. 'Rodney Neville. I'm sorry we didn't have an opportunity to speak yesterday. I gather you were doing an excellent job of dealing with our media friends.'

'Some of them were dealing with me, Sir.' She allowed herself an ironic smile. 'I expect you've seen today's press.'

'And intend to capitalise on it,' he said.

Her heart sank at his enthusiasm. It was better to say nothing. She stayed at as near attention as she could with his hands still enfolding hers. When she was finally released, she allowed herself to stand at ease, chin up, posture a model for any rookie who happened to be watching.

'Oh, do sit down, Sergeant.' If it was a command, it came from a relaxed and smiling face, the skin in the sort of condition that came, she suspected, from meticulous skin-care. He himself turned to a bookshelf supporting a coffee machine. Kate had met the machine's bigger and pricier brothers in Florence. If he offered her coffee it should be excellent.

He did. She accepted, placed the cup and saucer on his desk, and continued to wait.

'Now, Kate – I may call you Kate?'

'Sir,' she nodded.

'This meeting today is only one of many I intend to set up with members of my Command Unit. I believe absolutely in efficient communication – in fact, I want you to regard my office door as permanently open. True, the police service is necessarily hierarchical but that shouldn't deter you in any way.'

Hierarchical and patriarchal, she thought. But did not say. Instead she smiled and nodded.

'Now, it's quite clear that your communication skills are excellent,' he beamed.

If standing still, sitting upright and nodding were communication skills, no doubt it would be difficult to fault them. On the other hand, she had no idea on what other, more searching criteria, he'd made his judgement. She risked a cool, 'Sir?'

'You handled the Press very well yesterday, I understand. And you're clearly photogenic.' He tapped the *Guardian* and *The Times*. Some hack had made a great deal of profit out of Alan Grafton's death. 'The service is always on the look-out for people with original talent. Your future could lie in that direction. Think the media, Kate. Think televisual. Think *Crimewatch*, Kate. Think fronting that.'

'With respect, Sir, I'm a detective, not an actress.'

He looked at her in surprise. 'Have you never watched the programme?'

'Not recently.'

'Come, Sergeant, all work and no play!'

'My recent personal circumstances have not been conducive to watching television, Sir.'

He raised elegant but disbelieving eyebrows. 'Well, serving officers are involved at all levels, including in front of the cameras. Should a vacancy arise, I am minded to nominate you as a likely presenter. *The new face of the West Midlands Police.*' His fingers drew quotation marks round the sentence. 'You're personable, well-turned out and clearly intelligent.'

So the attribute she valued most was bottom of his list. She smiled politely.

He was waiting for her to say something, wasn't he?

'Thank you, Sir. I have to point out, though, Sir, that the same can be said for many of my colleagues. I'm new to the squad, to the area. I—'

'It would look well in your CV, Sergeant. Think career.' He smiled. 'And it doesn't hurt to let those dimples show.'

The interview was clearly over. Thank God.

'So much against my will, it'll be you and Colin who will start going through Grafton's effects.' Graham had called her into his office almost as soon as she'd returned from Neville's.

She nodded. 'It'll be better than the job the Super has in mind for me,' she said. 'Has he told you?'

'The Boy Wonder?' He shook his head. 'Enlighten me – unless it's confidential.'

'It is between you and me. I'd hate the others to get hold of it. He only wants me to go on the bloody telly, doesn't he? Fronting some crime programme. Bastard!'

'It would be a great opportunity,' Graham said mildly. 'Tea? Or are you full up with expensive espresso coffee?'

'I know he gave me some, but I don't actually recall getting a chance to drink it. I want to be a cop, Graham. Not a well-groomed doll.'

Another man might have told her to come off it. Graham smiled, but with restraint. 'The women on that programme are actually top-notch officers,' he said. 'And it certainly wouldn't do you any harm, career-wise.'

'Oh, don't you start using his lingo! *Minded, personable* – is it pompo-verbosity or verbo-pomposity?'

He stiffened. If she'd forgotten the difference between them in rank, he hadn't, had he? And then he smiled, his face softening, his eyes warm. 'Not many people have read Gowers' *Plain Words*, Kate. I think it's pompo-verbosity, though.'

'We had this brilliant English teacher,' she said, helping herself from the tin of biscuits he was shaking at her. 'She made us read Gower and that essay by Orwell, the one in which he listed all the rules no writer should break. Not part of the syllabus, but useful.'

'And it explains why your reports are always a pleasure to read. And I shall look forward, of course, to what you have to say about Grafton. The brother that ID'd him will be at Grafton's house to unlock it for you this afternoon.'

Colin looked up from his desk as she went back into the office. 'Harry says he thinks the woman who wouldn't talk may have called in again, but she spoke so quietly they couldn't make out what she was saying.'

'Get them to do something with the tape – enhance the quality.'

'Costs money,' he said, half-heartedly. He was feeding her a line, wasn't he?

'If she cares enough to call three times – what do you think, Gaffer?'

'You and your bloody hunches are going to bankrupt the Force,' Cope grunted. 'Beg your pardon, the Service. Go on, see what them boffins can do.'

She nodded. 'By the way, Gaffer – this Grafton business. Thanks for your support – I take it it was you that got me on to this Grafton case?'

'I like a woman with a bit of spirit,' he said.

'Whatever that's supposed to mean,' she said, as she and Colin headed for the stairs.

'"Yes", I suppose. Plus an implied criticism of Fatima.'

'Kate! Sergeant Power!'

She turned. It was Fatima herself, gesturing to the phone.

'Hell! I'd better get it, though!' Who on earth might that be?

Fatima covered the handset as Kate came through the door. She grinned, mouthing, 'A man. Personal.' As she passed it over, however, she added, 'Not the same one as the other day, if that's what you're wondering.'

Kate pulled a face. That was precisely what she had been wondering, hoping even. 'Kate Power,' she said, her disappointment making her curt.

'Detective Sergeant Power?' She recognised the voice but couldn't place it. 'Patrick here. Patrick Duncan. We met in fairly inauspicious circumstances yesterday. I wondered if you'd had any more thoughts about the deceased?'

'I'm checking out his papers and so on this afternoon,' she said.

'To help you with your theory that he had everything to live for?'

'We need as much background as we can get,' she said, noncommittally.

'Trying to blow my thesis out of the water, eh? Well, you won't succeed. But I think you should try. In the interests of truth. Why don't we talk things over – a drink, perhaps – this evening?'

'I'll check my diary.' All she had planned, of course, was a visit to Aunt Cassie. And a basketful of ironing. 'It couldn't be before eight-thirty,' she said.

'Shall we say nine, then? Any preferences for where we eat?'

'Eat?'

'Why not? After a day's work!'

She mustn't make a big deal out of this. 'OK. No preferences, anyway. The only places I've checked out so far socially are a pub near Symphony Hall, a Balti restaurant in Kings Heath – oh, and a wonderful Kings Heath chippie specialising in the most marvellous chicken tikka in a naan.'

'Are you based in Kings Heath then? Splendid – I know just where we'll eat.'

'It doesn't have to be Kings Heath—'

'But no reason why it shouldn't be. Giovanni's, that's where. Just off the High Street, opposite Safeway's car park. Would nine-ish suit you? Excellent. I'll look forward to that.'

Would she? His voice told her it wasn't a purely business meeting. Could she really want to go out socially with him? Biting her lip, she looked for the phone to replace the handset.

Fatima pointed, ironically. The phone was at the extreme edge of her desk. There was a barricade of files between it and Fatima's work-space. On top of the files was a styrofoam cup of greyish liquid which was probably the coffee that Selby had left there earlier. He himself was nowhere around.

'Is he being a pain?' What Kate couldn't ask was why Fatima simply didn't plonk it back on Selby's desk.

Fatima shook her head. 'He just finds it funny to leave a drink just where I might reach for it without thinking. When we were out yesterday, he kept offering me sweets and crisps.'

'You don't think he's just being generous?' Kate said, her heart not in the question.

'Do you?' Fatima asked.

Kate shook her head. 'I don't think he knows the meaning of the word.'

'Maybe he's just trying to proselytise? Turn me to the paths of Christian righteousness?'

'It would be nice to think he knew the meaning of those words. Oh, shit!' Kate shoved a chair over to Fatima's side. 'What are you going to do? Apart from resist temptation, that is?'

Fatima shrugged. 'What would you do?'

'Have you tried simply explaining and asking for his co-operation? No? I don't say that it'll succeed but you never know.'

'Too many people are hostile to Islam.'

'Do you really think it's anything as sophisticated as that?

Not just like some stupid prat thinking it's clever to offer a bacon sandwich to a vegetarian?'

Fatima looked her straight in the eye. 'He may be a prat, but that doesn't mean he can't be a malicious prat.' She smiled. 'Kate – that phone-call upset you, didn't it?'

Kate blinked. 'Not – well, yes, maybe. Not so much upset as unsettled me. My bloke was killed only a few months ago and this path's asked me out for a drink. Then it became a meal. After sunset,' she risked, to be rewarded with an answering grin.

'Is he nice?'

'I've only seen him in the morgue. He did yesterday's autopsy. Says he wants to discuss my theories about Alan Grafton's death.'

Fatima nodded. 'There's always the possibility that that's precisely what he wants to do.'

'Hm. He may be just a path. But that doesn't mean he can't be an amorous path.'

Fatima threw up her hand to acknowledge the hit. 'And what if he is an amorous path: is that a problem?'

Kate shook her head. 'I don't know. I really don't know.'

Chapter Seven

'Doesn't look much like a business tycoon's residence,' Colin said, as he and Kate stood under an inadequate porch waiting to be let into Alan Grafton's house.

'Remind me never even to contemplate moving into – where is this? Acocks Green?' She dashed a futile hand at a dollop of rain, presumably sloshing from a blocked gutter.

'It's not so bad when it's fine,' Colin said. 'Ah, do I hear action?'

'Can you *hear* action? Or only see it?'

'You know what I mean.'

The door was opened by a paler, more delicate version of Alan Grafton.

'Good afternoon. Mr Grafton, is it? Mr Adrian Grafton? I'm Detective Constable Colin Roper, and this is Detective Sergeant Kate Power.'

What had made Colin so voluble? He usually left this sort of introduction to her.

'Yes. Adrian Grafton. A.C. Grafton, as opposed to A.J. Grafton. Can't think what my parents were thinking of, giving us the same initials, well, nearly. Always got the wrong post, so embarrassing at times.'

Someone else too voluble – the sort of reaction to stress they were all familiar with in bereaved relatives and friends.

Another drip down her neck prompted Kate to speak. 'You'll know we're investigating the circumstances surrounding your brother's unfortunate death, Mr Grafton.'

'Oh, call me Adrian – everyone does!' He smiled. It was a horribly winsome smile.

'I will if you get us out of this rain.' Kate fancied her smile was bracing.

He stood aside, gesturing courteously.

He watched them as they wiped their feet, and took their coats to hang them on an old-fashioned hall-stand. Kate stepped forward to look more closely: in the elaborate woodwork of the back panel there was a brilliant turquoise enamel inlay in a copper plaque.

'Ah, you have an eye for a good piece, Sergeant,' Adrian said. 'Arts and Crafts. Lovely, isn't it?'

The plaque was. On the other hand the hall stand was too ornate, too heavy, and dominated the narrow hall.

'Now, Alan used the box-room as an office. Everything else is just a normal home. Except – well, you'll see what fine taste he had. Do you want to look round down here before you go up? Looking for Clues?' His winsome smile inserted a capital C.

Kate nodded. 'If you don't mind. What we're looking for is anything that will help us work out why he died as he did.'

'You put that very tactfully, Sergeant! Did he fall or was he pushed? Isn't that what you're wondering?'

She smiled. And waited.

'Firstly, as I told the other policemen, you know, the ones in uniform, as far as I know he didn't have a single enemy. Not one. But there again, he'd just done this fabulous business deal – why should anyone with his prospects want to – to kill himself?' Adrian's voice cracked. He turned briefly from them.

'This must be very upsetting for you, Sir,' Colin said quietly.

'I'm all right as long as I can be interested or angry. My poor kid brother – and some kinky bastard strings him up to die.'

Kate's eyes flickered to Colin's: he'd registered the word, too.

But Adrian noticed. 'Oh, you know, these guys and their funny sex. Strange underwear, plastic bags and oranges in their mouths.'

'Did Alan ...?' On the face of it, she'd have thought Adrian a more likely candidate.

'No, Sergeant, he did not. To the best of my knowledge – isn't that the phrase? – to the best of my knowledge, Alan was just a decent ordinary guy. To the best of my knowledge ... No, we weren't all that close. Talked on the phone, that sort of thing. Family Christmases—'

Was he cold or repressed? She must remember his brother had just died horribly.

'Your parents—?' Colin prompted.

'Dad had a stroke two years back. Like that.' He snapped his fingers. 'Pity Ma can't – she's got some sort of dementia. Only sixty-three.'

'I'm so sorry.' Kate meant it. Aunt Cassie might have her moments but thank God she had her full complement of marbles.

He shrugged. 'Tea or coffee? I suppose I can't offer you what I'm going to spend the afternoon sinking: a decent red wine. If one's got to pick over the bits and pieces, one might as well do it in style.' But there were tears in his eyes.

'I'll make it, shall I?' Colin pushed open a door which did in fact lead to the kitchen.

Kate followed. The place was immaculate – even to the J-cloth wrung out and hung to dry over the tap. The fridge was switched off, empty, door ajar. The freezer was still running, however, with a typed note of the contents stuck to it.

'Unbelievable, isn't it?' Colin gestured. 'Imagine, going through all this – leaving it as if you wanted to find it nice and clean when you came back from your holiday.'

'Maybe he did. Maybe he simply didn't use it when he got

back on Sunday – didn't have time to restock with milk and everything. D'you want to have black tea or black coffee?'

'Try that tin over there,' Adrian suggested, coming up behind them. He pointed, but wouldn't pass it.

They followed his finger. The hand-printed label said, POWERED MILK.

'It was one of the last things Ma wrote,' Adrian said. 'He said it made him smile every time he used it. He had this vision of Ma casting aside her zimmer, slipping her knickers outside her dress and taking off to right the world.' He spread his arms to demonstrate.

Colin winked affectionately at Kate, but didn't say anything. Kate screwed a ball of kitchen towel and passed it across to Adrian; Colin made coffee for three, stirring more sugar than was good for any of them into each mug.

'You know, Adrian,' Kate said at last, 'I really think it might be better if you didn't do very much down here. I'm certainly keeping an open mind about your brother's death—' Whatever the evidence might suggest.

'And that means not dusting his china and packing it away before some shitty little bastard breaks in and smashes it all?' His voice rose dangerously.

She hesitated. 'I take your point. I suppose it's statistically unlikely that anyone would have left prints on a vase rather than on a door or something. But—'

'I wear cotton gloves: eczema. I'm allergic to household dust. Amongst other things.'

'Pack them by all means, then. But don't wipe them.'

The box-room – Alan's office – was less intimidating, but still terribly tidy. There were stalks of filing-trays, several piles of envelope files on a shelf, an obvious system in the filing cabinet drawers.

They divided the work between them, Kate knowing that Colin's would be even more meticulous than her own. They would list each file, with a clear summary of its contents, and then one of them would work through the computer. Downstairs Adrian was listening to light music as he stowed china. She'd never known anyone who collected china until today. Was it like stamps, a matter of the rarity? Or like train spotting – collecting a whole series? Or maybe – she thought of the jewel-like enamel in that otherwise hideous hall-stand – it was for the sheer beauty of something? That would certainly fit what little picture she had of Alan – he'd spoken of his leather and wool with more enthusiasm than if they'd simply been investments. They were more than money in the bank.

Or overdraft in the bank. Top of one pile was a letter from his manager, informing him that his overdraft facility was withdrawn, as from – she checked her watch – Monday's date. Looking at the size of it, she could see why. But was that enough to make a man hang himself?

She checked another file. Trade references. Symphony Leather Products was worth £10,000 worth of credit, according to two other companies. There was also a bank reference – '...to the best of our knowledge ...' saying much the same thing. There was a collection of invoices, the earlier ones apparently paid with cash – did they get a discount? The later ones hadn't been paid – perhaps they were invoking their credit. Ah, here was a batch that had been paid after two months. She checked the dates. June, paid in August.

She turned to Colin. 'Can you make anything of this lot?'

He shook his head. 'They didn't teach us accounting where I went to school. How about you?'

'Me neither. Funny thing, though. I get this feeling that we're sitting on a gold mine here, pardon the pun. That everything's written on these papers if only we could understand them.' She slapped them against her open palm. At last she looked up. 'Got any decent contacts in Fraud?'

'Why not make an official approach?'

She shook her head in feigned shock. 'Cost centres, Constable, that's why not. Come on, there must be someone owes you a freebie.'

To her horror, he blushed. His horror, too. At last he smiled sheepishly. 'I'll see what we can do. Should we take this lot away or leave it locked up here?'

'I can just see Cope's face if we turn up with more clutter. Yes, we'll take it with us. And the computer and those disks.'

'In for a penny, in for a pound, eh?'

More morgue humour. She rolled her eyes. 'Are you sure that's in the best of taste?'

'No worse than your crack about gold mines.'

They suppressed their giggles – footsteps on the stairs. In a hurry and making for this room. Their raised eyebrows were mirror images of each other.

'Sergeant! Is it OK if I come in?'

'Sure – it's your brother's room,' she added, hoping he wouldn't notice the lack of logic.

'And these,' he said, flourishing them, 'are my brother's photos.'

At first sight, the photos didn't warrant such drama. Colin leafed through thirty assorted views of Florence. Michelangelo's David, outside the rain-drenched Palazzo Vecchio and indoors in the Accademia; Florence roofs in sunshine and in snow; several churches.

'I thought he was there on business,' Colin said.

'Let's just say he used his spare time efficiently,' Adrian said. 'Ah—'

'How did you get hold of them?' Kate cut in.

'The lunchtime's post. He always uses this quick postal service. And I thought – well, see what I mean?' He dabbed a forefinger on the next print.

They peered at a della Robbia bust.

'Ah. No, it must be the next one.' Carefully he eased the top photo sideways so it exposed half the next print. Another glazed terracotta della Robbia, this time a plaque with a young woman's head in three dimensions. As they watched he removed the top photo altogether. Beside the head was another, in exactly the same pose. A living woman's head. Kate's head.

'You seem to have taken it very calmly,' Colin said, as he shoved the last box of files into the boot. 'But I still think I ought to drive.'

She flicked him the keys. 'What else should I do?' She could think of a lot of things herself, but none of the options seemed appropriate.

'And you're sure he didn't say anything to you on the plane? About having seen you before?'

'I can't be positive ... I kept going deaf. He was kind and offered practical advice.' She pulled at her deaf ear. Any day now it would be worth a visit to a GP. 'But it was no more than a tentative suggestion we should meet for a meal. Tell you what: stop at that chemist's – I want some ear drops.'

Colin looked at her sideways. 'I don't buy that. No, more like a case of softly-softly. After all, what man's going to say to this woman dripping with cold: I fell in love with you in this museum?' He signalled and pulled over.

'I didn't have the cold then. Maybe I'd turned out to have feet of clay.'

'Or nose of snot. You'll have to tell Graham, though.' He slid another look at her 'What's the betting he won't like it?'

'No takers.' She cut him off abruptly. She had shared a moment with Graham that no one would ever know about, when, staring into the murky waters of a Birmingham canal he'd told her he could offer no more than friendship. Not that she'd asked for more. And there'd been a gulf between the words he'd used and the tone in which he spoke them. His pain had been tangible.

And meanwhile there was a joke running round the squad: Graham fancies Kate, OK. The graffiti level of tact and subtlety.

Would it have made any difference if any of them had really thought Graham loved her? Not much. For the Selbys of this world it would have made matters infinitely enjoyable, of course.

And Kate? Did Kate fancy Graham, OK? In the warmth and companionable silence of the car, she could admit to herself that if she'd ever been able to love anyone after Robin's death, it might have been Graham Harvey. When they'd stood together, that cold winter's day, it had been all she could do not to turn and hold him. There'd been moments since when she wanted to stretch her hand to the back of his head, where the hair tucked neatly into the neck. It was a good shape.

Like Robin's.

Since it was Colin beside her, she could say it. 'You think you're over it, don't you? And then something sets you off. A day like this, a glance down a dingy rush-hour street, and I think I see Robin. I pick up his aftershave in the queue at Sainsbury's. Damn it, even you wear it sometimes. It smelt different on him, though.'

Trying to open his door without having it removed by a passing juggernaut, he asked, 'How's the counselling going?'

She snorted. 'It turns out I've got myself in for the sort that deals not in emotions but in changing behaviour. So I have to look at pictures of bugs and maggots and any day now I've got to have the little bleeders crawling over my hands. To get myself habituated.'

'Even that's not the same as opening a tin full of them on your desk, though.'

'No. Oh, I'll stick it out, don't worry. But – and this really is for your ears only – I sometimes wonder if I need someone to poke round in the middle of my head. Help me sort out why I'm putting up with the problems with my house, for instance. Still, the kitchen floor should be laid tomorrow – I shall be in an hour or so late. I've warned Cope and Harvey.'

'Are you going to phone in and leave a message with Selby? Out of purest scientific curiosity, of course.'

'I'm tempted. Very tempted. I still have this gut-feeling that it was Grafton who tried to phone me the other day. And an equally strong feeling that it was Selby who "lost" the message.'

'With a view to simply messing things up for you? Or to land Fatima in it? You have to phone in, Kate. Mention it to Harvey when you tell him about the photo.'

She grunted assent.

The rain drove into their faces as they sprinted across to the chemist's. She stopped short in the porch. 'What are you doing here? I only wanted ear-drops!'

'I thought you might want to make it an official visit. It is a pharmacy, and we are supposed to be looking at pharmacy thefts.'

She nodded. 'My head must be even thicker than I thought.'

'Fancy that,' she said. 'Good job you came with me to prompt me, Colin.'

'Oh, you'd have got round to it sooner or later.'

'Better sooner. So now we've got another pharmacy that's been done over. Vitamin tablets again! Does this really make sense? Tell you what, as soon as I've got a moment I'm going to talk to someone in Drugs.'

The rain was now a steady downpour, and pedestrians wrestling with umbrellas were taking ludicrous risks dashing to buses across the road.

'Later than I realised,' Colin said at last. 'What do you say to briefing Harvey and then sitting this lot out over a snifter?'

'Snifter?'

'Sorry. Tipton for drink. Don't ask me why. Anyway—?' He pulled into one of several empty spaces.

'Rain-check time, I'm afraid.'

'Oh, it's football training tonight, isn't it?'

'Should be. But I've phoned the BB. I'm not hanging round wet car parks supervising teenage kids in this weather with this lot rattling round inside me: it'd be asking for trouble. The blokes who ran it while I was off sick will just have to do it again. No, I've promised to see Cassie instead. And I can't put that back because afterwards I'm having a drink with Pat the Path. A meal, actually. Don't ask me why.'

Unclipping his seatbelt he looked her in the eye. 'Because he's an attractive guy and there's no reason why you shouldn't. That's why.'

Harvey was running down the stairs as Kate and Colin pushed their way through the heavy doors. If Kate expected him to slow down long enough to ask how they'd got on, he didn't.

'My room first thing tomorrow,' he flung over his shoulder.

She shrugged at Colin and gave chase.

'Gaffer! I'm going to be late in – remember?'

He paused long enough to grimace in irritation. 'Soon as you can make it, then.'

'Sir!' she mouthed at his retreating back.

Chapter Eight

'I can't tell you how much I'm looking forward to having the new kitchen flooring laid,' she told Cassie, pouring her another vermouth.

'I don't know why you needed it,' Cassie said, indicating with a jerk of her head that she wanted her glass on the table beside her. She wasn't in bed, but was reclining on the day bed. 'Those quarry tiles would have polished up a treat.'

'They got badly damaged when they put the new membrane in,' Kate reminded her, wishing she could throw open a window, the room was so hot. 'The men discovered rising damp, remember, and I had to have the floor dug up and all that plaster taken off the walls.' It frightened her that she was having to go over all this again. 'Well, it's all dried out and the walls painted – you remember, that pale green? – and before I got to bed I shall sweep the concrete ready for the Vinolay. And the men come tomorrow!' It would be such a treat to be able to pad around in bare feet on something other than all that flaking concrete. All she had to do then was finish emptying those damned boxes and she'd have a home. 'I thought I might have a house-warming party when it's all finished,' she said. She'd said it idly, without any real thought, but, yes, it would be nice, to gather a few people together.

'I don't know where you'll put everyone,' Cassie said.

'Though come to think of it you can't have all that many friends up here – too busy gadding about. What with the chapel and the football and all this flying round Europe.'

Kate bit her lip. Which was worse, having to admit that her aunt was right about the lack of friends, or the injustice about her gadding? True, she'd had a holiday, but that was more or less on police orders, to speed her recuperation after the double trauma of the accident in which she'd hurt her leg. It had been dreadful to have almost a re-run of the accident which had injured her and killed Robin. And the man running her down with a van had been someone she'd thought was a friend. Yes, she'd needed a break. As for her involvement with the Baptist church, that had been on her aunt's instigation, and coaching the football team had simply arisen through that. But she hadn't made any friends amongst the congregation, had she?

'Who will you invite, anyway?' Cassie asked. 'That man you call gay, the queer, no doubt – you know he came to see me while you were away. Proper little charmer, isn't he? More like one of the male nurses they have here. Funny job for a man, if you ask me, nursing. Most of them queer, I suppose. Though I don't know what one of them's doing in the police.'

Trying as hard as he could not to let any of his colleagues know he was gay, that was what. 'Working hard,' she said out loud. 'He's an exceptionally good officer. And a very kind friend.'

'Hmph. I'd have thought they'd have wanted someone tough in the police. A proper man.'

Kate said nothing: however much her aunt was provoking her, she wouldn't be drawn. And she certainly wouldn't offer Selby as an example of just the sort of tough officer no one would want. Selby – outside work – wasn't worth the breath it would take to say his name.

'And there's that coloured woman next door,' Cassie pursued. 'That Jamaican. I suppose you'll have to have her.'

'I'm very fond of Zenia. She's good woman: I like her very

much. And despite her troubles, I know she's been to visit you here.'

'I don't know why she bothered. Mind you, she thinks the same as me about Rosie. You remember: her husband – so-called – is beating her up. You'll have to do something about it, Kate. She's got a huge bruise on her cheek. You ring the bell and get her up here – see for yourself.'

Kate shook her head. 'There's nothing I can do if she doesn't want me to. But I'll have a word with some of my colleagues in the Domestic Violence Unit – they may have some ideas.'

'Domestic – what?'

'Violence Unit. It's to protect women from their part-ners—'

'Unit. Partners. All these fancy terms. All these women need to do is walk out. I'd never have stood for a man trying to knock me about, I can tell you.'

Kate smiled. 'I'm sure you wouldn't. Nor would I. But some women—'

'Oh, you'll be telling me they've no choice. And you can stop sliding looks at your watch and thinking I don't notice.'

'OK. I'll look properly. And tell you I've got to go. I'm having a meal with someone tonight.'

Cassie heaved an exaggerated sigh. 'Don't tell me. He's coloured and queer and got only one leg.'

'He's a Home Office pathologist. White, middle-class, middle-aged. All I know about him is we disagree about a case I'm working on and he's got twinkly brown eyes and dimples.' She could have told her about Alan Grafton, she supposed. But she didn't relish discussing death, not in a place like this. And not with Cassie in this mood.

She stifled a sigh. Oh, it was fine to be tough, to be your own woman. But sometimes, just sometimes, it would be nice to have someone supporting you, sympathising with you, whatever happened.

In the corridor, she pulled herself together. There was Rosie, resplendent with her bruise. Kate stopped and smiled.

Rosie stopped too. 'The old woman's got the devil on her back today, all right,' she said.

Kate nodded: 'I suppose she's in a lot of pain.'

'Plain bad-tempered if you ask me.'

'What about you?' Kate asked, her eyes on the bruise.

'Door,' Rosie said shortly. And went on her way.

It was so good to have all her clothes to choose from! She'd had to leave them all in London while the major repairs were done on the house, and had only recently brought them up. She'd sorted them out while she was on sick leave, and she'd even had time to buy replacements for those she'd consigned to the hospice shop at the bottom of the road. How did she want to look tonight? She shook her hair free for a start. And reached for a dark red, semi-fitted dress that gave her height and took an inch or two off her hips. A pair of the soft Italian pumps that had worried Alan Grafton. No. Better be sensible: the rain was turning to sleet. Boots, then. Make-up. Jewellery – the ring Robin had given her less than a week before his death. She knew she looked good. She even gave a twirl in front of the wardrobe, as if she were a little girl going to a party. Or a young woman going on a date.

Walking up the High Street, she told herself she'd been infected by Aunt Cassie's irrepressible notions of romance. All she was doing was meeting a man who'd put her down in public.

Like Graham. It would be nice to know what was going on in his mind, these days. Kind to the point of tenderness one moment, next as authoritarian and bad-tempered as he'd been when they'd met on the stairs. And he was determined to keep her in her place – which was wherever he wanted to put her at the time, either as a delicate frail woman or as a subordinate to call to heel. Her reflection in Boots' window showed she was frowning unhappily, chewing off what remained of her lipstick. Bother Graham. Making her re-do her face in public like a Forties' vamp!

As she turned into Poplar Road she had a moment of unease: would she even recognise Patrick Duncan with his hair and face visible? Any more than he would recognise her? She crossed the road.

Running feet! Flipping her bag-strap over her head she prepared for whatever action was needed. But it was only Patrick Duncan.

'I was afraid you'd stand me up, I'm so late!' he said.

Her wristwatch told her he'd been prompt, but she smiled and let him open the door for her.

'Florence! But you won't be wanting Italian food again so soon!' Patrick slapped his forehead extravagantly.

'Why ever not? I couldn't taste anything while I was over there.'

'You can taste the Punt e Mes?'

'Hmm. Cheers!'

They were sitting in a tiny bar, having admired a tray of fresh fish flourished by an enthusiastic waiter. Despite Patrick's urgings, Kate had played safe, settling for steak rather than venturing into the gastronomic unknown.

They had to make conversation while they waited to be called through to their table: Kate felt a real effort was involved. In some ways it would make sense simply to give an account of her afternoon's work, which was, after all, the ostensible reason for his invitation. But Graham would want to be the first to know, especially about her appearance in one of Alan's photos.

'What are you doing for that sinusitis of yours?' Patrick reached across and touched her cheek.

It wasn't an intimate gesture, though: it was totally impersonal. He moved the fingertip slightly and pressed. She winced.

'See – I thought it was infected. Time to talk to your GP.'

'I shall feel such a failure if I do – I was talking to a pharmacist the other day who reckoned the only treatment I needed was steam.'

'If you use it often enough. Ah, do I detect a blush, Ms Power? How many times have you steamed it today, for instance?'

'Point taken. And this cold wind seems to be making it worse. It seemed to be blowing straight down the High Street.' It hadn't helped the deafness, either. She was having to lean intimately towards Patrick to hear what he said.

'"The North wind doth blow, And we shall have snow,"' he said. 'Up in Moseley it was already trying – nasty little flakes driving in the wind.'

'You live locally too, then?'

'Just off the main road.'

'So you'll have the same problem as me. Other people's cars.'

Obviously he didn't: the blank expression told her quite clearly that this was a man with a front drive and a garage. She had the feeling that this wasn't going to be an evening to remember.

Except in the end, it wasn't as bad as all that, though she was afraid some of its success might be attributed to the amount of alcohol they'd sunk. And the excellence of the food. Robin would have been in his element in a place like this – he'd have enjoyed the attractive pink and green decor, matching wine to food, savouring the liqueur at the end of the meal. Which was when, after talking almost non-stop about his passion for vintage motorcycles, Patrick had finally raised the question of Alan Grafton.

'And did you find anything to convince me that our friend was done in?' He passed her the plate of mints.

She shook her head. 'Do you really want to talk shop?' she parried, before she realised that such a question might well be wrongly construed.

'Only if it proves me right.'

'OK, I'm afraid you could be right. Except it seems odd, a man preparing to die spring-cleaning his kitchen. Leaving his fridge defrosted, that sort of thing.'

'Odd? Eminently practical, if you ask me. Particularly if he had family who'd have to come and sort everything out. Quite a generous gesture. What about his paperwork?'

'Neat and methodical to the point of anal retentive, if I remember my psychology classes.'

And he plunged her into talk of her degree and then her master's, fleshing out her account of her life in Manchester with accounts of his own stint there.

She became more and more aware of his physical presence – his maleness. Hell, it was the booze, wasn't it, converting an ordinary middle-aged man – yes, he must be older than Graham, in his mid-forties – into someone who was all too desirable.

And then she remembered she had to prepare her kitchen floor.

He out-flashed her with his credit card, his idea of compromise being that she should pay next time. But no, his hands didn't linger as he helped her into her coat. It was the Maitre d' who kissed her hand. When they got outside, it was definitely snowing. And the snow was definitely lying.

'Are you walking too?' she asked. 'Because it's going to be driving into your face all the way back.'

They walked the twenty yards or so back to the High Street together. As they left the shelter of the side road, the wind blasted the words from their mouths. No time for tenderness, then.

His face gave him away. 'Look, I must walk you back,' he said, clearly wishing he didn't have to.

'Nonsense. I'm only four roads away from home.'

'But—' he protested without any strength.

'What's a quarter of a mile after my years on the beat? Thanks, Patrick, for a lovely evening.'

'We'll do it again soon – yes?'

'Lovely.'

They kissed – once on both cheeks, very formal.

She wished they hadn't. It reminded her of the warmth and smell of a male face, and all her scurry home couldn't eradicate her longing for more.

Chapter Nine

'There's no way I can lay it on this, me love,' the young man said, jabbing his toe into the concrete of her kitchen floor.

He didn't look old enough to have left school, let alone to cast such a final opinion.

'But—'

He shook his head sadly. 'It's your surface, love. Look at it, all breaking up. See?' He bent and scraped a bit more away with his finger nail. 'Now, if I lay it on that, you'll have lumps and hollows in your Vinolay, too – and where it's proud, it'll wear through quick as you like. Well, a bloody sight quicker.'

He was right, of course. 'So what—'

'What I need to do is skim it – put a levelling compound on it, leave it to set overnight and then come in first thing the next morning to put the Vinolay straight down. Don't worry. The boss should have told you this. I'll sort it out with him when I get back. It'll cost you a bit more, but when we've done it, it'll look a treat. Good quality stuff you've chosen. Last you years.'

Kate reached for her diary. 'But what about the washing machine and the freezer? Won't they have to be moved if you're going to skim the whole floor?'

'I've got some industrial polythene'll cover the washer. It'll have to spend the night outside, see. But we'll have to cox and box with that freezer. What d'you keep in there? Bodies?'

'I'll make sure there aren't any left,' she said. 'Now, how soon can you come?'

'As soon as you can fix up to spend the night somewhere else. Once that stuff's down, you mustn't even think of coming in here or the whole lot'll ripple summat shocking! Joking,' he added. 'But you really can't use the kitchen at all. Not till we've got the flooring down. Now, the earliest I can do – let's see . . . End of next week suit you? If I come in Thursday night and again Friday morning?'

She shook her head. 'I can't guarantee what time I shall get home.'

Another kind smile. 'No probs. You drop your key round to the boss whenever it's convenient. I'll use it to let me and me mate in, Thursday and Friday. Then I'll lock up and drop it through your front door when I go out. Either that or you leave it with a neighbour.'

Zenia, when well, worked shifts. Her husband Joe was a teacher. There was the burglar alarm . . . She pulled a face.

'Well, we have to be honest, don't we? The Old Bill'd soon be on to us if every house we laid flooring in got burgled!'

'I very much hope so,' she said.

She couldn't stop crying. No matter how she told herself it only meant another week before she had her floor, she couldn't stop crying. She sat on the stairs, hugging the phone like a comforting toy and willed herself to stop crying long enough to phone into work. Yes, she'd reminded Graham she'd be late, but she wanted to leave a message with Selby just to see if it would get through. And she would, as soon as she could stop crying.

At last she put down the phone and trudged upstairs. Cold water then hot tea. With the call to Selby in between.

A glance at her face was enough to tell her that it would be at least half an hour before her eyes returned to anything like normal. God, she looked a mess. And damn it if the tears didn't start all over again, almost as if they came from somewhere outside her. Grabbing loo roll, she perched on the edge of the bath.

If she could work out what she was crying for, maybe she'd regain control. Robin? Dead these six months. But the pain of waking to find him not there, the pain of turning to him and finding him not there — yes, the pain was still very much alive. But it was diminishing, if imperceptibly. Look at last night. She'd have welcomed far more contact with Patrick than he'd seemed keen on. And look at her relationship with Graham. Six weeks ago she'd fancied she might be falling in love with him. A nasty little bitch on heat, that was what she was turning into. Just what Selby and his laddish friends would have predicted. With their coarse gestures and obscene language, they'd have been right.

Up to a point.

It wasn't — surely it wasn't — just sex she wanted? It was companionship. Surely. A friend. The sort of friend Cassie had been, someone you could talk to, enjoy being with. Now Cassie was becoming an irascible old woman, critical of whatever she did. Fatima? Still a very cool colleague. Colin, now, he was a friend. Yes. But he showed no signs at all of wanting to include Kate in his private hours, however much he was prepared to enter hers. She managed a rueful snort of laughter — perhaps it was Colin she should invite herself to for the night she had to leave home. That was better. She pulled herself upright.

And just for the record she ought to see if any burglaries had taken place in houses the flooring men had visited. Oughtn't she? Despite the transparent honesty of the young man? She'd compromise — rustle the grapevine.

The first thing to do was phone in with Selby's little test. She got through after enough rings to get her fingers tapping with frustration. Don't say the silly bugger was playing solitaire on his computer again. If she caught him at it, she'd have to make an issue of it.

He answered at last.

She gave her message: that she'd been delayed but would be in as soon as she could.

'You all right?' Selby asked.

'Fine.'

'Only if I didn't know you better, Ma'am, I'd say you were having a cry, like.'

Bastard! It wasn't sympathy that motivated him, but nosiness and a bit of good gossip for the lads.

'I suppose you haven't noticed the fact I've had a cold ever since I came back off leave? And it seems to have turned to sinusitis.'

'No wonder you've been having a cry, then. Nasty thing, sinusitis. Or is it the time of the month, then? What shall I tell the gaffer?'

'You'll tell him that I've been delayed and I shall be in as soon as I can. Full-stop.'

Still fuming, she tried to phone her GP for an appointment: maybe this would legitimise her lateness. To herself. OK, perhaps to Graham, too. The line was engaged. She jabbed the re-dial button with increasing irritation while she made and drank a coffee. OK, the only answer was to stop off at the surgery and get into work even later.

Kate had done no more than hang up her jacket and notice that the dead coffee – what point was Fatima trying to make, for God's sake? – still lurked on Fatima's desk when Graham appeared at the office door, gesturing with his head.

She followed immediately.

Unsure of his mood, she remained standing. If he offered her tea she could take the upholstered chair; otherwise the upright wooden one might be a more tactful option. He lifted the kettle; she sat comfortably.

While he waited for the kettle to boil, Graham leaned on the back of his chair, eyes amused. 'And how are your period pains, DS Power?'

She grimaced. 'So at least Selby deigned to pass on some message!'

'Indirectly, shall we say?' He turned back to the kettle and made two mugs of drinking chocolate. 'There was still snow on the ground when I came in,' he said, as if justifying the extravagance.

Kate hadn't noticed, didn't want to pursue discussion about the weather. 'So what's this about my period pains?'

'Just a loud and public announcement about women and their habits, with the word bloody much in evidence. He's had a bollocking, Kate – in public and again in private.'

'Did he remember – I use the word loosely! – to pass on my message? To you or Cope?'

He shook his head. 'Apart from the public joking, no. Been setting traps again?' His voice was serious.

She nodded, unrepentant. 'Looks like a long-term problem, doesn't it? When I joined your squad, you tried to persuade me to grass him up. I said I'd rather deal with it myself. But I've a nasty suspicion that – while not actually giving up on me! – he may be harassing Fatima now. You know it's Ramadan and she's fasting. He keeps tempting her with food and drink.'

'Which she has left on her desk. Well, it's not a hanging offence.'

Her eyebrows shot up. The man had just been on an equal opportunities course, for God's sake.

Graham shifted under her gaze. 'OK. This time I want proof positive and he'll be out of here sooner than he can say "disciplinary". I'm not asking you, Kate. I'm telling you.'

She nodded.

'Are you all right, by the way? You do look peaky.'

'See how bloody insinuations stick! OK, sorry. Actually I've tried to see my doctor, but he's booked up till next week. I'll just have to be more conscientious with my steam inhalations. Sinusitis,' she explained, trying not to laugh at the expression on his face. 'Meanwhile,' she continued, 'yesterday afternoon was interesting. Colin and I had a look at Alan Grafton's house and contents.'

'And?'

'Nineteen-thirties semi. Some oldish furniture: the same age as the house, I suppose. He collected antiques. He had an enormous overdraft the bank was foreclosing on. And before you shrug and tell me it's obviously suicide, I'd like someone who knows about accounts to have a look at his papers. Maybe someone in Fraud. I did ask Colin if he knew anyone who owed us a favour. But there might be a lot of work and maybe it ought to be official.'

He shook his head. 'I was afraid you'd take this too seriously.'

'I think I have to. The other thing we found at his house, you see, was a photograph of me.'

He stared. 'You're joking.'

'You think I'd joke about a thing like that?' She gave him the details.

'What do you make of it?'

'I'm not sure there's anything to make of it. It might just be that he caught me standing beside that head and thought it would make a good shot.'

'But he sat next to you on the plane: did he mention seeing you before?'

'It's all so hazy . . . I reckon he did say something very vague about having seen me there. I made some silly joke. You know how you do—'

'If you're being chatted up by someone you don't fancy.' He leant on the last word slightly.

She grinned slightly, to acknowledge the reference. 'He did talk of taking me out to dinner; but he might have been joking. And he did say other things but I missed them – I was so deaf.'

'And did he try to contact you again?'

She got up and walked to the window. Fine snow was slicing across the sky. 'He may have tried to phone me here. Someone did. Fatima took a message. The message disappeared.'

'Fatima lost it?'

'Possibly. Or possibly not.'

'You mean someone might have "disappeared" it?' He was beside her at the window. The harsh light delved into his frown lines, making his skin look tired and unhealthy. 'Bloody hell! We're supposed to be fighting crime here and all some stupid bastard can do is play silly pranks.'

'If that's all they are.'

'Nail him, Kate. Just nail him. soon. OK?' He moved back to the desk.

'What do you want to do about the message not getting through this morning?' she asked.

'Your word against Selby's.'

'Unless you want me to get Telecom to send me an itemised list of today's outgoing calls from my number?'

'Proves you made a phone-call, doesn't prove you gave a message. Leave me to think about this.'

'Can I ask a favour?'

Shocked eyes caught hers. She held them.

'Don't consult anything except your own instincts, Graham. If you talk to the Super he'll see it as a wonderful chance to ship me off to the media.'

'For God's sake, I wouldn't want him to know about this. I keep dirty linen very private, Kate. If I talked to anyone, it'd be Cope.'

'Exactly.'

'For God's sake, Cope may be a rough diamond but he's the salt of the earth. And one of your fans.'

She stared at him, eyebrow raised.

He gave a sudden embarrassed grin. 'I suppose I mixed my metaphors.'

'I'm no school-teacher. You can split your infinitives and leave your participles hanging as far as I'm concerned.'

'But not rate Cope?'

'Just regard him as I do. A funny bugger. Hard one moment, vulnerable another. Human and fallible. Certainly a bully.'

Graham shook his head, more in disbelief than disagreement.

She looked at him under her brows and held his gaze. And then smiled. 'Thanks. And I can talk to Fraud and see what they say about Alan Grafton's accounts?'

'If this goes over budget—'

'OK. I'll see if Colin will call in that favour. By the way, have we got any unsolved break-ins?' Almost against her will she told him about her flooring.

'Worth a quick check. Get Fatima and Selby on to it. OK?' He looked at his watch. 'Meeting. Budgeting.'

'Great. See you, Graham, and – thanks.'

If her smile was sunny, his was troubled. One day she would ask him if he hated meetings that much. But what she would not ask him about was the latest addition to his desk. No, not a snazzy computer. A very large, heavy, silver frame. She'd not seen what it held, of course. But she'd bet her Christmas overtime it would be a photo of his wife.

Chapter Ten

Perhaps it was that heavy frame that put the idea of domestic strife into Kate's head. Not that she could imagine Graham lifting a hand in anger. Not even his voice. Though perhaps the cold withdrawal he'd specialised in recently was a means of control at home, too.

It was other means that she was thinking about, however. The sort that put bruises on the face of that care assistant at Cassie's home. Rosie, that was it. Angry with herself for not thinking about it earlier, she reached for the phone, though their office was only a corridor or two away.

'Domestic Violence Unit.' The woman's voice at the other end was cheery and positive. 'What do you do for lunch?' it asked, when Kate had introduced herself.

'Strong coffee.'

'Well, why don't you stretch a point and make it a sarnie? Come down and join us – then we'll go down to the pub for half an hour. Me – I'm Lorraine – and Midge. Go on, do you good.'

Any other day it might. But it felt as if the wind were slicing into her sinuses, and her eyes poured tears. Again. At least this time she wasn't crying, if such a distinction could be made. Her two DVU colleagues looked at her with obvious anxiety but seemed reassured. And relaxed visibly when they reached the shelter of a pub and her tears stopped. Presumably every day they heard nervous victims giving fictitious explanations involving friends being beaten. Not themselves, no way!

Both women would be in their late thirties, Lorraine white, Midge African-Caribbean. Lorraine, the sergeant and the older by a couple of years, sank heavily into a deep chintzy chair, before looking round. 'Hmph. All these familiar faces – it gets more like the police canteen every day. Except for the furniture. Funny, trying to pretend this is a country cottage bang in the middle of Brum. Still, it's a break, isn't it? And you can have a salad.' She gripped the pads of fat on her hips.

'*You* can have a salad,' Midge observed. '*I* shall have – oh, their chilli con carne's not bad.'

Kate had expected anyone sporting the nickname Midge to be grossly overweight, but in fact she was slight to the point of thinness. She was also surprisingly short. Both women were in plain clothes, but whereas Kate tried to look business-like, sometimes, she thought, adopting her own severely tailored uniform, these women obviously dressed to reassure their clients: cheerful tops and informal skirts.

She bought the first round – mineral waters for all – and settled for the chilli con carne with side salad. And, as an afterthought, chips.

'There's this nurse at the nursing home where my great-aunt's staying,' she said. She paused, catching a look flung from one woman to the other. 'No. If someone was knocking me around I wouldn't stay. I'll put up with a lot of things, but not, repeat not, violence. It really is, like I said on the phone, information for someone else.'

Lorraine gave an apologetic smile: 'We have this sort of double act. We go into it automatically, almost. So if we sound a bit heavy, a bit obvious, you will forgive us?'

Kate nodded. 'No need to apologise.'

'OK. For starters, you know we can't intervene – can't just turn up on the front door and offer to sort the bloke out

– without being invited. By someone or other,' Midge added, grinning. 'By the beat officer, often as not. And we can't wave magic wands. The woman's got to want to protect herself. Which means not continuing in the relationship as it is.'

'Who'd want to, if you were being beaten up?' Kate led with her chin. She knew many of the answers already – no money, no place to stay. 'You can't tell me many women actually enjoy it – ask for it?'

Lorraine looked hard at her over the rim of her glass. 'You batter away at a woman's self-esteem long enough, she'll think she does deserve bad treatment. Ah! Here's the food. Now, before I forget, you give that nurse one of these.'

Kate took what looked like a credit or a loyalty card.

'See? A woman can slip it into her purse, and no one will be any the wiser. You don't even have to talk to her about it – everything's pretty self-explicit – but if she does ask you can point out that that's our number. There.'

'My phone: some people get all the fun,' Midge observed.

'The thing to remember, Kate, is that brutality isn't always a matter of breaking bones. Some people do seem to thrive in really explosive relationships. But some men seem able to grind their partners down in unbelievable ways without ever hitting them.'

'Or without needing to hit them any more,' Midge put in dryly. She dabbed crisp-looking chips into the chilli con carne.

Kate followed suit. The chips were excellent.

'So what's it like in the hallowed halls of CID? For a woman?' Lorraine asked, as if to take her mind off her salad. She'd allowed herself a puny-looking slice of ham.

'A bit male.'

'What! After the Met? I'd have thought anything else would be a holiday after a stint down in the Smoke!'

Kate shrugged. 'I never had anything there but a bit of teasing. Not sexual harassment, ever. And we got very close, some of us. Maybe I'll make friends up here eventually.' It slipped out before she could stop it.

'Not so good up here?' Midge asked.

It wasn't worth prevaricating. She'd heard her voice give her away. 'I'm actually quite lonely. I got quite friendly with one couple, but we've rather drifted apart. Her brother was implicated in a very nasty case and – I think she rather blamed me. I've got a lovely next-door neighbour but she's got my cold squared – flu, really. Anyway, she works shifts. I do run a football team for the local Boys' Brigade but—'

'You don't go in for cradle-snatching. And I suppose the boys' parents are – all parents?'

'And solidly married.'

'And you don't do married men? Very wise.' Lorraine nodded sagely.

Except that she did, didn't she? Kate didn't reply.

Fatima was looking very pale when Kate got back, warmed by a brisk walk and the promise of some more time with Lorraine and Midge. It was a long time since she'd held a tennis racket in her hand, but Midge assured her she'd soon manage again, and promised to coach her at an indoor centre. Lorraine promised to take her cooking in hand, just as soon, that was, as she'd reached her WeightWatchers' target.

Selby, an indefinably cocky air about him, was clicking away so assiduously with his mouse that Kate wanted to pounce, there and then. But she didn't want to sink to his level and humiliate him by bawling him out in front of anyone else, and in any case, maybe she should be finding out what ailed Fatima. It could be sheer hunger. She sniffed. There was a strong smell of food in the room – cheese and onion sandwiches, and something fried. A sandwich at your desk was one thing, chips and burgers quite another. But so far as she knew there were no rules apart from those of courtesy and common sense. Or, at the other end of the spectrum, loud, crude complaints if someone's tuna on brown was deemed too smelly.

Anything was too smelly for someone on a dawn-to-dusk fast.

Hell, she'd taken food so much for granted. Should she have salad or a portion of chips with her meal? Why not both? Pile them on! And there was this woman allowing herself not so much as a glass of water, never mind whether it was still or sparkling or plain Severn-Trent H_2O.

Still, it was no good appealing to Selby's non-existent sense of humanity. No good either going over his head to Cope, who probably thought a thick pork chop with crackling would do Fatima good.

It would have to be something to float when she and Graham had another moment.

Meanwhile Fatima was digging in her desk. 'A couple of messages for you, Kate.'

'And she hasn't lost either of them. Bloody hell, this must be a first!'

'Shut it, Selby. Anything interesting?'

'Two. Harry Carter says someone's phoned and will you go down. The other was from a man who didn't give his name but asked you to call back.' Fatima waited until Kate was between her and Selby. 'Pat the Path.' she mouthed.

'Probably the Chief Constable – only Fatty's forgotten his name,' Selby offered.

Kate clenched her fists. 'You're way out of line,' she said, rounding on him. 'Way out. For God's sake, man, can't you remember the simple rule that you always support your partner? If you can't rely on each other in the bloody office, how can you trust each other in life or death situations? A bit of decent, human loyalty, please.'

'Ma'am.'

Damn the man. Impossible to tell how much submission, how much insolence the single syllable carried. And here were some of the others coming into the room. She didn't want a yelling match in front of them. If she didn't lose dignity, he'd lose face. Neither a good scenario for the squad.

She held out her hand for the notes. There was no doubting the anger in Fatima's eyes.

Trusting she could lip-read, Kate mouthed, 'The loo. Five minutes. OK?'

Pat the Path.'s answering service invited Kate to leave a message. She did. Then, picking up a couple of quite irrelevant files, she strolled out of the office, fetching up in the loo. The evil lighting made her hair look green and increased the swelling under her eyes to the size of weekend bags. Some of the skin round her lips and nose was flaking badly: she scraped at it irritably. She was so engrossed that she jumped when the door opened. Fatima, of course.

'I don't want any favours,' she said, before she'd shut the door properly. 'Ramadan is a time of temptation. We choose to undertake the fast. We don't expect other people to fast. Or even to be particularly considerate,' she added, breaking into a faint smile.

'But not to leave coffee on your desk or to wave food under your nose.'

'It shouldn't matter.' Fatima's face was stubborn again. It wouldn't matter. But—'

'But?' What else has he been doing, Fatima?'

Fatima wouldn't meet her eyes in the mirror. 'Let's just call it violating my personal space.'

'Groping you!'

Fatima turned away, shaking her head. 'Not quite.' She turned abruptly. 'Look, Sarge, I don't want to make a big deal out of this. OK?'

Kate looked straight at her, holding her gaze. 'If it's not a big problem we don't make a big deal out of it. But you looked awful in there just now and—'

'I just felt a bit sick. You get used to it.'

'The smell of food or something else that stinks? Look, Fatima, I meant what I said in there. Out there we have to trust each other with our lives? How can you function as partners if Selby's bullying you?'

'How can he trust me if I grass on him?'

How many times had Kate used the same specious argument to Graham? No wonder he'd been angry. She pushed her hands through her hair in exasperation before trying again. 'You'll tell me – please – if things get any worse. Not because I'm "Sarge" but because I—' She tailed off. If she'd said, *I'd like to be your friend* that would have all the wrong connotations. The most brutal of the men she'd worked with had thought all women officers were bikes or dikes. Selby might even have suggested to Fatima that Kate was one of the latter. She tried again. 'Because I believe in what I'm doing and I don't like little fuckwits like Selby giving the service a bad name.' God, she sounded pretentious even to her own ears. 'Sorry,' she added lamely.

Fatima looked uncomfortable, as well she might.

Kate tried one last tack. 'I also think the service is the better for having women in it. The woman who you replaced left. Altogether. I don't want you to leave. Or the next woman in the squad.'

This time Fatima smiled faintly. 'If it gets any worse ...' But she didn't promise to tell her.

The message Harry Carter had for her was much clearer, in tape quality and in content. They listened to it in the room set aside for the incoming calls, a minute or two from the front desk. A woman's voice said, 'Good morning. If you want to know who was responsible for Alan Grafton's death, ask Howard Sanderson.'

'That's it.' Harry said. 'Time I went back to my desk, love.'

'It's a lot,' she said, walking back with him. 'Middle-class, probably white, well-educated. An accusation against a possible killer. Harry, I could kiss you. Giving up your lunchtime like that.'

'I'm only the messenger,' he said. 'I mean, it was young Mandy on the switchboard who picked them all up. Like I said, she's a bright kid. But that doesn't mean I won't take you up on your offer when there's no one around.' He grinned, looking over her shoulder.

'Won the pools, Kate?' It was Graham, winking at Harry and then smiling at her with an almost frightening intensity, given the lightness of his words.

'Better,' she said. 'We've got a lead in the Alan Grafton business.'

'Some woman says that one Howard Sanderson killed him,' Harry added.

Should she correct him? Or would it be pedantic? She compromised. 'Or can help us with our enquiries,' she said dryly.

'Funny thing,' said Harry, with the air of someone pulling a rabbit from his hat, 'her voice sounds ever so like that woman we've had on the blower before. The one we were talking about, Kate.'

'Why didn't you tell me before, Sergeant?' Graham demanded, his face rigid once again. 'OK, Harry – give me the tapes.'

Chapter Eleven

Graham took the stairs two at a time. Kate followed a pace behind, as if he were royalty. He didn't speak until they reached his office.

There wasn't any question about which chair to take. Kate stood.

'Other tapes? Other tapes? There's something going on here that a civilian receptionist knows about that you haven't bothered to tell me?'

'Or DI Cope hasn't bothered to tell you,' Kate said quietly. 'He was going to try to authorise the funds to have the tapes improved. As it was they were virtually inaudible.'

'And?'

'And he hasn't told me what the current situation is.' One of them had to defuse the situation, even if it meant taking a risk. It had better be her. She went over to the kettle. Empty. At least there was water in the plastic bottle. 'Tea or coffee?'

He flung over to the window: had he been a teenage girl she'd have called the movement a flounce. She could see his knuckles whitening as he gripped the sill. OK. Herbal tea: something to calm him down, even though she found it disgusting. Leaving the tea bag to stew, as he preferred, she placed the mug beside one of the pots of geranium cuttings. He left it where it was.

So did she tiptoe away like a nurse leaving a patient? She had an idea he wanted to be alone with a capital A. Or she could confront him? Risky, in the circumstances. Or she could embark on a possibly futile wait, knowing, meanwhile, that waiting for her out there was an office full of paper she ought to be sifting through. Or some tapes to listen to.

She took the first tape from where he'd abandoned it, the corner of his desk, and slipped it into the tape-recorder on one of the filing cabinets. 'Good morning – I want—' That was all. Then the next two. Much the same. Then the most recent. 'Good morning. If you want to know who was responsible for Alan Grafton's death, ask Howard Sanderson.'

'Any idea where she was calling from?' he asked, as if he'd never hurtled up the stairs in fury.

'One-four-one'd the first. I don't know about the others.' Well, she wouldn't, would she? Hadn't had time to ask, thanks to his tantrums. Except she had. She'd forgotten in the heat of the moment. She dialled down to Reception. No, she'd better not ask Harry for information. Just for Mandy's internal phone number.

Mandy's number was engaged.

'All calls made about twelve,' she said, reading the information from the cassettes. 'Two of them two minutes before the hour, one two minutes after. One spot on.'

'I wonder if that's more than a coincidence,' he said, moving over to examine the cassettes himself.

'And this Howard Sanderson?'

'If it's the Howard Sanderson I know, you can't just turn up on his front doorstep and ask questions. He's got all sorts of contacts with very senior officers indeed, and is your classic pillar of the community committee man.'

'You *know* him?'

'Know of, more accurately.' He did not elaborate.

'There might be more than one Howard Sanderson?' She picked up the phone books. 'Who was it had the bright idea that Brum needed three residential volumes? And you only get one delivered, as if you only need to phone people in your immediate area. Aren't people in Birmingham South West supposed to know people in Birmingham North or Birmingham South East?'

'Only if they're rich enough to pay for a third volume – you get a second free if you ask. Anyway, the Howard Sanderson I know of will grace yours – South West.'

She passed it to him, running quick fingers down the entries in the other volumes herself. 'No. No one here.'

'And only the one I know here. But there may be other Sandersons ex-directory. Check, will you? I want a complete list.'

It was on the tip of her tongue to ask what would happen if there were only the one in the whole of Birmingham, but a look at his face, anxious, drawn, told her that this was not the moment. 'I'll get Colin on to it, shall I?'

'Get him and Cope in here. I want to make sure everyone knows what everyone else knows. And – Kate!'

She stopped, hand on the doorknob. 'Gaffer?'

'Nothing. We'll – I'll—'

No. Not an apology. Well, she'd have to live without one. But he was just opening his mouth to say something else when his phone rang. He seized it as if it were a life-line.

She closed the door quietly behind her.

'Kate! Kate! Phone for you!' Fatima waved the handset as Kate walked into the room.

'Hello?'

'Kate. Patrick here. You got home safely?'

Another tart comment, bitten back quickly. *I usually do* wasn't especially conducive to building relationships, even one with a man with whom she didn't especially want a relationship. 'Fine,' she said.

'Good. Now, if I promise a door-to-door service, might I have the pleasure of your company again? There's a party tomorrow night – it'll be a bit of a crush but you might find it not unamusing.'

What did a woman detective do on her Saturday nights? Stay in and unpack more boxes? Wash her smalls?

'It's not impossible,' she said, sounding, she hoped, as if she were working her way down a long list of other potential engagements and eventually choosing his.

'Excellent. Excellent.' She could hear his dimples coming through. 'May I collect you about nine? I'll come by taxi. Oh, and before you ask, it's not the sort of do you take a bottle to.' She could hear someone speaking to him, and his muttered response. 'Nine, then, Kate. I'm really looking forward to it.'

'And I am.' She held the handset from her: had she bothered to put so much warmth into her voice just for a dead phone?

Colin had heard, if Patrick hadn't. His eyebrows headed for his hairline. 'Oooh,' he began.

'None of that, DC Roper, if you don't mind!' she snarled, winking. 'Now, the DCI wants you and me and DI Cope in his room. Now. Will you collect Cope? I'm going to the loo.'

Their meeting was sweetness and light itself. Cope revealed that his experts didn't think the tapes worth enhancing. The last tape was clear enough, anyway. They'd check how many Howard Sandersons lived in the area and then – on Monday – start a few preliminary enquiries. Kate would alert all the switchboard staff to the importance of the unknown woman's calls. And they should all go home and have a nice peaceful weekend because when things started up on Monday their feet wouldn't touch the floor.

'You don't want us to get stuck in tomorrow?' Colin put in.

Kate glanced at him: it wasn't like him to want extra work, and there was something in his voice that worried her.

'I don't think something as tenuous as this justifies the overtime. If it does build, it would be nice to have fresh minds and bodies attacking it. OK, everyone. Have a good weekend.'

'Not that it's started yet,' Cope reminded them. 'I'd like an up-date on your *Grass on your Neighbour* investigations. It should only take five minutes, if you've been doing your jobs. Afternoon, then, Gaffer.' He nodded at Graham and ushered his underlings out.

Kate decided to celebrate with one of her cough sweets. She repeated the dose several times in the course of the afternoon, so the whole room was pulsating with creosote fumes.

Despite that, it was well after five when she and Colin escaped.

'Fancy that snifter?' Kate asked. She really ought to see Cassie again, just for a few minutes, and then there were her boxes. If she found the state of her home offensive, how would Patrick see it, with his judging, stranger's eyes? But she owed Colin. And yes, he was the closest she'd got in Birmingham to a friend.

'You sure you've got time?'

The tone; the body language: there was something the matter.

'Of course. We might as well let the rush hour thin out anyway.'

He nodded. They created spaces on their desks – the nearest they ever got to clearing them – as a gesture to the new week, and set off.

'Don't forget,' Graham's voice stopped them as they headed for the stairs, 'have a good weekend.'

With one accord they turned. 'Thanks, Gaffer. And you.'

'Not that there's much chance of it for him, poor bugger,' Colin muttered, as soon as they were out of earshot.

Kate shook her head, sighing. It would have been good to tell Colin all about Graham's tantrums, but she found she couldn't. What she did offer up was the picture on Graham's desk. 'Like a bloody albatross, isn't it?' With Graham as the Ancient Mariner? Not a good comparison, all in all.

Colin said, 'She's very attractive, isn't she? Lovely neck, and really nice little ears?'

She bit. '*Attractive?*'

'They make a good-looking pair.' At last he relented: 'Mind you, I don't fancy the expression on her face.'

'I haven't actually looked at the photo, to be honest,' she said, loftily. 'The circumstances haven't arisen ... Hey, how did you manage to see it?' she added, succumbing to his grin.

'Accidentally knocked it with a file.'

'Accidentally on purpose, I suppose! What's the matter with her expression, anyway?'

'I wouldn't want to prejudice your impressions.'

'Bother you, then. I'll look at it myself, said the Little Red Hen. God, what's happened to the weather?'

They peered into a bank of fog.

'Perhaps it means it might get a bit warmer,' Colin said doubtfully. 'Come on: I can hear that half calling me.'

Except he didn't stick to halves. He embarked on pints with whisky chasers. Kate, on mineral water after a dry white wine, looked at him anxiously and then decided to risk it.

'You'd better tell me,' she said, laying her hand gently on his. 'There's something up, isn't there? Oh, come on: it's pretty obvious.' She nodded at his third pint, already half gone.

He shook his head. He looked horribly close to tears.

'Tell me at home, then.' She gathered up her bag and coat. 'I'll stand you a balti. You can't drive after that lot anyway.'

'I'll be—'

'Come on. It's easier to sink that stuff than it is to stop sinking it. Trust me. I've been there.'

'You're not an alcoholic though. You stuck at the one glass.'

'There but for the grace of God.'

'Oh, don't bring Him in! OK. Stop looking like my mum with a headache. Let's go.'

✼   ✼   ✼

'Tell you what,' he said, 'we'll clear – three? make it four? – boxes before we go and eat. And then we'll come back and finish the rest. And run the vac round. So at least your bloke can see the potential of the place.' He gestured expansively.

'He's not my bloke.' She hung her coat up, passing him a hanger too. 'Anyway, I'd rather hear about whatever it is that's getting you down.'

'Look, it's no big deal. It's just that – OK, it is a big deal. I've been with Clive for nearly five years now. The house is in his name, but – you know, we're partners. And I get home Wednesday night to find him shagging his bollocks off with this kid from the Greek chippie. And when I make a token protest, he tells me I'm out. I thought he was joking. Well, we both over-reacted, maybe.'

'So what's the present state of play?'

'We'll just have to see.'

She couldn't press him. Not with his face wearing that expression. 'My ears are here whenever you want them. And a waterproof shoulder. OK?'

'OK. Thanks. In the meantime, I can see a hell of a lot of mess and – you know – my ears must be particularly alert tonight! – I can hear that balti calling me.'

Chapter Twelve

———◇———

'Did you have a good day?' Patrick asked, as they fastened their taxi seat belts.

'Excellent. My Boys' Brigade football team had a home win. One-nil, but the ref re-invented the off-side rule specially for the occasion. And I've at last unpacked the last of my goods and chattels from London. The carpet-layer will appear next Friday.' The young man who was going to lay her kitchen floor would do the downstairs carpets too. She hoped his record – and his boss's – would be immaculate. 'And you?'

'I did some Christmas shopping, played a round of golf and started to put the gearbox back together on that Triumph I was telling you about. Highly satisfactory, in other words.'

Golf. Gearboxes. Christmas shopping. She hoped their host went in for loud music because this evening didn't promise much conversationally. The Christmas shopping seemed the best conversational opening, but that meant exposing her own weakness here – hardly anyone to buy a present for, and, conversely, hardly any to receive. Which reminded her: she might as well volunteer for Christmas Day duty – it would free up people with families. Cassie could be morose with her fellow patients until Kate could make an evening appearance. She'd been morose when Kate had dropped in for half an hour after the match to pass the plastic information card as casually as she could to Rosie.

Patrick was waiting for her to pat the conversational ball back to him.

'So how many shopping days is it to Christmas?' she asked.

'It depends whether you count Sundays, I suppose. Which you have to, these days. Worse than weekdays – all those families with the biggest push-chairs in the western world ... Then it'll be one day of gorging, and Boxing Day sales. Poor sods. And they won't be off to the piste as compensation. Where are you ski-ing this year?'

'Not one of my things, Patrick, I'm afraid. I've been to the Cairngorms, but each time I've contrived to bring about a thaw.'

The house to which they were delivered was in an affluent looking road in Moseley, a suburb which embraced extremes of housing. Many of the huge Victorian piles had been converted, multi-occupation taking its toll, but this road's houses, slightly smaller but still imposing and mostly detached, seemed owner-occupied. Chantry Road.

'They've closed off access from Salisbury Road at the bottom of Park Hill,' Patrick said. 'Originally to stop kerb crawlers. It's had the effect of stopping through traffic. Much more pleasant now.'

Kate thought about her street. No doubt hands would be flung in horror if anyone suggested closing one end of that. True, there was no right turn from the High Street, but she had a strong suspicion that that was to prevent traffic jams, not protect the residents. And it was noticeable that the roads with speed-bumps were those lined not with terraced houses like her own but with comfortable semis, of various eras. What was it called, the Inverse Care Law? At least Chantry Road residents were suffering parking problems tonight – but the cars were of a different order from those crammed into her street.

The house they approached sported in its front garden a fir tree of some sort, already lit up with large fairy lights. No throbbing music, though – she'd have to find something to talk about then, with the owners of the loud, confident voices which gushed from the front door as it opened to admit other guests. This was not going to be an evening to remember, either.

'Kate doesn't want to play with your trainset, darling,' her hostess, Daphne, was saying.

'But she does!' Mark, her son, insisted. He'd be about eight, and although someone had imposed a white shirt and a bow tie on him, the tie was blessedly askew and the shirt several buttons adrift. 'She's a friend of Tim's – you know, Tim—'

'From the Baptist Church?' Daphne asked.

'—and she knows all about them. Don't you, Kate?'

'I can tell my GWR from my LNER,' she admitted. And after all this smiling and yelling platitudes at complete strangers a few minutes' quiet might not be a bad thing. Particularly as her furred up ear made it hard to work out their responses unless she could watch their mouths.

'You wouldn't know a diesel from a steam train, would you, Isobel?' laughed one of the group Patrick had joined, a tall well-built man with a golfer's suntan.

Isobel, a woman in her later forties, shook her head in self-deprecation, as if she had shaken it that way many times before.

'Actually, they're not trains, they're locomotives,' Mark said. 'Aren't they, Kate?'

'They are indeed,' she agreed. 'And – if you'll all excuse me – I really would like to see Mark's layout. I want to be able to discuss it with Tim when I see him.'

'And you'll come up too, won't you, Patrick? I need someone to fix a loose bogie, you see.'

Kate would have loved Isobel to observe that her husband thought bogies were things small boys picked from their noses, but she didn't. Neither did Kate.

'And Dad's busy, you see,' Mark added. 'With all these

people. And you know about engineering, don't you? You've got all those wicked motorbikes.'

'It ought to be Howard,' Patrick said, clearly not keen to leave the adult company. 'He's the engineer really.'

Sod him, she thought. 'If you've got some tools, I'll see what I can do.' Meanwhile her brain was in gear. *Howard? Lots of Howards in Birmingham, Kate. But I ought to find out – You ought to help that kid. You've offered.*

'Plenty upstairs,' Mark said.

'Well,' she said slowly, but trying to think quickly, 'if we can't rely on manpower, we'd better see what womanpower can do. Do you fancy helping, Isobel?'

'Her! She can't change a light bulb without blowing all the fuses! You've asked the wrong lady there, dear.'

Kate smiled back an angry retort. Isobel smiled at her feet again. Mark put his hand out to tug Kate's skirt, but withdrew it.

Patrick gestured with his glass. 'I'll be up in a minute. OK?'

Suit yourself. 'Fine.'

What sort of money did people have if they could furnish a child's play room like this? True, it was an attic room, but it was newly-decorated and had thick heavy curtains which must have cost for one pair what Kate had paid for all of hers combined. And it was well-heated – as warm as a living room. She sat on a bed-settee with a cushion on her lap, a model engine – Evening Star – upside down on the cushion, and Mark sitting rather too close to her, ostensibly passing her tiny tools when she asked for them but actually putting his head between her eyes and her hands.

'Tim has his trainset in his bedroom,' she said.

'Daddy plays with this sometimes. Sometimes.'

'Now, which man is your daddy? The man Patrick and I were talking to?'

She deserved the scorn in his voice. 'Daddy was the one

who let you in and gave you your wine. You were talking to Mummy and Howard-and-Isobel.'

'So who are they?'

'Howard-and-Isobel live in Oxford Road. They've got a smashing garden – big enough for cricket on the back lawn. And a tree house. It used to be for their son – that's Nigel, but he's grown up. Nearly. He used to play cricket with me. But his dad—'

'That's Howard?'

'Right – you won't make that too tight, will you?'

She pushed his head gently out of the way. 'Not if you let me see what I'm doing! What about his dad?'

'Sorry. Oh, he makes him do his homework.'

That seemed reasonable. 'Have you got a tree house?'

'No. Daddy says I've got to put up with my fort. Is that done, now? Let's try it!'

She thought, as she made her way down the thickly carpeted stairs, that maybe she could have pumped Mark more. But he was a child wanting his engine to work. A nice little boy, too. He'd promised she could come round whenever she wanted to play with him.

Pausing at a turn in the stairs, she looked down. No, she was too smart to be Cinderella – her little black dress had cost an arm and a leg even in the sales – and this wasn't a ball, but she felt uneasy. No sign of Prince Charming at the moment. She'd better insinuate herself through the mass to find him and a drink. Not necessarily in that order. And try to talk to Howard-and-Isobel again. She had the best excuse that they were the only guests she knew. Patrick, she suspected, might not like it if she did her usual thing – her usual pre-Robin thing – and swanned round talking to people he hadn't introduced her to.

Daphne saw her first. 'Food and drink through there, darling!'

Kate nodded and followed the pointing finger.

This must be the breakfast room, rather Laura Ashley, perhaps, but bright without being a killer on a sunny morning. It was crowded with brightly yelling guests. And this the kitchen – mercifully almost empty. She would have died for this kitchen. Even though she was getting ready to love her own – floor permitting – this was magic, the sort that appeared in *Homes and Gardens*. At the far end, on a peninsula fitting, were the drinks. All the bottles, red or white, bore the same label.

A middle-aged man was just opening a bottle of red. Balding, thickening round the waist. A very expensive signet ring. Her host. Had she ever known his name?

'It's a good job this doesn't need to breathe too long. There's some white chilled if you'd rather?'

'The red will be fine. I'm Kate, by the way. I came with Patrick. I'm sorry – I don't know—'

'John.'

They shook hands. He seemed quite happy to lean against the working surface and talk. 'It's not very good, I'm afraid.' He smelt his glass. 'But it's from our own vineyard and I have a sentimental attachment to it. The wine and the vineyard. There!' He passed her a glass and pointed to a large framed colour photo of terraced hillsides.

'Cheers.' She gave an appreciative smile. 'Apart from growing vines, what do you do, John?'

'I'm a health service manager,' he whispered. 'The sort that's loathed by the media.'

No wonder he was loathed if he earned the sort of salary needed to support this place! She touched the side of her nose: 'Your secret's safe with me. I've been playing with Mark: he's a lovely little boy. He lacks only a tree house to be perfectly happy, he tells me.'

'Ah, he's been talking about the Sandersons', has he? They're so patient with him. Well, Isobel.'

Yes! 'She seems a very nice woman. Very quiet.'

'Too quiet. I like a woman – I don't know. This is going

to be misinterpreted, I can see by the gleam in your eye! But a woman with a bit of spirit. I work with high-powered professional women all the time, Kate. They can look you in the eye and say their say. Not Isobel. She worries me. God, how much of this have I drunk?'

'Oh, I like it when people are indiscreet,' she said, cosily, sitting on a stool beside him as if to make her point. 'Now, what does — what's his name? Howard? — do? Is he a manager too?'

'Runs his own business. He was an engineer — had his own factory in the Black Country but when the recession struck he branched out. Doing very well, by all accounts. They've got a bit of trouble with their son. You know what teenage lads are: full of it, aren't they? Anyway, they've got him on a tighter rein, now — he stays at home studying more than he goes out, by all accounts. Look, if I'm being this indiscreet, I'd better give you another, so you can be indiscreet too. And then — you look as if you're the sort of woman who likes dancing.'

If the price of these nuggets was a cheek to cheek with him, then so be it. She released her dimples in a beatific smile. What she wanted to do was drag herself into conversation with Isobel: not to confirm the voice on the phone was hers — in this crowd she'd never be able to, not with this persistent foggy hearing — but because she seemed the sort of woman who'd spend a long time at parties listening with downcast eyes to her husband snubbing her.

Once she had a purpose, she started to enjoy the party much more. She ran into Patrick as she and John were heading for the room where John had promised music. She disentangled herself from her host, acquiring Patrick's arm with the skill of a Russian vine. Kittenish wasn't her usual style, but it looked as if he was too pissed to notice. John kissed her hand extravagantly as he surrendered her.

'John was taking me to dance,' she said.

'Well he can't, can he? I'm taking you to dance. Sorry, John, but you know how it is!' He didn't take her hand, but propelled her forwards with pressure in the small of her back.

What she wanted to do was see the Sandersons again, together or singly. The odds were heavily on the former, of course. She was sure she could re-insert herself into conversation somehow. But at the moment they were nowhere to be seen. She hoped that the music would be restrained and that Patrick was a good dancer.

It was. He was.

And damn it if she didn't find herself getting aroused.

Which was a pity: he didn't seem to be.

They agreed, after several numbers, that they needed another drink, and, this time with him holding her hand, moved back through the hall. Something was up. People were moving ultra-casually away, or, more honestly, peering over other shoulders to see what was happening. Should she squeeze Patrick's hand to bring him to a standstill or disengage hers?

A fellow-guest – a man in a DJ, no less – seemed to be the source of the trouble: loud and thrashing away the hands of people brave enough to try to steady him. She'd better do something. That's what the police were for. Except someone else was doing something. Howard Sanderson was fishing fivers from his wallet.

By now the front door was open, and a young Asian man, the cab driver, she supposed, was standing looking in, bemused. Howard stepped forward, thrusting the money at him, muttering confidentially so no one could quite hear what he said, particularly as his fellow guest was still giving voice – though this had now sunk to an aggrieved whine. Any moment now he would start to cry.

'And you'll come straight back here to collect us,' Kate picked up as she inched forward.

The driver did no more than look at the wad of notes before Howard added some more.

'See you later, then, mate. Sir,' he corrected himself when he fingered the extra notes. He turned to the drunk. 'OK, guv?' He linked arms easily with him and headed off down the drive. Presumably he'd been given enough to cope with swabbing vomit from his cab if necessary.

Howard shut the door. Kate felt she should congratulate him, but waited. What next?

As if he'd simply tipped a carol singer fifty pence he turned and picked up his glass. Catching Patrick's eye, he lifted an ironic eyebrow. 'Christmas spirits,' he said, dismissively.

Patrick gestured him towards the kitchen. Kate made as if to follow and then pulled Patrick back. 'I was afraid I was going to have risk my dress in a bit of crowd control,' she said.

'That would have been a great pity. You know, seeing you in mufti, no one would guess you were a cop.'

'The same could be said of you,' she said, dimpling.

He looked round, almost furtively. 'I tend not to talk about my work. Any more than you seem to,' he added, looking at her shrewdly.

For answer she smiled. 'Maybe we both remember that old *Punch* cartoon with these two men at a party. And one of them was stripping off his shoe and sock—'

'—saying, "So you're a chiropodist, are you?" Oh yes! The weird thing is—' he dropped his voice to an almost inaudible level '—some women seem to find it a real turn on.'

'Something to do with stiffness,' Kate suggested, raising an eyebrow. 'Whereas no one would find my job a turn on, and they're quite likely to ask me why their burglar hasn't been caught. Tell you what, I won't split if you don't.'

For answer, he kissed her lightly on the lips.

Both the Sandersons were in the kitchen so it was natural to join them in the knot waiting for wine. She'd have liked to congratulate him on a job well done, but judicious praise might have sounded as if she knew what she was doing. Neither could she coo, as Daphne was cooing. So she smiled and nodded as the others chorused.

Howard shrugged, almost with irritation, but certainly with the sort of gesture she made when people rabbited on about things she'd rather brush off.

'Look,' he said at last, 'it's over now. I just wish I'd stepped in earlier, before he spoilt the evening. Now why don't you come round for drinks tomorrow evening.' He gestured round the small group. 'You and a few others. Just a few nibbles – would that be OK, Isobel?'

She nodded at her feet, but managed to sweep a smile around the circle.

'Oh, but it's such short notice! You can't expect her to conjure even nibbles out of thin air!' Daphne expostulated.

Kate nodded in sympathy.

'Thin air! She'll despatch me off to Sainsbury's the moment morning service is over. And I'll come back to find her feet sticking out of the deep-freeze.' He smiled at his wife with apparent affection. 'The pity of it is that at this time of year you won't be able to see the garden.'

'I gather from young Mark that it's well worth seeing,' Kate said.

Isobel shook her head at her feet.

'Indeed it is!' Daphne insisted. 'It puts us all to shame.'

'Sometimes I think she lives out there,' Howard smiled, putting an arm round her shoulders.

His wife shot him an extraordinary look: it lasted the briefest of nano-seconds, but Kate was sure she saw it. Within a blink, however, her smile was much in evidence, if still self-deprecating. She hadn't, of course, spoken during the whole of the exchange.

'Why don't we bring some of our left-overs? There are still several trays of canapés hiding in the pantry,' Daphne said.

'What? Deprive me of my chase round Sainsbury's?' It

was impossible to tell what Howard felt about Daphne's intervention.

'If Patrick promises to haul me out of my deep-freeze, I'd love to contribute some cheese-straws,' Kate heard herself say. She couldn't retract the offer, even though she and Robin had made them together the weekend before he was killed. What had she meant to do, she asked herself, preserve them till the anniversary of his death? No, she must not give way to nausea, not here, not now.

She gulped at her wine.

'That would be so kind—' Isobel began.

'It really isn't necessary—' Howard said at the same time.

Before Isobel could add 'but', Daphne jumped in. 'That's settled, then. What time, Howard? Tell you what, since you've been deprived of your dash round Sainsbury's, why don't you take John out for a game of golf? It's such a long time since he played, poor dear, and I know I can rely on you to be patient with him.'

The Sandersons' taxi arrived at the same time as Patrick's. During the short journey home, Kate wondered how she could deal with the coffee issue. Why not with the truth?

'Any day now,' she said, 'I shall have carpets on my floors. Friday, to be precise.'

'In that case,' he said, kissing her lightly on the cheek, 'I shall have to wait till then for a cup of coffee.'

Chapter Thirteen

It might be Sunday morning but the office, as Colin would have put it, called. Loudly enough for even her bunged up ears to hear. Loudly enough to get her out of bed, despite the late – and solitary – night.

Fatima had obviously been busy, despite Graham's instructions that they were all to have the weekend off, which everybody else seemed to be obeying. Even the pair rostered for the weekend were nowhere to be seen.

Three files, neatly marked in Fatima's handwriting, occupied pride of place on Kate's desk.

CARPET-LAYERS

SANDERSON

PHARMACY BREAK-INS

Kate picked up the one she didn't want to have anything in it. CARPET-LAYERS. Of the unsolved breaking and enterings in the whole of the West Midlands area, only four households had had carpets laid recently. None by the firm that had done Kate's. She wanted to dance with relief. But, the note continued, Fatima and Selby were going to follow up the incidents on Monday. Fine, she wrote on the note she clipped to it.

PHARMACY BREAK-INS. There had been a couple more. On one occasion the intruders had been disturbed: they'd taken only unimportant items.

Unimportant? Let her be the judge of that! Resisting the urge to scrawl, she wrote a note in extremely clear block capitals and stapled it – twice – to the folder: EXACTLY WHAT DID THEY TAKE?

Right. Now to the interesting one.

Sanderson. Three Howard Sandersons in Birmingham itself. Fatima seemed to have covered the whole area in which the *Local Crime Watchers* programme could be picked up: there were four more there.

She sat down to leaf through the sheets. One on each Howard Sanderson. There was a potted biography of each. One was black, two under eighteen, one in a gay partnership. Not that any of them was to be ruled out entirely, Selby's scrawl informed her. Colin would no doubt enjoy that. The others included a man in a geriatric hospital and one in HMP Winson Green, both of whom probably could. And a Howard Sanderson of Oxford Road, Moseley. M. to Isobel. One s., Nigel. There was a list of his business activities – he seemed to be involved in some nine firms, what with directorships and joint ownerships.

If this was indeed Graham's Howard Sanderson, Graham and she needed to talk. Whatever Mrs Harvey might say. And preferably before the drinks party at the Sandersons' tonight.

She flicked a look at her watch. Eleven-thirty. No use phoning him yet. No one knew quite which sect he was attached to but probably he'd still be in whatever church it was. As she ought to be. It was one thing shedding the job of organist, another to drift away from the chapel altogether, especially after the parson and his wife had been so kind to her.

Enough of that. What she'd do was compare the firms on Sanderson's list with the firms in Alan Grafton's files. And check them all out at Companies House. Tomorrow's job. As soon as the Central Ref, which housed Companies House, opened its doors. Meanwhile, she'd better return the folders. She'd keep the one on Sanderson herself, to refer to when she spoke to Graham. She couldn't snub Selby by not acknowledging his part of the work, so she dropped the carpet layers folder on his desk. She'd leave the one needing specific attention on Fatima's. Except she wouldn't. It would be much better to leave it somewhere less obvious to the squad file-nicker like Fatima's filing trays or even her chair. Maybe the stacking filing system . . . .

And here was a memo from Graham. To Fatima? Graham? He was a man for conversations or notes. Rarely anything as official as a memo. Almost against her will, certainly against her conscience, her fingers reached for it, slid it forward till it was within reading range but still in the tray. And pulled back, as if bitten.

MEMO

TO: DC Khalid   FROM: DCI Harvey

EQUAL OPPORTUNITIES TRAINING

Subsequent to the course I have just attended, it has been decided that all non-European female personnel will be required to be experienced in the normal sexual practices of uncircumcised men. Please let me have a list of dates when you are free from your normal duties and can undergo the appropriate training, which I will personally attend to.

Shit! No, it wasn't from Graham. Of course it wasn't. Not Graham. Not the man she liked and respected. Her friend. No. It was a cruel, wicked spoof. Perpetrated by none other than the delightful Selby, no doubt. Who else would still right justify the text? Well, there was Cope, but surely he wouldn't be party to this sort of thing. Not a man in his position.

She laid a sheet of paper on top of the memo, and then picked up it, the memo and the sheet underneath the memo too. Even Selby probably hadn't been stupid enough to leave prints but she sure as hell didn't want hers to stand out. Or perhaps there would be prints — whoever had perpetrated this would not doubt claim it was only a joke. To the photocopier — so far so good. And two clear copies. Then back to her desk. She slid the original into an envelope, which she sealed. Then she slipped it into another, larger envelope together with a note.

Fatima
I happened to see this on your desk. I'm sure it's not from the person it's supposed to be from. Please let me help.
Kate.

And put the lot back where she'd found it. She was breathing horribly hard. And there were footsteps in the corridor. Back to her desk. Fast. She was burrowing in the bottom drawer when her colleagues came in.

They acknowledged her briefly but were too busy arguing about some case she wasn't involved in to do anything more than greet her. She responded with a flap of the hand. She managed a short laugh: their raised voices would provide an authentic background if it was Mrs Harvey who happened to answer the phone.

An hour later, in his office, Graham flung his hands in the air. 'Don't you realise what a risk you were taking? Removing it and photocopying it? What if someone had seen you!'

Damn it, she hadn't emptied the whole desk! She shot back, 'Don't you realise the risk you ran as long as it was visible? No. No. Sorry. I was out of order there. Your reputation would have carried you through. But mud tends to stick, Graham, for however short a time. And I couldn't just remove the thing altogether – she had to receive it or she couldn't complain about it.' She filled the kettle from the plastic water bottle.

'But will she anyway?' He joined her by the kettle and dug in the caddy for a herbal tea bag. Then he shoved it back, dropping a fully-caffeinated one in his mug instead. He poked it with a teaspoon as she poured the water. Then – they had a good routine by now – he transferred it to her mug and poked it again. They exchanged what she thought was a comradely smile. It didn't do much to wipe the anger or anxiety from his face. It probably didn't do much more for her own, particularly as she still had to tell him about Sanderson.

'It strikes me she's already taken some shit and isn't prepared to talk about it,' he continued.

'Not to me, anyway. She doesn't want to snitch. Any more than I would in her position. Not that I'd keep quiet if I'd had something like that.'

He turned so he could look her straight in the eye. 'What happened to you on your first day here? Not just that business of sending you hither and there for those files. When Cope and I came into the office we interrupted something. It's time you told me, Kate.'

Somehow he infused into his voice a blend of kindness – tenderness, even – and authority. The mixture was compelling.

'You came in just after Colin had stopped – stopped what I suppose I'd have to call a simulated rape.' Trying to make her voice business-like made it sound gruff. She turned away from his gaze, and looked towards the window. 'Selby pushed me face down on the desk and—'

'Attempted penetration or merely feigned it?' His voice sounded very dry, very forensic.

Why didn't he show some emotion? Some anger? Outrage? 'He didn't lift my skirt,' she said flatly.

'But you're his superior officer.'

His comment so took her aback it was a moment before she

could continue. 'That's not the point. The point is I'm a woman. And – yes – I'll go before any tribunal you want – provided it's to support Fatima. Not on my own account. I'm too busy pursuing him over something completely different,' she added, trying for a rueful grin and succeeding. 'I'll tell you all about it when I've managed it.'

Not the wisest thing to say to Graham, knowing his belief in the hierarchy. 'You'll tell me now. You're not the Lone Ranger riding the range avenging ills.'

'Oh, it's all quite trivial in one sense. But it wastes so much time. He's got this habit of playing patience on his computer. Not just the odd game when we're quiet. All the time.'

'You've warned him?'

'In private.'

'You see him at it again get him in here so quick his feet don't touch the ground.'

'What about evidence? My word against his.'

'Get evidence. This week.'

'Evidence? Even with all this urgent stuff going on?'

'Allow me to be the judge of what's urgent. OK, if you can't get evidence, bollock him again – you're well within your rights, Kate – and warn him it's three strikes and he's outside my door.'

'Fair enough. Now: the urgent stuff. I've been invited to drinkies at Howard Sanderson's tonight. I'm supplying the cheese straws,' she added, enjoying the expression the irrelevance brought to his face.

'You're not going and you're not supplying anything.'

'I've been invited to go with Patrick Duncan,' she said, carefully.

'Duncan! Oh, yes. I could see he was after you. And I suppose you like his flashy car and executive house.'

'I've seen neither yet. I've heard all about his motorbikes,' she said. She tried for a mocking smile. '*All* about them.'

'So if you don't like him why are you going out with him?'

Turning back to the window she took a deep breath. It had been all too easy to be frank with her DVU colleagues. Opening up to Graham wouldn't be. Not the way he was these days, bouncing from one emotion to another, like a badly balanced ball. She put her hands on to the sill to steady them.

Graham didn't prompt her, but she could feel him willing her on.

If she turned back her face would be in shadow: her distress wouldn't be quite as humiliatingly obvious. 'If I don't go out with Patrick who do I go out with?'

He flung up his hands. 'That chapel you go to. There must be a social life there. And that nice neighbour of yours. Zenia. Colin.'

'I'm not specially *persona grata* at the chapel. And, given some of the congregation, I'm not so sure I'd want to be,' she added, chin in the air. 'Zenia's just getting over flu. Colin's a dear but we tend not to clutter each other's lives.'

'You wouldn't get very far with him anyway.'

She bit her lip.

'OK, it's not the sort of remark I'd make in general. And never in front of Selby.'

'Nor,' she added, before she could stop herself, 'in front of Cope. Or anyone in the squad. I'm reasonably sure that homosexuality isn't the flavour of the month round here. Even in these enlightened days of Equal Opportunities courses.' She looked him straight in the eye.

For once he accepted the implied criticism. 'So you're saying you're a bit lonely?'

'A lot lonely. I mean, circumstances haven't helped – the bad knee, going on leave and so on. And I probably haven't helped. I've probably been pretty prickly.' She smiled, as if in apology.

He didn't contradict her.

As if she hadn't paused to let him, she continued, 'So you can see why, even if a man bores me silly with his gearboxes, I'm not going to turn down invitations for parties and so on. I need to build up a network of contacts. Midge from the DVU's going to teach me how to—'

'DVU: why have you been down there?' He jumped in very quickly.

'One of Cassie's nurses is getting beaten up. I got one of those help cards to give her. And besides,' she added more slowly, 'it occurs to me that it's odd for a woman who phones in to try and report a crime to cut her complaint off in mid-breath. Not once, but several times. She may be phoning illicitly from work, of course, and have the boss come in unexpectedly. Or she may be phoning from somewhere else and have someone else come in unexpectedly.'

'You mean her husband?' If his voice was harsh it might be because he recognised the secrecy to which he was driven if he phoned Kate. And that one-four-one business if she phoned him from her home. The fact she mustn't pick up the phone immediately he'd made a call to her, lest his wife press the redial button to check up on him.

Poor bastard. And don't tell him he should use the term 'partner', either.

'Spot on,' she said lightly. 'So I wanted to talk to Lorraine and Midge to find out what a woman could do to get out from such a situation. What I'd like to do is have another talk with them about the sort of man that bullies his wife. You see, I saw a really cowed woman the other night – no, not a bruise in sight – and I wondered how affluent, respectable men might torment their wives.'

She'd tried to keep her voice neutral, but he picked up on it. 'Are you talking Isobel Sanderson here?'

'Would it worry you if I were?'

'You don't mean you think she made that call! For God's sake, Kate!' He turned on his heel, and strode back to his desk. He flung himself into his chair.

What was with this man? She followed, taking a chair opposite. Just in case, the hard one.

For a long time he said nothing, staring at the files on his desk as if they would open up to provide him with a solution. Even if he wasn't entirely sure what the problem was. At last, still at a loss, she took the initiative.

'How well do you know this guy?'

'Well enough. I may even be at the party tonight.'

She produced a huge sarcastic beam. 'Well, won't that be cosy? I'll hear you talking shop in the intervals of Patrick talking motorbikes.'

He pushed away from the desk, prowling back to the window. 'Do they have any inkling of your job?'

'I shouldn't think so. Patrick and I made a pact not to broadcast our respective occupations to those not already in the know. All they know about me for definite is that I can mend double-0 locomotives. But that may connect me back to the Baptists via Tim.'

'Tim? Oh, the parson's son. And they certainly know what you do.'

'I doubt if anyone's interested enough to find out. They may ask me directly, in which case I shall have to give a direct answer. But no one seemed overly interested. Apart from John, our host last night, people tended to regard me as just someone Patrick had brought with him.'

'Apart from John?'

'He wanted a gentle flirt. Actually, there was a bit of trouble – I have to say I thought Sanderson handled it very well.' She explained. 'It all goes to show you can solve any problem provided you've got enough money.' When he didn't react, she added, 'And there was an awful lot of money around at that house last night. Well, look at the house itself. You could have got the whole of my place in their ground floor – with room to spare!' How did he fit in if he was one of their circle? She had a pretty good idea of how much he earned. If his wife wasn't working and he had a big mortgage to pay on that nice house of his, he couldn't be anywhere near their league.

'OK. Go to the party tonight. Keep your mouth shut and your eyes and ears open. If they should invite my wife and me I'll find an excuse not to go. She rarely goes anywhere anyway, with those migraines of hers.'

'What,' she risked, 'if she wants to go to this particular party?'

'In that case I shall have to claim pressure of work – maybe even come in here.'

'She could go by herself – recognise me?'

'She never goes anywhere like that by herself,' he said, with absolute finality.

Chapter Fourteen

Eight-thirty in the morning, and this was the third time Graham was picking over Kate's account of her evening at the Sandersons. They were on their second mug of tea, him ensconced behind his desk, her on the comfortable chair opposite him.

'So we have no bruises and no verbal violence to support your theory of domestic bullying.'

She shook her head. Even Howard's tone had been right: affectionate, proud, even, of a wife who could conjure a feast from nowhere.

'And nothing to show that Isobel could be responsible for the phone-calls,' he concluded.

'But we have her cowed demeanour,' she insisted. 'And, incidentally, that of their son. Most teenage kids I know run a mile if their parents have a party. But Nigel passed drinks and nuts like a waiter. A pretty obsequious waiter.' Horribly well-scrubbed and neatly dressed for a kid of his age. But she had a feeling that Graham might prefer sanitised teenagers to the usual sort.

'They had some trouble with him, I gather. The wrong crowd. His father had to come the heavy.'

'That figures. Oh, I know the place is very nice.' She'd better not favour him with her views on the Sandersons' taste in interior decor: all that designer furniture and carpets you need a machete to slice a way through – more of a conference centre than a home. It was perilously close to that of his own home. 'But there's something funny there, Guv, honest. Know wot I mean, sniff, Squire?'

He cocked a quizzical eyebrow, grinning as if in spite of himself. 'I love it when you talk London. You bleedin' Savvernas.' His cockney accent was atrocious. 'Funny thing, my wife was saying she didn't think Isobel was a very happy woman. But you should see their garden. It's magnificent.'

It was. 'I saw some of it: it's even floodlit.' Where did these people get their money? 'Does Isobel really do it all herself? But then,' she added sourly, 'I suppose she's got nothing else to do. Except for housework – such a big house for three people ...'

'Don't you believe it. Committee woman, that's Isobel.'

'*Committees!* But the woman never opens her mouth! Or just not with Howard there?'

He shrugged. 'The word is she's remarkably effective, in an apologetic sort of way.' He leaned back in his chair. 'I'm going to have to declare an interest in this, Kate. Which means either you'll report direct to Rodney Neville or that he'll take the case off us altogether. Don't look like that: the wind may change and you wouldn't want your face stuck like that forever.'

In response she crossed her eyes and stuck out her tongue.

When they'd stopped laughing, she asked, 'Have you had any more thoughts about that memo you're alleged to have sent?'

He shook his head, his face sad-lined again. 'Have a word with Fatima if you can. Try and persuade her to come to me. Or to go, if she must, to an FCA.'

She stared. Yet another new acronym!

'First Contact Adviser. The latest initiative to stamp out harassment. If you have a problem you phone one for support and advice. These are their cards.' He produced a sheaf. The cards were bigger than the credit-type DVU contact cards, the size of an A4 sheet folded into quarters. 'Drop one on to each desk, will you? Perhaps the knowledge that such people exist will be enough to curb Selby.'

'You'd rather stop him than stamp on him?' she asked.

He shrugged. 'He's not a bad officer. Overall. And if neither you nor Fatima will make a complaint I don't see any other way. Oh, Kate.' Hands covering his face, he sounded exhausted already. No, he sounded as if he was crying for help.

Anyone else and she'd have been round the desk to put her arms round him. Already on her feet, she stopped herself. In the eyes of that photo on the desk, a hug might have been a hanging offence. And no doubt Graham had put the photo there to remind him of exactly that.

Perhaps they'd both been praying for it: the phone started to ring. He clicked it on to hold.

'I'll see you at lunchtime for a quick half,' she said. 'You need a break.'

He bent to burrow in his briefcase, coming up with a neat sandwich box full of neat sandwiches. 'I've got lunch.'

She bent to pick up and shake his waste-bin. 'I've got just the place for it.'

It was while she was distributing the First Contact Advisers cards that it occurred to her that she'd forgotten to mention to Graham that she'd left at the Sandersons' the box in which she'd taken the cheese straws. She'd told Isobel she'd come and collect it at some unspecified 'sometime'. Isobel had simply told her her phone number: 'If I'm in the garden I don't always hear the front door bell.'

'Yes, she's always out there — all weathers,' Howard had said. 'The evening's the best time to catch us.'

All very affable. Except that he'd said 'us'.

So it would have been good to have Graham's advice.

'Wonderful!' Cope exploded, charging into the office with a note. 'The wretched woman's only been in the squad five minutes and now she's gone home sick. You women – you've got no stamina, have you?'

'I'd like to see any of us fasting all day and still managing to shift the work she does,' Colin said.

'Ah! That'll be it, I suppose. No food. Never did anyone any good trying to work on an empty stomach. Can't she have a few nibbles and not tell the priest?'

Colin laughed: 'I think you've missed the point, Gaffer.'

'Is there any indication that it's the fasting that's the problem?' Kate asked. 'I must say, if it is, we probably haven't made it any easier for her, feeding our faces in here at all hours.' She picked up the styrofoam cup from Fatima's desk. 'And leaving this sort of "present" – my God, it's more like a specimen for the Path. Lab. than coffee.' She shuddered and – OK, it would destroy whatever point Fatima had been trying to make – put it down on Selby's desk.

'Are you saying we ought to manage without a cup of coffee all day? You got to be joking.'

'Did I say that, Selby? No, I said there were ways of making it easier – if, indeed, that's what the problem is.'

'It could be,' Colin said, seriously. 'After all, she came in here right as rain twenty minutes ago, sat down at her desk and seemed to be working. And then you come in with your bacon buttie, Merv, and off she goes.'

It took Kate a moment to register that Merv was Selby: she'd never heard anyone use his first name before.

'Did she say anything to you before she went off? After all, you were on your own with her when she actually went,' Colin asked.

'If you're saying I had anything to do with it—'

'I'm not saying anything. I'm just asking. She's a nice kid. We're just trying to see if we can do anything that'll make it easier for her to come back to work. Anyone know when Ramadan ends?' Colin looked round.

'Round about Christmas, I think,' Kate said. 'But all this is speculation. I'll get her address from Personnel and pop round and see her tonight. We might as well know where we stand before we start agonising about coffee. But maybe we ought to have a self-denying ordinance where food's concerned. The place smelt worse than a chippie the other day. Eating sarnies at our desk's one thing: but the canteen's the place if we want a full fry-up.'

'Better to eat away from our desks, anyway,' Colin added.

Cope looked round the room. No one seemed to have anything to say against that. He nodded. 'OK. Seems reasonable. Now, it's time we did a bit of work. Kate—'

Selby pulled himself upright in his chair. 'Are you saying that's an order, Gaffer?'

Cope shifted. Wriggled, more like. 'It can't be an order, like, can it? Because it's just between ourselves.'

'So there's no one can say it's wrong if anyone does eat up here?'

'Well – not really.'

'What about a bit of democracy, Sir?' Kate chipped in. Clearly the man had the backbone of the average louse. 'If it's what everyone else in the office wants, it doesn't seem right for one person to go against them.'

'Show of hands?' Colin prompted. 'Right. A clear majority, I'd say. And – before you ask – not just when Fatima's fasting.'

'Hmph, I don't know. Next you'll be wanting a non-smoking office,' Cope muttered. 'Hey, how long are you going to let that phone ring? We're supposed to be working, not chafing the fat.'

Kate fielded it, but covered the mouthpiece. 'One more thing. I don't think it's on, calling Fatima "Fatty". It's personal and hurtful even if it patently isn't true. OK, everyone?'

Most people looked plain puzzled, but there was general muttered agreement. And she returned to the call.

It was Rodney Neville's secretary. Kate was to present herself at ten-thirty prompt.

'She didn't quite tell me to clean my teeth and brush my hair,' Kate grumbled to Colin as she redistributed the work she'd hoped Fatima would do that day. 'But she might as well have done.'

'Don't forget to polish your shoes, either. What's this abrupt little note about precise lists of the items stolen from this chemist's? You don't want to embarrass me by making me list Tampax and suppositories, do you?'

'If that's what it takes, you can mention Dutch caps and incontinence knickers.' She turned to Selby. 'Thanks for your work on the carpet fitters: it looks as if you're on to something interesting. Now, can you follow up what you've done so far? Names of the firms, employees at the time? You know the sort of thing.'

'I've got this lot to work through!' He gestured. It was a large pile of files.

'What are your priorities?'

'All of them. Cope's dumped a load of them *Grass up your Neighbours* messages on me.' He patted the files almost affectionately and tipped back his chair. 'And I'd say a DI ranked above a DS, wouldn't you? Ma'am?' He stuck his hands in his pockets, ostentatiously moving his fingers. His eyes drifted to the top button of her shirt and stayed there.

Her fingers itched to slap him. On impulse she tapped the mouse he'd been using. The screen-saver evaporated to show a game of patience, half way through. As coolly as she could, she caught his eyes and held them, before raising a slow, ironic eyebrow.

'Well, I'd say a sergeant ranked above a constable. And you won't have forgotten I warned you about this weeks ago. OK, Selby. One more strike and you're out.'

'You can't do that.' He sat up.

'I know a man who can. Understand? Selby?'

'Ma'am.' This time the syllable was barely audible. The resentment in it wasn't, though.

'And if you have too much to do, now Fatima's off, then we'll talk it over with Cope. Together. Right?'

'Ma'am.'

Much support she'd get from Cope, of course, she reflected, as she tidied herself in the loo. The squad in general had been great – very quick on the uptake and apparently well-disposed to Fatima. Decent, caring men. On the surface, of course. What they'd be like over a few pints in a male bar was another matter. And if Selby went running to Cope, as he'd done in the past, complaining that she was a bad manager, she knew who Cope would back. And he'd probably trot off to Graham and Neville. Hell, how she hated fighting for dominance. Look at her: she was still trembling after even the short encounter with Selby, although she'd won every round so far. Well, she'd better win the next, too.

Kate supposed it was the Superintendent's prerogative to keep her standing like a lemon while he finished whatever he was tapping into his computer. Eventually he finished with a flourish, and moved and clicked his mouse with panache.

At last he looked up as if surprised she were there, switched his hundred-watt smile on, and gestured expansively to a chair. There was a smell of coffee to go with his aftershave. Two pictures graced the walls: they were in clip-frames so they were obviously prints but they weren't the usual bland waiting-room wall stuff.

She allowed her eyes to linger.

'Ah, you're an art aficionado, too, Kate. Feininger, as you've probably guessed. I picked them up at the exhibition in Berlin this summer.'

'Florence was bulging with those wretched bored cherubs,' she countered.

'You're over that dreadful cold, are you?'

'Pretty well.' Actually, she was much better. The sinuses had responded to frequent steamings over the weekend, and the ear-drops might just be working, too.

'Excellent. Because I have in mind for you a slight change of function.'

She blinked: it didn't take someone that far up the tree to give her different work.

'In fact, you won't be working here for a while. You'll be transferred to the Fraud Squad. For how long I'm not sure. Maybe a matter of a few days only. Maybe longer.' He allowed himself a kindly smile, as if to reassure her. 'You are, of course, on the Accelerated Promotion Scheme, so it behoves us to give you as many – and varied – assignments as possible.'

Behoves? One moment the man talked like Mr Media, the next he was in Victorian headmaster mode! She hoped her smile and nod adequately disguised a distress that hit her like a blow to her stomach. Hell, she was just beginning to feel her way here; there was the Fatima problem, all that unfinished business with Selby. 'May I ask how this has come about, Sir?'

'I believe DC Roper made contact with a colleague in Fraud to help with some accounts. This colleague was sufficiently intrigued to talk about them with his colleagues, because they tied in with another enquiry. My opposite number's response was to ask to take over the case completely. I gather you wouldn't have been happy with this?'

'You gather right, Sir. I really am committed—'

He smiled, but then his face chilled. 'There are reasons why I'd prefer you out of the squad at the moment, Kate. I understand that you don't enjoy the best of relationships with one or two of your colleagues—'

'Sir?'

He tipped back in his chair, putting his hands behind his head and staring at the ceiling. 'Human resource management's always a delicate area. Maybe this will give time for passions to cool.'

'If we're talking about who I think we're talking about, Sir, the man's a bully—'

'Kate, Kate! I hear what you're saying. I also hear that there is a feeling that he may be responsible for some very nasty racial abuse. But while you're here he may well allege that you're producing the material that you've shown DCI Harvey in order to frame him. So if the abuse continues in your absence, we shall know it's not from you.'

'One flaw, Sir. Fatima's gone off sick If she's not there the abuse will cease anyway.'

'I was coming to Fatima.' He pulled himself upright and put his elbows on his desk, supporting his jaw on loosely clasped hands. Hell, he was trying to smooth away a double chin! 'You will not attempt to contact her while this is going on. Is that understood?'

'With respect, Sir, I'm the only thing she's got approaching a friend in the squad. I'd feel awful if I didn't phone up to find out how she is: she's gone home sick, after all.'

'You'd risk contaminating evidence for the sake of offering a bit of comfort? We have a whole welfare department able and willing to do just that.'

'You're suggesting she's forged that memo herself?'

'No. Nor even—' He stopped abruptly. 'As far as the Alan Grafton case is concerned, it's better that it should conducted from elsewhere anyway. Graham Harvey knows the man alleged to be involved—'

'Howard Sanderson, Sir.'

'He tells me I can rely on your discretion. I hope I can.'

'Sir.'

'I've arranged for you to meet your new colleagues at twelve-thirty. No problems with that, I take it?'

'I'm afraid I'm committed at that time, Sir. Could it be at two?'

His fine eyebrows convulsed, but he smiled almost immediately. 'A full diary! Now, I have a window at two-thirty: we'll make it then. My opposite number and the DI you'll be responsible to.'

Kate stood. 'Two-thirty, Sir.'

Chapter Fifteen

'So apparently I'm an art aficionado. All I did was look at those prints on his wall while he finished playing silly-buggers on his computer and now I'm an expert!' Kate drained her cup and set it down with a slight tap.

Graham laughed, as she hoped he would.

She'd taken him not to any of the pubs used by the police, but for a sandwich at a place Colin had recommended. Not a sandwich bar – by no means! – but a cross between a cosy Thirties' living room and an up-market café, with the daily papers and laminated copies of the *Beano* for reading matter. Hudson's was in one of Birmingham's more up-market shopping malls, the Plaza, where, she was delighted to inform Graham, they had the best public loos she'd ever come across. His embarrassment added significantly to her pleasure, particularly when she sent him off to test the men's for himself.

'And he talks to me about this picture as if I know who the artist is. Apparently Neville went to the exhibition in Germany this summer.'

Graham was still smiling. 'And did you enlighten him?'

'Would I? Actually,' she became serious, 'I know nothing about art. Furniture like Alan Grafton's, pictures: I'm a total ignoramus. But I've got this terrible feeling I ought to know more. No, not ought – want. You know, when I think of a lovely bit of enamel at Grafton's—'

'Enamel? Like in baths and things?'

'Enamel as in purely decorative. This bit was a beautiful turquoise and in the middle of a hideous hall-stand. Except I don't know whether it really is hideous or if it's just my bad taste. But I covet that bit of enamel.'

'What do you think of Neville's pictures?'

'Gorgeous. Especially the one with reddy-orange sailing boats.'

'In that case I think your taste's impeccable.' His voice was warm as his smile.

Think about the Gorgon's eyes, Kate. He's got to go home to them. And live with them.

'Meanwhile,' she said, brisk, with the teapot poised above his cup, 'have you heard about Neville's plans for me?'

'He's not back to that media rubbish again, is he?'

'Not yet. But he's moving me out of the squad.'

'What?' He sounded thunderously angry. Almost. 'I thought he was supposed to be an expert on human resource management,' he said at last.

'Only for a bit. He's got this idea I may be trying to fit Selby up by firing off memos that bear his stamp.'

'Memos?' There was no doubt about his embarrassment.

'Well, one – hang on. That's it! He nearly let something slip. And now you – come on, you're not a good actor. There's been another one, hasn't there?'

'Kate, you do not know about this. In any circumstances.' He touched a fold in the tablecloth with his index finger. 'See that line? There's my job.' Then he put the next finger beside the first. 'And there's yours.'

She put her finger to her lips. 'You know me, silent as the grave.' So why was he telling her? To get it off his chest, to share it with someone?

'There's been a reply to that one I didn't send. Word-processed, of course, so we can always get it off the hard disk. Even if it's not been saved, they say. Well, the experts can.' He smiled, as if to acknowledge her superior knowledge. 'The contents are appalling. About wanting experience with nice big—'

'—big dicks,' she prompted.

'—and going into all sorts of detail. Vile. The sort of thing you'd get in a porn mag. The trouble is, it arrived immediately after you'd left my office. So *in theory* Fatima just had time to write it and bugger off.'

'Is "yours" still in her in-tray?'

'I take it your handwriting would be on the envelope? In that case, no. It's gone. And, for your ears only, Selby's gone to Cope alleging that you've got it in for him and are making his life a misery. Thank God you told me about it, Kate. You've got to watch your back in something like this.'

She nodded. 'And you yours, Graham. Maybe Neville is actually doing me a favour getting me out for a bit.'

He nodded. 'I think he's OK. After all, you don't get to be as high as he is in such a short time without being good at your job. All this business about painting and so on: I think it's genuine. And he's come out *maxima cum laude*—' he grinned in response to Kate's flying eyebrows '—from all the courses he's been on – which, of course, is a lot. Plus he's got a reputation for putting in a lot of hours, coming up with plenty of good ideas. Maybe this was one of them. Though I—' He looked away, pretended to check the hot water jug.

Though he'll miss me. As much as I'll miss him. In this mood, at least.

'Tell you what,' she jumped in. 'If I'm going to be off with Fraud long, couldn't we do this again? Well, quite often. I don't want to lose touch. With everybody,' she added.

'Good idea.'

But even as he smiled she saw the fear creep over his face. It was those eyes on his desk, wasn't it?

✳　　✳　　✳

The Fraud Squad was based at Lloyd House, West Midlands Police's administrative hub. They had to wait to be collected from the foyer. Kate was aware of a preponderance of tall middle-aged men in anonymous grey suits passing through. Somehow they seemed as menacing as anything she'd read about in the fastnesses of the Kremlin or the White House. Yes, there was something reassuring about navy serge.

The rooms were modern and anonymous, apart from some highly complex computer screen-savers, displaying a story Kate feared she wouldn't ever have time to watch to the end. The main thing that distinguished them from her squad's territory was, however, the tidiness. Extreme tidiness. Graham Harvey's meticulous wife would be at home here. Kate, however, had a terrible fear that she wouldn't.

There was quite a little party in Detective Chief Inspector Dyson's office: the DCI himself, looking, with his greyish, cadaverous face more like her former philosophy professor than a cop, Rodney Neville, Graham, and a woman DI in her early forties with the most unruly mane of auburn hair Kate had ever seen, Lizzie King. She was introduced as the Officer in Charge of the Corporate Fraud Section.

'Not that your name ought to be King,' Neville had said, lingering over her hand as he shook it. 'It ought to be Siddal.'

'That's how I got to be called Lizzie,' the woman grinned. 'I'm really Lydia, but I suppose I do look like a perambulating pre-Raphaelite model – though without the goitre, I hope.'

The allusions were lost on Kate. Something else to look up – and she'd not made it this morning to Companies House to check on Sanderson's connections, had she?

Once Neville had abandoned King's hand and everyone was seated, coffee was produced by a woman who wasn't introduced. Or thanked. Secretary or colleague? Kate's stomach sank. But this was not the time to get on what Cope would no doubt have dismissed as her equal opportunities high horse.

Nor to wonder why there were so many people involved.

Left to herself, she'd have settled for a quiet chat with Lizzie over – with luck – better coffee than this. It must be one of the games management played. And yet she could understand that Neville, new in post, would need to make contacts, and she could see that Graham, his eye, no doubt, on promotion, wouldn't want to be left out. Maybe he even wanted to see her settled here.

Soon enough, anyway, they had an action plan and her brief was drawn up. She was to be responsible – and she tried not to beam when she heard the word – for pursuing the investigations into Alan Grafton's death, and the financial debacle that surrounded, if not prompted it. Because Fraud knew of other cases – 'a positive rash' – of similar ends to small firms, she would work closely with Lizzie, and she'd be allocated a couple of experienced constables. Although two departments were at work, neither woman was to regard the collar, if any, as hers. Co-operation was to be the name of the game. But the Fraud Squad would have discretion in day-to-day decision making.

Kate didn't have a problem with that. Lizzie's expertise, her footslog – that seemed a good combination. She said so.

'What about my contacts with this guy Sanderson and his wife?' she asked.

Graham explained briefly: yes, there was a spot of back-watching there. Her transfer might almost have been his idea.

'Maintain them. Develop them,' Dyson said, before Neville could speak. 'Especially with the wife.'

'As a matter of fact, I may have a good way in there,' Kate said. She explained about the freezer box.

'Good! What I'd really like is an informer. Maybe we could even sign her up. Find out what committees she's on. Join one if necessary. I'd like to see the two of you like this.' He linked his index fingers and tugged: neither yielded. 'OK, Neville?'

'Fine by me. Harvey? King?'

And, by default, fine by Kate.

*   *   *

Kate and Graham walked together the short distance back to base. Neville had dawdled behind with his opposite number. Lizzie had given her a flap of the hand and a promise to find her a desk by eight-thirty the following morning.

'This means my spying on a friend of yours,' Kate said. 'And trying to persuade his wife to sing.'

'Not a friend. An acquaintance. And as far as Isobel's concerned – if it was she who made those calls, well, she's too intelligent not to see the end of the process she's started.'

'You never said whether you thought it was she.'

'How grammatical! I'm not good on voices. I wouldn't be able to swear on oath.'

'What do you *think?* If I'm on a wild-goose chase I'd like to know.'

They'd been walking slowly. Now he stopped altogether.

Head on one side, he said, 'If I thought you were, I'd tell you. What I'm very much afraid is that you'll end up chasing something infinitely more lethal. Sanderson's a powerful man, with endless resources. He's got friends in very high places too. Believe me.'

'Funny handshake brigade?' Was Graham one, too?

'I wouldn't know,' he said stiffly.

Well, it was a silly thing to ask, wasn't it, of a policeman? She'd better think of a way out of the little silence that was accumulating around them.

'There's something else I need to know,' she said.

His face softened again, but not much.

'Who's this Lizzie Siddal woman?'

He stared but then burst out laughing. 'Kate! Surely you know that! I mean, it's more general knowledge than art'.

She shook her head. 'Something about pre-Raphaelite? And a goitre?'

'Well done. You've heard of the pre-Raphaelite Brotherhood? Victorian artists? Come on, you must have done. Heavens, what do they teach young people these days? She was the model and then the wife of one of them. Rossetti, I think.' He stopped, and frowned. 'Tell me: you really don't know what I'm on about, do you?'

She shook her head. 'You know how it is: you've heard the name but it doesn't really register.'

'And you did your degree in Manchester! They've got an art gallery there with lots of pre-Raph. stuff. Didn't you ever go in? Even to get out of the rain?'

'I don't ever remember it raining all the time I was up there,' she said, straight-faced.

He laughed. 'OK. It's not raining now, but I do think ten minutes' education is called for. We can work late tonight to make up for it.'

Can we indeed? She nodded noncommittally.

'Just along Colmore Row, here. The Museum and Art Gallery. And if we don't find Lizzie Siddal there I'll – I'll buy you a cup of tea.'

'And if we do?'

'You buy me one.'

Most people had left by now, but Kate was still staring at the lists of items stolen from pharmacies. This was a case she didn't want to let go of. She knew there was something staring her in the face that she couldn't see. She put a note on Colin's desk: would he get one of the inputters to put the material through a computer check to see which items figured in every single theft. If he had time, could he also phone a sample of chemists' shops to see if they'd had minor thefts they'd not bothered to report.

She reached for the phone: one of her Met Drugs Squad contacts might still be working.

It rang so long she was just about to give up.

'DI Thomas.'

'Dai? Kate Power.'

'Kate my old love! Corn in Egypt! The first daffodil

of spring. How are you?' The Welsh voice rose and fell like the sea.

'All the better for hearing your voice!'

'You'd have heard it before this, only I've been in the States, see. And then there was that big trial. No, truth is, love, I should have phoned. You know how it is. Never know what to say. And are you getting over – everything?'

'It's a slow business, Dai. But I'll get there one day. Now, I want to pick your brains. Such as they are.' She gave him a resume of the pharmacy thefts.

'Well, your Crime Prevention people should be getting busy. They've been so active down here, what with CCTV and metal grilles, the rate's been cut down a great deal. Maybe they're knocking stuff off up there and bringing it down to us. But I can't see why. They make the stuff they want, these days, on their home chemistry sets or whatever. Or bring it in from abroad. However we try to stop it, they seem to keep bringing it in. Big people. What you've got sounds dead amateurish, girl. What d'you expect, out in the sticks, there?'

What had Graham said when she'd first joined? She'd use that on Dai. 'They don't all wear woad, here. And – strictly between ourselves – I quite like the place. Someone's found some money from somewhere and the city centre's as nice as you'd wish to find.' She wouldn't say she still couldn't believe how tiny the shopping centre was or how she hated the accent. Pride? Loyalty? Who could tell? She told him about her present cases, picked up a bit of the London gossip and rang off.

There was just time to phone Isobel Sanderson. She even had her hand poised to dial. Then she thought better of it. They wouldn't rate anyone who had an urgent need of freezer boxes. She'd have to find a reason for wanting it – batch cooking mince pies for the Boys' Brigade or something. So she'd wait just a couple of days.

She glanced at her watch. Eight-thirty. Plenty of food in her freezer, and a microwave ready for action. But on the whole, she thought she'd stop off at her favourite chippie. Not for fish and chips: for a wonderful concoction, chicken tikka in a naan bread, with salad and spicy mint sauce. A feast. Not because she had to: because she wanted to. And just to round it off, a cup of that milky drink full of sweet noodles they'd started to sell. Faluda, that was it. Yes, there were a lot of good things about Brum.

Chapter Sixteen

'It's a lovely morning,' Lizzie had observed almost as soon as Kate had got into the office. 'Just the sort of morning it'd be nice to go and look at the firms which said Alan Grafton could give credit to Symphony Leather. They're not all that far apart. Let's go straightaway. Then we can talk to the accountants looking at the books later this afternoon and make sure we can ask them the right questions. You can sort out your desk later.'

When she had one, that is.

'What I also want to sort out is all Howard Sanderson's business links: can you drop me off at Companies House on the way back?' Kate gulped her coffee, and stowed the KitKat she'd meant to eat with it in her bag.

'If you want the walk! But we've got on-line here practically all the information they've got there. We use the Dunn and Bradstreet system: modem-linked to Companies House in Cardiff. Why stretch your legs when you can stretch your arm?'

'Great.' Better to learn to fish than wait to be fed. But it occurred to her that so far she'd only heard about the tackle.

After the recent damp greyness, it was good to be out, even if the bright sun made it awkward for Lizzie to drive. They were heading almost due east and the sun was still too low for her visor to be effective. Kate burrowed in the depths of her bag, producing the sunglasses that always lurked there, whatever the time of year.

'Proper little Girl Guide, aren't we?' Lizzie observed, putting them on, nonetheless.

'Boys' Brigade, actually,' Kate said, wondering if she was imagining the edge in Lizzie's voice. 'I coach their football team. Under some duress.'

'How on earth did you get involved with that?'

'It's not getting involved that's the problem. It's getting dis-involved. Turn right – just where that lorry's coming out.'

This was the opening to a tatty industrial estate. It had been awkward to get to, partly because of the rush-hour traffic and partly because the roads weren't well signed. Now it promised very little in the way of reward.

'Welcome, Kate, to Stechford,' Lizzie said, parking on a badly broken factory forecourt. 'Or probably Garretts Green.'

'Familiar territory,' Kate said, grinning. 'I worked undercover in Yardley a couple of years ago. It hasn't got any more attractive, though.'

'Was it ever? Fancy siting buildings almost directly under a well-used railway line. Not to mention,' Lizzie added, putting her hands to her ears, 'one of Birmingham Airport's main flight paths. Not, I suppose, that they'd want to put anything else under the railway line. And there are lots of things under this flight path. Oh, and it seems to be right by a bus stop, too.'

'You wonder what sort of organisation would want to base itself here,' Kate said. 'It wouldn't inspire me with confidence, I can tell you. I mean, the buildings are practically derelict.'

'Sixties disposable,' Lizzie nodded. 'Time they disposed of them, too. But not until we've run – what do they call themselves? – to earth.'

'Minim Products. They're not exactly trumpeting their whereabouts, are they?'

After five minutes they admitted defeat.

Lizzie looked around her. 'We need a friendly native.'

'There's a postie – he should know.'

It was hardly surprising they hadn't run it to earth. The postie, warning them they were wasting their time, directed them round the back of a warehouse specialising in the distribution of pet food, where they found a small name-plate, one of a collection. Entrance was via an intercom, of course. And no one from Minim responded.

'What a surprise,' Lizzie said. 'Still, *nil desperandum*. Try another button.'

A young woman responded and they were buzzed into two yards of passageway leading straight up steep stairs.

'These must violate health and safety regulations,' Kate said. 'Look, these tiles are loose and those things that wrap round the treads are dangerous.' She picked up the end of one. As she let it go, it subsided gently.

'They're called noses, I believe,' Lizzie said. 'No, wrench the thing up. Better no nose than one that trips someone. Give it to the kid who let us in.'

They'd got themselves admitted to the tiny office of a firm rejoicing under the name of Meedja Contax. The young black woman at the desk stood up quickly when she saw their bounty, her beaded braids clicking with agitation.

'If I've told them once I've told them a thousand times,' she said. 'Did either of you hurt yourself? Because—' she leaned towards them confidentially – 'if I were you I'd take legal action. Look.' She fished a notebook from a desk drawer. 'Those are the dates I've complained. Me, personally, right?'

Lizzie nodded. 'Well done. You want to watch your step, though.'

The woman groaned. Kate did likewise.

Lizzie didn't respond. 'OK. Now, we're trying to speak to someone at Minim Products. No one answered. That's why we bothered you.'

The young woman's shrug wouldn't have been out of place in a silent movie. 'Law unto themselves, they are. Mind you,

I reckon they've done a moonlight – it's been like the grave up there the last couple of weeks. I used to hear their phone ringing – on and on it went, for ages. Now it doesn't. Either Telecom have done their stuff or someone got tired of hearing it and pulled it themselves.'

Lizzie jerked her head at Kate, who took it as a hint that she was to go up a further flight of hazardous stairs and see what she could see. Which was a locked door. Applying an eye to the letter box, she could make out nothing except a dusty desk. She reported back to Lizzie.

'Hell, this means going back to the landlord to try and trace them.'

The black woman dug in another drawer. 'Here's his address. You could take that thing if you go to see him.' She pointed a green-tipped finger at the detached nose. 'What do you want them for, anyway? Up to no good, are they?'

'What makes you think that?' Kate asked.

The girl spread her hands. 'Come off it. I wasn't born yesterday. Someone rents so-called business premises in a tatty dump like this. They never have deliveries, never have callers. I popped up one day to see if their receptionist would like to come to lunch with me – you know, just to be friendly, like. No receptionist, just this bloke in a suit so sharp I'm surprised he didn't cut himself.'

'Your organisation's based here,' Kate said.

'So it is. And it's legit, too. Just poor. Oh, it's quiet enough now, but these music kids are never up before twelve. Hots up after the early afternoon *Neighbours*. Really busy half-five. Just when I want to push off to feed my cat.' She looked at the other women. 'Tell me, what's it like being in the fuzz? Often fancied it. I reckon I'd look good in a uniform.'

'You'd look great,' Lizzie agreed. 'And we need sparky women like you.'

'Black ones and all?'

'Especially black women,' Lizzie assured her.

Kate thought of Fatima, and merely smiled.

The next address, near a canal in Selly Oak, was equally elusive. They were looking for Breve Fancy Goods.

'Breve sounds a bit exotic for Selly Oak,' Lizzie observed, pronouncing it with two syllables. 'They favour homelier names round here. Look at them. Lottie Road, Winnie Road. Even a Katie Road!'

Kate nodded, abstracted. A narrow boat was puttering its way along the canal, coal powered, by the smell coming from the chimney stack, and laden with coal. The man leaning on the huge tiller might be living in the Thirties. She'd never realised that — what had Graham called them? Cuts? — that cuts were still used by working vessels. As if to make a point, another narrow boat nosed into view, in its full panoply of painted kettles and buckets and lovingly picked-out woodwork. In the bows, an elderly woman, wrapped up, true, against the cold, was basking in the winter sun. A cat sat on the cabin roof, and an elderly man steered. She could have done with a camera.

'Sorry?'

Lizzie coughed, ironically. 'I was saying we'd better find another postie. And they seem to be like hen's teeth.'

They came on the place themselves, however, down an unadopted road near a car-breaker's yard.

'Highly salubrious,' Kate said. 'I wouldn't want to work out here, either.'

'You wouldn't work anyway. You'd spend all your life looking at boats.'

Kate blinked. The tone wasn't jokey: it was critical. Like the Girl Guide comment. Wrong side of bed morning? Or something more serious?

'Maybe sell my house and live on one: end of parking problems,' she said lightly. 'Here we are, anyway. Not that it looks as if anyone's at home.' She rattled the doorknob.

The door flew open. A youth dashed out. Lizzie grabbed and grounded him. Kate checked inside.

'Nothing in here,' she said. 'Unless you count a flea-ridden sleeping-bag. And a *Big Issue* bag.'

'I'm just dossing. Honest. Honest, Miss. Look in the bag. Me ID's in there.'

Lizzie let him up, slowly. 'Is it, Sergeant?'

'Yes, Ma'am. Even looks like him, a bit,' Kate grinned. She passed the card. 'How long have you been here?'

'Couple of weeks. That's all. Honest. I didn't even break and enter. Door was wide open. Well, a little bit open.'

'Was there anything in here when you arrived?'

'Some paper in the bin. That's all.' He turned to Lizzie. 'As God is my witness, that's all.' His voice rose.

Lizzie continued to watch him implacably.

'What sort of paper in the bin?' Kate asked.

'Just screwed up rubbish.'

'Like you, eh, Simon,' Lizzie said. 'Screwed up rubbish.' She shoved him hard away from her so he staggered against the wall.

It must be a wrong-side-of-bed morning, Kate decided. Lizzie was definitely out of order there.

'Hang on. You don't have to say that. I started my A levels once. And I'm clean, now. Look.' He pushed up his sleeves. There were no new tracks. He glared resentfully, and turned to Kate again. 'Like, letters, you know. Some torn across, some – some paper balls,' he said, clearly to the point of insolence. 'And no, I didn't read them. Not because I can't read. Because I'm honest. They weren't mine to read. Right? Anyway, I used them as bog paper. There's a bog up them steps.' He pointed to a door at the back of the office. 'Through there. But watch yourself. The whole place is falling to bits.'

Kate grinned. 'Come on, Simon, you're sitting having a quiet crap. Surely you'd have a quiet read, too?'

'Blank paper. Just the heading on it.'

'Heading?'

'Hmm. Something foreign. Breve. Doesn't it mean short, or something? La vida breve.'

Did the average *Big Issue* seller speak Spanish? Kate was about to take him up on it when Lizzie spoke.

'I suppose you haven't any left in your loo?'

'Sainsbury's recycled, that's what I'm on now. Mind you, the bog isn't flushing all that well.'

'And you've been here exactly how long?' Kate asked. She dug in her bag and gave him the KitKat.

'Two weeks and three days. Cheers. I watched them go, actually. In this big motor.'

'Any idea what sort?'

'Flash.' He obviously knew exactly what car had been used, probably down to the last digit of the number-plate.

'When did you last eat, Simon?'

He looked affronted. 'Last night. I try and eat regular.'

'So you're not hungry now. You couldn't use a burger at that café back on the main road.'

'I'm supposed to be a veggie – Oh, go on. Twist my arm.'

'So we know it was a grey Merc with this year's plates, driven by a middle-aged bloke with a funny accent, not quite Brum but not not Brum. That bit'll help, I don't think. Looked well-off. Not fat, not thin. And that there was a secretary some days of the week and an answerphone. It's not a lot, is it?' Kate said. Though it was more than Lizzie would have got with her tactics. What was wrong with the woman? She didn't have to prove anything to Kate.

She and Lizzie were stuck in a traffic jam heading back towards the city. The early brightness had given way to gusting cloud and rain was spattering the windscreen.

'It's enough to make me think we've got a long firm fraud on here,' Lizzie said.

'Long-term fraud?' Kate repeated. She'd thought her ears were clearing at last, but that defeated them.

'Long *firm* fraud. It's a well-known scam. You set up a company by buying a named limited company. In this case it was probably trading in fancy goods, clothes, whatever. You open a bank account. Then you acquire a warehouse to receive the goods you acquire. At this stage you play by the book – cash up front, or prompt payment of invoices. All very boring, so far. Then you set up a couple of false companies. Let's call them Minim and Breve, for the sake of argument. So when you start expanding you can supply credit references. You're buying from lots of small firms. Then you start asking for credit – you know, cash flow crisis, that sort of thing. And you pay prompt to the minute. You tell them you're tripling your orders. You need to extend your credit. You've no intention of paying, of course, but they don't know that because you've been such a prompt payer before. And then you – and your credit referees – do a flit.'

'So what happens to all the stuff you've acquired?'

'Lots of outlets within motorway distance of here. Worcester, Lichfield, Warwick – they'll all have tatty premises you can rent on a short lease. Just right for the Christmas rush.'

'Tatty premises? Alan Grafton was talking about high-class leather wear. You'd want to flog that somewhere quite nice, wouldn't you? Nice big mark-up?'

Lizzie sighed and cut the engine. 'Why bother about nice big mark-ups when you're getting the stuff for free? Come on, even you Londoners must have the places. Everything under a fiver. You'd shift even high-class leather wear there.'

Kate hadn't been sure whether the sigh was directed at her. But she knew the sarcasm was. Before she could take her up on it, Lizzie fished out her phone, asking the voice at the other end about traffic.

'Solid into the city.' Lizzie repeated, drumming on the steering wheel and looking at her watch.

Kate looked at hers. Then she pointed. 'There's a pub over there. Why don't we stop off for a sarnie? Maybe it'll clear.'

'If you want.' Lizzie started the engine, signalled, and nudged towards a gap in the inside lane. 'And if you try to close on me, you fucking bastard, I'll do you for bleeding careless driving.'

The driver gave two fingers and closed the difficult gap. Kate got out, flashed her ID and pointed. He reversed. Smartly.

She got back in. 'Seems a bit of an anticlimax to park quietly in a pub after all that,' she said.

'I can always try and pick my way along the rat runs,' Lizzie said, 'if you're in a hurry to get back.'

'Why should I be? We can always have a working lunch.'

'I thought you might be meeting someone.' Lizzie parked, not very well.

Kate shook her head. 'Who should I be meeting?'

'How about Graham Harvey?'

'Why should I be meeting Graham, for goodness' sake?' Kate felt her anger rising.

'Well, Kate, the word on the street is that you and he—'

'I don't give a fuck about the word on the street.'

'You bloody should, then. He's a good, decent man, and mud sticks in this job.'

It didn't make her feel any better that she'd said exactly the same thing to him already. 'It seems to be sticking to me already,' she said, keeping her voice level with an effort. 'Without reason.'

'Why have you come swanning over here to us, then, unless it's to get you out of his hair?'

'Didn't you hear what we said yesterday? He knows Sanderson – and you people wanted to follow up Alan Grafton's bankruptcy. Full-stop.' She let her voice rise to match Lizzie's.

'Rodney Neville told Ted Dyson there was another reason he wanted you out of the office. A man-woman thing. And I'm telling you, Graham Harvey's as decent a cop as you'd wish to find and the last thing he needs is some silly bitch sleeping with him to get herself speedy promotion. Except – pardon me – I'd forgotten you were a Butterfly.'

'I may be on the accelerated promotion scheme but that doesn't mean I've ever been a PC CV. Neither does it mean I'm sleeping with Graham. I'm going out with another bloke, as it happens. And, though I don't know why I'm telling you this, the man-woman thing is a major case of sexual harassment. And the guy that's doing the harassing has complained, I gather, that I'm framing him.' She reached for the door-handle and got out of the car.

'Where the fuck are you going?' Lizzie ran after her, and pulled her arm. 'For Christ's sake, woman, if you want to go by bus, fine – but just wait until I've apologised and done a decent grovel.'

Kate stared, swallowing her anger, and at last softened. 'OK. So long as you can grovel inside over half a pint.'

Chapter Seventeen

Two messages awaited Kate: one from Harry, asking her to call, and one from Graham, telling her to call. Lizzie, on whose desk they'd been put, since Kate was still homeless, passed them to her with an ironic smile.

She responded with an equally ironic bow. Well, even if she was still angry, at least she understood a bit more about Lizzie's attitude now. If you'd joined the force as a career cop without the cachet of being seen as a high-flyer, you could be forgiven, perhaps, for disliking people like Kate apparently flitting in and out. It didn't help knowing that they were guaranteed to go upwards and onwards while you had to slog every inch of the way. And as a woman, who'd no doubt endured years of stuff every bit as bad as Selby could dish out, and maybe worse, you had twice the reason. Furthermore — and she couldn't bring herself to ask Lizzie point blank why — Lizzie was clearly a fully-paid up member of the Graham Harvey Fan Club: he was a man who could do no wrong and still be handsome and heroic. Kate supposed that if you worked alongside Ted Dyson, a bit of male pulchritude wouldn't come amiss. And Lizzie must be quite close in age to Graham: she might not see him, as Kate saw him, as middle-aged, however attractive and kind he might be. When he was kind, that is. When she picked up the phone to dial, she was all too aware that she could be on the receiving end of a bollocking just as well as a bouquet. And it never helped if you didn't know in advance what the bollocking was for.

'Kate!' He sounded pleased to the point of delighted. 'Tell me, have you had lunch yet?'

Keeping her voice rock steady, she explained she'd already eaten with Lizzie. At the sound of her name Lizzie looked up. She might have looked down again but Kate was damned sure she was still listening.

'Pity. Well, do you have time for a quick half after work? Very quick. I want to up-date you on developments here. Have you arranged to collect that freezer box yet?'

'Not yet. I didn't want to look too obvious. I mean, people with their money might think I'm a bit odd wanting it back at all.'

'Don't you believe it: most wealthy people I know watch every penny. Anyway – the place you and Colin usually drink? Six?'

'Fine.' She cut the call. With Lizzie's ears flapping, there was no way she could tell him she was looking forward to seeing him. Nor would she ask if Colin would be there too.

Harry's news was so exciting she told him to phone Graham straightaway – might even have sounded irritated that he hadn't told him already. Or – more appropriately – that the woman logging the calls hadn't told him already. The woman who'd fingered Sanderson had made another accusation. That Sanderson knew about those tablets, those—. That was all. The call had started and terminated at twelve noon. Which tablets might they be?

She made another call. 'Colin: any news on those pharmacy break-ins?'

'Hello, and it's lovely to speak to you, too. I'm very well, thanks. How are you?'

'Sorry, Colin. My brain's ahead of my manners, I gather. I'm fine and missing you and all the others, though not as much as you, of course. And how *are* you? Seriously.' She'd never even asked him about his home life, had she!

'Back together, as it happens. Ish, I'd say, if pressed. But there you go. And no, the civilian in-putter – I've asked Rona to do them, by the way, since she's the most efficient – hasn't done them yet. Late this afternoon, early tomorrow, I'd say. Anyone else, Friday.'

'Remind me I owe you. You're an angel.'

'I know. Isn't it lucky you know me. Bye, sweetie! Sorry: Ma'am.'

'Oh, Sweetie will do. So long as you stand to attention while you're saying it.' She replaced the phone.

Lizzie coughed. 'Nice to see standards of discipline being maintained at all times. Is that that gorgeous Colin Roper? No wonder you're not interested in Graham! Colin's got the nicest bum in the West Midlands Police. Hmm,' she growled, predatory.

Kate hesitated. Was it OK for women to refer to men in the terms they'd have found offensive had the roles been reversed? Not that Lizzie would have made the remark had she known Colin was gay. But as long as Kate was Colin's beard, she'd stay that way. 'He's my closest friend,' she said firmly.

From the flicker of her eyebrows, Lizzie must have registered the rebuff, but she said nothing. She interrupted the desert-island screen-saver in the middle of the protagonist's swim, and brought up the Dunn and Bradstreet programme. 'Hey, aren't you supposed to be the bee's knees where computers are concerned? Your actual geek?'

Kate wrinkled her nose. 'A couple of courses. But I've yet to make the acquaintance of Messrs Dunn and Bradstreet. If you'd care to introduce me?'

Lizzie said, 'When a firm is registered at Companies House, it has to list all its directors. And they have to list all their other directorates and interests. So all we have to do is start our trail and you can trace a man through all his legitimate business connections. Provided he declares them. What I'd like to see is a bit of serious cross-referencing where you can type in someone's name and watch all their activities appear before your eyes. It'll be the next development, I hope, but it ain't here yet. So we know of Symphony Leather. So let's just hope he appears there. What a strange thing: we have a Mrs Isobel Sanderson here. But no Howard Sanderson. I wonder why not.'

'I believe he had a manufacturing company in the Black Country that went down the tubes.'

'So he may have gone bankrupt and be ineligible to hold any more directorates till he's been discharged. Hmm. No idea of the name of the firm? No? Well, that's a little job for Bill and Ben.' She waved an airy hand in the direction of two thirty-something men, who responded with equally off-hand nods. They looked decent enough – Kate would have been glad of the chance to make a friendlier overture.

'So what about Minim and Breve?' Kate tapped Minim into the computer. And came up with names, but not Sanderson's. The same applied to Breve. She flung up her hands in despair: everything she needed must be in there somewhere, but she didn't know how to dig it out. Yet. And from their expressions, neither Bill nor Ben wanted to come over and help.

'The trouble with accountants,' Lizzie said, an hour later, 'is that they go all round the Wrekin and still—'

'"Wrekin"?'

'Bloody big hill in Shropshire. Brum's version of "round the houses" – more graphic, I always think.'

Kate nodded. 'And still—' she prompted.

'—still don't give you the answers you want. OK, all we're after now, right, is to know whether, all things being equal, Alan Grafton was a decent business man, who, had he not have been diddled, would still have his bank behind him and would therefore be solvent.'

'And alive,' Kate added. 'If, that is – and you know I

want him to have been murdered, Lizzie – he was driven to suicide.'

'There you go then. That's what we tell them to find out. Anything else? Right. Now here's a list of other firms that have gone under recently.' She laid a print-out on her desk. 'Any common factors: could you check through and see if our friends Breve and Minim feature amongst the credit referees?'

She'd just settled to the task, working on a spare table brought in from the DCI's room, when she was summoned to the phone on Lizzie's desk. Lizzie passed her the handset with a sigh, which might have been humorous.

'Kate? I had to tell you. It's me: Patrick. I'm calling from Paris. I've just got hold of the most marvellous machine and simply had to tell someone. Kate: I've got my hands on – wait for it! – an MV Augusta. The most beautiful, fire engine red MV Augusta!'

She had to say something. She hoped she expressed more enthusiasm than she felt. 'That's great. Wonderful! Well done!'

'I knew you'd be pleased. Look, as soon as I've arranged for shipment, I'll get back to you. This calls for the most super celebration!'

'Count me in.'

'I'll be in touch!'

Kate replaced the handset.

'I have to say,' Lizzie observed, 'that while your voice gushed with enthusiasm, your eyes did not.'

'I challenge anyone to get truly passionate about an MV Augusta,' Kate retorted. 'It's a red motorcycle.'

'Didn't Mike Hailwood ride one? Oh, before your time. Before mine, really. But I had a big brother.'

'Well, now I really regret not having one.' And Kate headed back to the table.

'Who have you got, then? This man who lusts for big red bikes?'

No reason why she should temporise. 'Patrick Duncan.'

'Pat the Path? My word! Well, Kate, I'd say you were in for some interesting times.' And Lizzie got up and swept from the room.

What about phoning Isobel, on the off-chance that she might be at home? Kate paused, hand above the figures: what if all she got was an answerphone? What message should she leave? Simply that she'd pop round that evening? That she'd phone back that evening? Or should she risk leaving her own home number? There was no way she could leave the CID or the Fraud Squad numbers, lest anyone happily – and correctly – announce themselves as West Midlands Police. She replaced the phone. How did she feel about giving anyone her home number? Isobel, yes – it was an excellent idea. But not Howard.

What about another phone line? She'd better set one up. For that she'd need authority. Lizzie shook her head: it was beyond hers.

'But a DCI could do it,' she added helpfully. 'Why not ask Graham if you're seeing him tonight.'

'I might just do that. Unless Ted Dyson would oblige?'

'Depends whether he's on speaking terms with his stomach ulcer. Happy hunting – I'm off to the dentist.'

Professionally speaking, she'd rather have asked Dyson. It would have meant she could get on with the job more quickly. But if he'd decided against it, she wouldn't have wanted to go on to ask Graham. Graham it would be, then. Meanwhile, on the merest off-chance, she dialled Isobel's number. And got the answerphone. She left a message saying she'd phone back: it was good to know that her number was denied anyone dialling 1471.

The best thing to do now, with the room relatively quiet, was to go through the list of credit referees. Not a Minim or a Breve amongst them. BrightSparks, Brio, Clef, Concerto, Darling, Gifts4All, Prettyware – right down to Zappideal.

'Some will be bona fide, of course,' said Dyson, over her

shoulder. 'Sorry, didn't mean to make you jump. That one there – see, they only guaranteed a thousand pounds, though. It's those with the highest ratings that you want to look for. Now, Kate, I forgot to say this this morning. Keep a copy. Of everything. One for the records. One for your records. One for me. OK, they say Fraud cut down more forests than any other department, but remember we're talking evidence, here. Evidence a jury has to understand. They see it written down, they're more likely to believe you. Time and date. Graham tells me you're a decent detective, but in Fraud you've got to be more than decent. You've got to be obsessive over detail. And that's the first detail to remember. Copies.'

Was that ulcerous behaviour? She decided to risk asking for a phone extension and an answerphone. And got both, with a wave of the hand. 'Just keep a note of when and why you requested it. That's all. Oh, and a copy for me.'

Kate was poring over the list while she waited for Graham, who was uncharacteristically late. She wondered if in fact she was being stood up: had fear of his wife's displeasure overcome his desire to meet her? And though she was happy to flap a matey hand at any coppers who happened to be using the place, she didn't want to invite company. Not until her standing up was definite.

'Another one?' Graham's hand hovered over her glass.

She knew her smile was unguarded, saw him register, return it with one equally open. And then their faces returned to formality.

'Cast your beadies over this while I get you one,' she said. 'Your usual bitter?'

'I think I'll settle for half of mild tonight. Why don't you try it? Midlands speciality.'

It was only as she ordered that she realised what they'd said might have two meanings.

'What's the problem?' Graham asked, putting the list down on the table so he could take both glasses from her.

She stood by his shoulder, pointing. 'We know Minim and Breve look pretty dodgy. What I want to guess is which of the others to go for first. Limited time, limited money. Oh, and keep copies of everything.'

He ran an index finger down the column, stopping to point from time to time. The wedding ring he wore, much wider, much heavier than average, glinted in the cosy lighting. 'Easy. That one. That one.' And so on.

He made a minute gesture with his head. She sat, at right angles to him, but pulled her chair round closer to his to watch his progress.

'Why those?'

'Breve.' He pronounced it as one syllable. 'Minim.'

'We thought it was – Oh, God!'

'And you're supposed to be the chapel organist! OK, retired.'

'So we should go for the ones that sound musical first. I should have noticed: they figure more frequently than some of the others, too. Graham, you're a genius.' She clasped his forearm briefly, in what she'd meant to be congratulation. It was the sort of gesture she made to Colin without thinking. Even beneath the layers of fabric, she felt his muscles tense. She released him as quickly as she could without appearing to snatch back.

She willed him to respond lightly. He had to carry the moment.

'Fully paid up member of Mensa,' he said. 'That's me. Or I will be as soon as I pass the entrance test. What now?'

'I check out a few of your choices, then I put it to Lizzie that we trace the person who let out their premises – almost certainly unoccupied by now.'

'How are you getting on with Lizzie?'

'She's not exactly a founder member of the Kate Appreci-
ation Society. Maybe it's because I'm a Butterfly,' she added, to
the tune of 'Maybe it's because I'm a Londoner'.

'She's had a tough time. You and she should be singing
from the same hymn sheet.'

'Do you know her well?'

'She was a neighbour of ours for a while. When we lived
out in Quinton. She was there – she was very helpful – when
my wife lost her baby.'

'I'm so sorry.'

'Hmm. It was a difficult time. She lost it very late, you
see.'

Kate nodded, but said nothing. Perhaps her silence was
sympathetic, but it was also a pause for rapid thinking. He'd
said 'her baby' – not 'our baby'. And he'd called it 'it'. Not
very warm. And had his wife – never a first name! – then had
post-natal depression? Had she still got it?

'You didn't try for another baby?' she asked eventually.

'My wife – no, she said she didn't want to risk it again.
She'd been quite ill, you see. And she's not been what you'd
call strong ever since. She has support, of course. The people
at the church ... Sometimes,' he added, dropping his voice so
low it was hard to hear him though the conversations buzzing
around them, 'sometimes it's not easy. Knowing what to do.
Knowing whether to stay. Knowing whether by being there you
make things worse.'

'You stayed.'

'Twenty years. Every time you work with a woman she's
sure you're having a relationship. Sometimes you feel driven to
do just that. A lot of attractive women in the police, Kate.'

Colin had said something once, hadn't he? About Graham
and another officer? He'd broken it off, not her.

'Anyway, I'd better be getting home to her now,' The life
had gone out of his voice. It wasn't the voice of a man who
wanted a woman to say 'Come home with me instead', was it?

Kate groped for something to say. Robin's wife had been plain nasty. So she'd always thought. It was easier to go on if you thought that. But Graham's wife might not be simply a Gorgon. She might be a sick woman.

'Another half?' Even to her ears the question sounded lame.

'Another night,' he said. 'If you've got time.'

'I've always got time,' she said, 'for a friend.'

Kate couldn't face going back home, not yet. She made her way back to Lloyd House, to find not only a new desk but also an answerphone sitting on it. Dyson had worked fast. She moved her file from the table, and put it in the middle of the desk. No chair yet. The one she'd used earlier had disappeared. No problem. She could record her incoming message sitting on the desk. No fluffs – right on the first take.

What about phoning Isobel?

No reply. This time she left a message on their machine asking her to call back. And crossed her fingers as she replaced the handset. OK, time to head for home and cook up some fish.

As she passed it, she saw yet another phone message on Lizzie's desk.

> *Kate*
> *Please phone me as soon as you can.*
> *Fatima.*

Great. Breaking a promise or disobeying a direct order? And the order one not without good reason. Hell, why couldn't this have come in an hour ago, so she could have chewed it over with Graham?

She was heading back to her desk when she was aware of movement behind her.

'You're working very late, Kate.' It was Dyson. 'And – if I may say so – you don't look very happy about it.'

'It's not the working late, Sir. Not when you've whistled up all this lot so quickly.' She gestured. 'Thanks. No, I've got a problem.'

'This squad or your own?'

'My own.' Funny how good that sounded.

'Take it back there, then. If I know him, Graham Harvey'll still be there. Or failing him, Superintendent Neville. Go on, Kate: that's what he's paid for – to make decisions. And to take the rap if they're the wrong ones.'

Chapter Eighteen

Although Kate had set out to follow Dyson's advice, she turned for home instead. She knew Neville started his days early – she'd catch him before she went into Lloyd House next morning. In what little was left of this evening, she ought to pop in to see Cassie.

There was very little indeed left by the time she eventually got home, and she was far from cheered by the nose-to-tail ranks of cars in her road. So the local school was having a parents' evening, and it was of course a biological fact that parents were incapable of approaching a school without the protection of a car. Cursing, she parked in an adjoining road, no doubt in someone else's cherished spot.

Still the same old concrete floor of course. Roll on Thursday. And a decision about what she did to let the floorers in. She'd have to get Cope to chase Selby on that one. The thought of having her own house open to possible burglars hadn't concentrated her mind as wonderfully as she'd have expected.

Suddenly cooking for herself didn't seem an option. So what was it to be – another chicken tikka naan or something out of the freezer? No contest: the chicken tikka naan meant turning out again.

She still had some wine in her glass when on the off-chance

she phoned Isobel's number. Three rings, and Howard replied. She introduced herself and asked for Isobel.

'I just want to find out when it would be most convenient for me to collect that freezer box I left behind the other evening,' she added.

'I'll call her – if you want. But I'm sure she'll say what I said the other day: the evening's the best time to catch us.'

Kate held on for some time. She could hear Sanderson calling his wife, perhaps even detected a murmured reply. What she didn't hear, as she heard an extension being picked up, was the sound of the first line being closed down. Had Howard simply forgotten, or was he still listening?

Isobel certainly repeated what Howard had declared. 'An evening is probably the best. I'm out so much in the day. It's very hard for me to tell you a time. But another evening this week – Thursday perhaps?'

Why not say that was the night she coached the football team? 'I'm afraid I'm tied up then,' she said. 'Tomorrow?'

There was a minute's hesitation. 'I believe Howard and I may already be committed.'

'Tell you what,' Kate said, not quite ingenuously, 'why don't I drop by anyway – your son could give it me. It's no big deal, after all – just a plastic box.'

'Nigel's very busy. School work. A levels.'

'It's a difficult time for these kids, isn't it?' she agreed, affably. 'So how about Friday?' Not that she'd really want to do anything except dance on her kitchen floor, would she?

'Oh. I believe we're going out on Friday. Perhaps – perhaps we could drop it round to you? On the way?'

Oh, no, you don't. 'Well, I was going to collect it from you on the way to somewhere else,' Kate said. 'Look, it's not that important. I can get another. It's just that I promised a huge batch of mince pies for the Boys' Brigade. Tell you what, maybe if I'm passing I'll just pop round on the off-chance. And if you get a spare hour, you could always phone me and I'll see if I can skive off work for five minutes.' She gave her new number and settled down for an hour in front of the TV.

'I'd like you to make the call with me as a witness,' Neville said, perhaps as Howard had said to Isobel last night. 'I can quite appreciate you want to support Fatima, and that she might be upset if you fail to return the call.' He smiled. 'But you must see why I don't want to do anything that might muddy our waters here. What appears to be happening is a violation of the Race Relations Act, and after the Stephen Lawrence affair I for one am not prepared to let such a thing happen within my area of responsibility. The fact it's sexual harassment as well makes the whole thing even more reprehensible. Put it this way, Kate – I want to nail the bastard.'

That was language Kate could understand. She reached for the phone.

And drew an alarming blank. A woman at the other end told her Fatima had gone to Bradford. Kate left a message.

'Though I'm not sure she'll get it. The person at the other end didn't speak much English.'

'You know Fatima spoke no English when she came over here? Until she was nine, that is? Makes her subsequent achievements even more remarkable, I'd say,' Neville said.

Kate nodded. 'She's a wonderful role model for Asian women,' she said.

Neville rubbed his chin, speculatively. Kate could almost see him thinking, *And she's young and attractive enough to be extremely televisual. And wouldn't that be a good bit of multi-cultural PR for the service?* Out loud he said, 'Absolutely. I'd like to see her going a long way. When this business is over, I'm sure she'll shoot onwards and upwards.'

'If we can stop her resigning. I don't like the sound of this return to Bradford. I really don't.'

Neville smiled, and poured her coffee. It was good, the caffeine firing her immediately.

'I know what you'd like to do, Kate. You'd like to drop everything and go up to see her. This morning. Am I right?'

Kate took another sip. 'Someone ought to,' she said at last.

'You're right. In fact, I think I may well go up myself, provided Welfare approve sufficiently to provide a senior woman officer to accompany me. Sooner, rather than later, before you ask.' He clicked his computer mouse. 'I can make an opportunity – yes, nothing I can't clear. Now, Kate, how are you finding Fraud?'

'I'm missing the jobs I'd started on here. And one has particular urgency, now I come to think of it. There are some burglaries associated with people having carpets fitted. I'm supposed to be having some laid at my place this Friday. I want to know how safe I'd be handing over my keys. I was going to discuss it with DI Cope.'

'Fine. Anything else you're working on? I like to know what people are doing even if I can't maintain daily contact.'

'There are some pharmacy break-ins that interest me. I've spoken to one of my mates from the Met. since I don't know anyone in Drugs up here. I've not set up a nice circle of contacts yet.'

He smiled. 'It takes time and effort, doesn't it? And still the work piles up on your desk.'

'And yet you make time to go to Bradford.' She was rather shocked she had said it out loud.

'It's what I joined the police for: helping people. What about you?' The directness of his gaze startled her. No, he wasn't just a promotion chaser.

She nodded. 'Funny thing. I did too.'

'God, you can tell you're a bleeding high-flyer – breakfast meetings with top brass while the rest of us poor mortals are still trying to park.' Cope was by the coat hooks in his office, struggling out of his raincoat. 'And now you've sorted out our

problems, I suppose you'll be dashing back off to Fraud to sort
out theirs. Drugs, tomorrow, I wouldn't be surprised. Next thing
is you'll be an inspector running a nick of your own.'

It was best to ignore Cope's charm. 'I've got a problem of
my own to sort out first, Gaffer. I'm afraid I may be giving my
house keys to Burglar Bill.' She explained briefly.

'You want to watch that,' he agreed. 'Who's working on
the case?'

'Merv Selby.' She braced herself for a torrent of criticism.
Selby and Cope got on too well for her liking.

'Well, that should be all right. Mind you, he's been busy
doing things for me. That bloody telly programme. Have a word
before you go.' He sat down at his desk, opened a drawer which
he rooted through.

Was she being cowardly or pragmatic? 'Look, Gaffer,' she
said, 'you know what's important and what isn't. I wouldn't
want to take him off some of your stuff if you don't think this
break-in business isn't important.'

'In my book having your mate's house broken into rates
quite high. Is Selby in yet? We'll have him in here and have a
word if you like. Here, sit yourself down.'

Cowardice. Yes. But it had worked.

'You hadn't thought of just taking a couple of hours off
so you could be there with them?' Cope asked.

'What would you have said if I'd asked, Gaffer?' She looked
at him through narrowed eyes.

He roared with laughter. 'Get on with you, wench! OK. But
I wouldn't like you to have that new house of yours done over.
It's not a nice experience, having someone in your place without
you asking them in. What's he like, this carpet-layer?'

'A really nice young man. But I have to leave the keys with
his boss, you see.'

'You know what I'd say, Kate, me love? I'd say, take the time
off. Even really nice young men can be crooks and swindlers. But
we'll see how – Ah! young Merv. Just the lad we wanted . . . .'

Selby lounged in, and leaned one arm against the nearest filing cabinet. He towered over Kate. She knew without looking that his eyes would be focused on her breasts. He jiggled change in his trousers pocket, his finger movements ostentatious.

He clearly hadn't made much progress on any of the files Cope had left him, and Kate sensed that without her in the room he'd have been on the receiving end of one of Cope's bollockings. But then, without her, Cope wouldn't have known he needed a bollocking – and he could always save it up for later. With a bit of interest, all being well.

'So you'll get on to that now, OK? All that piddling stuff the telly viewers have told us – that'll have to wait. I'm not having one of my squad put herself at risk.'

'OK, Gaffer. I'll get on to that for you.' There was a slight but inescapable emphasis on the last word. 'Good result the Blues got last night. Did you see it on the box? That last goal – fancy calling that off-side!' Now he was leaning his back against the cabinet, arms folded. Man to man conversation.

'I'd have called it off-side, myself,' Cope said. 'Commentator seemed to think it was.'

'Biased and blind. They always are. Bloody southerners.'

Including Kate, no doubt. Who was waiting her moment.

'No – he comes up here; passes over there – OK? – so then he comes up here. How can he be off-side?'

'Why don't you come along to my Boys' Brigade practice on Thursday?' Kate asked. 'I'm explaining the off-side rule then.'

Cope was so busy cackling, he didn't notice Selby leaving the room.

'You bitch: dropping me in it like that.'

She'd been expecting this: even his silent emergence from the doorway of another office just down the corridor from Cope's didn't faze her.

'I haven't dropped you in anything. Put your hands down and address me by my name or my rank. I will not tolerate bullying. You are answerable to me; I am answerable to Cope. That's the way it is. Like it or lump it.'

'You—'

'Shut up or you'll be in real trouble. Even Cope realised you've not been pulling your weight. I've said nothing except I need that list of carpet-layers checked for my own peace of mind. Now, go back and get on with your work. I'm going to get on with mine.'

He was ready to strike her but she stared him down. At last his arms sank to his sides again, but he dropped his face to hers. 'Sergeant,' he spat.

She watched him go back to the office. And then she let go her breath.

Time to go to Lloyd House. She turned. And practically walked into Graham Harvey, who was standing arms folded behind her. How long had he been there? And who, then, had Selby obeyed?

'I thought this place was off-limits,' he said.

'I was here to see Neville. And then I had to see Cope.' Was he angry because she was there at all or simply because he didn't know?

His nod was noncommittal. What he might have said was interrupted by Neville, striding past and beaming. 'Tomorrow morning: it's fixed!' he said, without stopping.

'He's going to go and talk to Fatima,' Kate said. 'She's gone back home and he's concerned.'

'I'm surprised he didn't send you.'

'He thought it was too important, perhaps.' She spoke without irony, but he frowned. 'I'd better be off, Gaffer. I don't want Lizzie on my back.' Did she hope for a cup of tea with him? On the whole, probably not, not with his face set like that.

To her surprise, he started to walk with her but at the top of the stairs seemed to think better of it. At last he asked, 'Did you have any luck with Isobel?'

'Her life seems one long social whirl. But all the calls to the switchboard were made about midday. Perhaps it might be worth trying then.'

'Could be. Kate – don't get her into any sort of trouble, will you?'

Lizzie despatched Bill and Ben to check whether the other firms with musical names had similar premises to those she and Kate had been to yesterday. Kate could spend a happy morning on the computer, chasing up connections between directors of Symphony Leather and other companies. Her main aim, however, was to be outside Isobel's house just before twelve.

'Each of the calls we've had has been made at that time. As if she comes in from one of her committees, perhaps, and tried to sneak an opportunity just before someone else arrives.' Kate rested her bum on her desk, facing Lizzie across the room.

'Like Howard?' Lizzie sat back in her chair, arms behind her head.

'Like Howard.'

But there was no sign of anyone when Kate turned up outside the Sandersons' house in Moseley. Unaccompanied by Patrick Duncan, she could spend more time looking round. Yes, it was an affluent area, but the houses were all turn of the century or earlier. Modern equivalents would be much more expensive. But they wouldn't have the heating bills associated with three storeys of high-ceilinged rooms.

The Sandersons' front garden was less impressive than the back, newly blocked to allow maximum parking, no doubt. Tubs with pansies and evergreens broke the monotony. No lit-up Christmas tree, though.

But the dancing red light of a burglar alarm. And, now she came to look more closely, well-positioned surveillance cameras, a make she knew was expensive and reliable. Howard had managed to keep something back from his failed company, then.

What was odd was someone working in the Black Country choosing to live in this area, with an awkward rush-hour drive across the city. Why choose an area the dominant population of which seemed to be health and other professionals, not entrepreneurs?

Shrugging, she pressed the bell. And glanced up to find a security camera, small and discreet, inspecting her make-up, which never had been flawless.

No curtains fluttered. No footsteps sounded within. But she had the strongest sense that someone was in that house. She rang again. And then, suspecting that whatever she did was being recorded, she turned on her heel and walked away.

Chapter Nineteen

Lizzie, sipping take-away tomato soup, greeted her with a flap of the hand and the news that Bill and Ben had found the same sort of uninspired and abandoned premises as she and Kate had found yesterday.

'So I think we'll talk to the landlord of some of them: a cross-section should do. And the lads can get on the phone this afternoon to our colleagues in any local town where there may be one of these cheap-jack stores. Especially new ones. With a bit of luck they'll run a couple to earth and you and I can have a nice girlie day out in Warwick, or Worcester, or wherever, seeing if the merchandise happens to tally with the stuff you reckon this Alan was dealing in.'

'It'll be a bit of a bummer if I find my pricey new bag up for a fiver somewhere, won't it?'

It was better to respond to Lizzie in the off-hand tone she used herself. She couldn't imagine herself ever positively liking the woman, but she knew her stuff and Kate was there both to sort out this Grafton business and to learn. She wished Lizzie had a little of the warmth of the DVU women, though. If she hadn't been so rough with Simon, the lad squatting in the abandoned office in Selly Oak, they might have got a lot more information. In fact, she might just look him up again – see if another meal might help him find more information to divulge. She could always take in a mega-shop at the Sainsbury's he bought his loo rolls from: maybe she might even find him flogging *Big Issues* there. Something for this evening on the way home: new route, new traffic jam. She could look at it that way.

Thanks to the Meedja Contax receptionist, they didn't have far to hunt for one landlord at least. His address was a city centre street near Summer Row. They walked the long way round. Someone had laid a bunch of flowers on the bridge where Grafton had hanged. Kate shivered, not just because there was a chill wind. What if she'd dismissed Colin's suggestion of Cosa Nostra involvement too glibly? They should be exploring every avenue, not just the obvious ones.

'Come off it! With our budgets, and with the likelihood that it was suicide, there'd be no justification whatsoever,' Lizzie said. 'Come on, we're talking nasty small-time crooks, not the big ones like the Mafia! I hope,' she added, with a rare smile. 'Over there. One of those buildings that have been tarted up. Not that they'll stay clean long, not in all this pollution.'

The buildings were attractive inside, too, full of curlicues and twirls in the wood and the plasterwork.

'He likes a bit of home comfort himself, even if the stuff he lets out warrants a demolition order,' Lizzie said. 'Come on, dear,' she said, rapping the counter with her car keys, 'you know you should always put seeing live clients before answering the phone.'

The receptionist tossed her hair and agreed that they had an appointment with Mr Carr. But he was running late. She gestured vaguely at some low chairs.

'Just how late?' Lizzie might have been an irate headmistress.

'Oh, half an hour or so.' Insouciance or bravado?

'I don't think he'll be that late, do you? You buzz through and tell him we're here, there's a good girl. Plump lump,' Lizzie added, turning away.

As terms of abuse – and Lizzie's in particular – went, it was innocuous enough, but the woman flushed crimson.

They were admitted to Mr Carr's office within three minutes, not, incidentally, having seen anyone come out. He was neat, middle-aged, nondescript. Co-operative, even in the face of Lizzie's abruptness.

'This is the file you requested, ladies.' He tapped a file on his desk. 'Our client paid in advance in cash. We did ask for references to establish that he could be trusted to move himself out when he said he would. But – well, this is quite unusual and not what I would recommend – my colleague Mr Bevan accepted an extra two months' rent instead. And they did vacate the premises on the agreed date.'

'So you don't have anything in writing about them?'

He shook his head.

Lizzie produced the list of other premises. 'Are any of these on your books?'

'Allow me.' He tapped into the computer on his desk. His eyebrows rose. 'Mr Bevan seems to have come to a similar arrangement with these four lettings.'

'I don't have to tell you how unwise that was,' Kate said. 'Even though there's a cease-fire in Northern Ireland, you still want to know who's doing what in places you own. What if this had turned out to be a chemicals factory – turning out drugs or arms?'

Carr tightened his lips. 'I've already told you this is most irregular. I'll have a word with Bevan.'

'Don't worry, Mr Carr. We'll do that. Where is he?' Lizzie was on her feet, ready.

He shook his head. 'In the Algarve. Playing golf. Inspector, he's done nothing wrong. Just not met our usual high standards.'

'And just deprived us of a possible source of information. Sod 'em and begorrah.' Lizzie was setting a cracking pace back along Colmore Row. 'Hey, that tomato soup's really lying heavy on my stomach. And I didn't notice your eating anything at lunchtime, which is foolish. First it lowers your blood-sugar so you can't think. And then it leads to indigestion and ulcers and things. So I prefer my team to have lunch-breaks and to eat properly.'

'Do as I say, not as I do?' Kate grinned.

'Touché. Anyway, I'm for a coffee and a cake. Druckers.'

Despite the answerphone, there were some written messages for Kate, both left, irritatingly, on Lizzie's desk. One from Cary Grant, the PC who'd mopped her mascara the morning of Alan's death and got them both plastered over all the papers. He was suggesting a drink sometime. The other was from Patrick Duncan, suggesting the same. Yes to both: why not? But there was a light flashing on her answerphone and she was across the room dabbing her hand on the play button before she could respond to Lizzie's jeers. It had to be Isobel!

And was. So faint she was almost drowned by traffic noises, she said, 'I'd much rather you didn't phone me again at home. I can't...' Her voice faded. 'I have a committee meeting tomorrow in Bournville. It should finish at eleven-thirty. I could spare you two minutes then. Meet me – oh, dear. I've no change. The car park. The Quaker—'

'Yes!' Kate was punching and jumping in the air.

As traffic jams went, the Selly Oak one was probably worse than Kings Heath's, especially when you had to turn right to park behind Sainsbury's. Not a *Big Issue* seller in sight. Rather than battle with the traffic again, Kate left the car where it was, walking down towards the canal and Simon's room. The damp had become a steady drizzle: she was glad he had protection, no matter how rudimentary.

But he wasn't at home in the squat. The door was secured by a cheap padlock which wouldn't have deterred anyone serious. She turned to make the slippery journey back up the unmetalled road, regretting the lack of street lighting. But the figure approaching her was friendly enough.

'You've come without your mate, this time, have you?'

'Hi, Simon. Yes, I had to do a bit of shopping at Sainsbury's and thought I'd look you up. Fancy a coffee?'

He turned to walk back up the road. 'What, in their little shop? It's not cheap, like – er—'

'I'm Kate Power. I'm actually a detective sergeant, but off-duty I'm happy with Kate. Thanks!' He'd grasped her arm as she slid sideways on dead leaves.

'How off-duty are you?'

'Fairly. Just wait till you see me pushing that trolley – then you'll know that in real life I'm actually a grand prix driver.'

'So you really want to do a bit more snooping. Without that cow being there to push me around. Hey, what's a nice girl like you doing in a set-up like the – the police,' he corrected himself.

'Earning a crust. Picking people's brains. Like, why aren't there any shops in Selly Oak?'

'Big business killed them all off. Down there, see, there's a Comet and Homebase and all that – people can nip into their car park, do everything they need, and never hit the main road. Or walk. I suppose you'll want to wait till it's nice and legal to cross.'

'Do you really fancy playing hedgehogs? I wouldn't rate my chances getting through this lot in one piece.'

Some of the women in Sainsbury's coffee area greeted Simon by name.

'Usually sell here,' he said, selecting a couple of packets of sandwiches then putting one back.

Kate retrieved it, and another, and pulled out bottles of fresh orange juice before ordering the coffee.

'Hollow legs?'

'How old are you? Twenty, twenty-one?' He nodded. 'Then I reckon you're at least a stone under your ideal weight. And the boss can pay for this lot.'

He grinned and dodged back for a bowl of soup and a couple of cakes. 'Reckon she can pay for these, too. My mum used to say there was nothing better with coffee than a nice cream cake.'

Kate paid and they found a table. He toasted her with his cup. 'She used to say, "Enjoy!" And smile. Lovely smile.'

'I bet her cakes were nicer than these will turn out to be. Go on – dig in.'

He started on the soup before he looked at her. 'You said "were".'

'Was I wrong?'

He shook his head. 'The big C. I'd be about fifteen. My dad was already dead, so I had to go to foster parents, see. No one Mum's side would touch me. She'd married out, you see. Trouble is, when you're sixteen, you're on your own. No mum and dad to keep an eye out for you.'

'Or fund you.'

He mimed a spit. 'Don't talk to me about the Social. Tory bastards.'

'So you got hooked on heroin, but now you're off it. And trying to get off the streets. You've got guts, Simon.'

'What I want is a job, like. Can't get a job until I've got an address, can't get me dole without an address, can't get an address till I get a job or some dole.'

Kate nodded, thinking of her empty bedroom. But no. Nice kid Simon might be, you couldn't just go inviting people to share. Could you? 'I'll keep my ears open,' she said.

'Thanks. Now,' he said, with the air of a chair gathering his committee's attention, 'I don't reckon your boss will pay for this lot without something in return. What are you after, Kate?'

'A proper description of the man using that little office. And his car number. And details of anyone else you saw using the place.'

To his dictation, she wrote down the exact model of the Mercedes, almost the entire number, a description of a nice middle-aged woman who always smiled as if she didn't like to show her teeth, but was really nicely dressed, better than Simon's mum could ever have afforded, and this good-looking bloke with a suntan. If only she had photos of the Sandersons.

'You could identify them in a parade if necessary?'

'I get it: no form so no photo. Yeah, I could ID them. Or I could do a photofit, if they give me decent coffee. Want a refill? Go on, my shout. I got a few donations today. Not supposed to accept them, but you know how it is.'

'Keep your donations for the phone. For when you remember anything else. Or see anything else. Anything. OK?' She gave him her card, and then added in her home number and her new answerphone number.

'You do want this help bad, don't you?'

'Enough to buy you another coffee. And something for breakfast, too.'

And home, bags less full of goodies than if she hadn't just been with Simon, for a domestic evening with the microwave, the freezer, the washing machine, the phone and the ironing board for company. As she hung the stuff in her front bedroom to air, she pondered on the justice of having or not having. She might not have a Sanderson-sized mansion. But she had a newly-solid roof over her head. Even if it would be more sensible to share it with Colin than with Simon.

Chapter Twenty

Isobel was sitting in the driving seat of her own car, a new, mid-price Rover, her eyes flicking from mirror to mirror to her watch and back again.

'Three minutes. I have to start back in three minutes. I have to.'

'Or?' Kate twisted in the passenger seat so she could see something of Isobel's face.

'Or his lunch isn't on the table in time.'

'And he'll be angry?'

'He may not even come back for it. But it has to be there or he knows.'

'Surely—'

'The cameras.'

Kate nodded. 'Start driving then. I can always get the bus back. And you can drop me off some road he won't drive up. Even if he comes.'

'But – the rain.'

'It's OK. A drop of rain won't harm me. None of the women here will say anything, will they?'

'Oh, they could – just drop it out. Oh, dear—'

Kate slipped the domestic violence card into Isobel's hand. 'Put this in with your credit cards. When's your next committee meeting? And where?'

'Tomorrow. Eleven. I know the chairwoman. You could come to her house.' She gave an address in Shirley.

'What's it about?'

'A work project for homeless youngsters.' She had the keys in the ignition, and was looking round with increasing anguish.

'In that case, Isobel, I shall be round quite legitimately. I know someone in desperate need. See you then.'

'Why don't we simply have her in? Talk to her up-front, like?'

Bill — or was it Ben? — earned a sigh from Lizzie.

'Don't you lads ever listen? Pity we can't hurry it on a bit, though. I'd love to find why her name's on the board of directors of half a dozen of these dodgy firms, and her husband's not at all. OK, hear it from her own lips. This pair established that Sanderson's last firm did go bankrupt, poor sod,' she explained. 'But he doesn't seem overly poor, so we can guess he'd protected his house and various other assets.'

'Including, we reckon, a warehouse,' put in Ben. 'Industrial estate, not far from Dudley. We tried sniffing around, but it was locked.'

'That's never stopped you before,' Lizzie grinned.

'Very locked. No accessible windows. But with a bit of equipment—' He grinned, gesturing a key turning.

'OK. Any signs that it's in use?'

'Tyre marks, quite recent.'

'Hmm. So they've got themselves this warehouse conveniently close to a motorway junction,' said Kate, happy to show off her local knowledge. 'Any news of out-of-town cheapo shops?'

'Funny you should ask that, Kate', Bill said. 'There's a number in county towns — Warwick, Worcester, Stafford. And then throw in Lichfield, Tamworth and Redditch for good measure. All recent, all selling good stuff at discount, according to the locals.'

'Good. Kate and I can go shopping for handbags one day.

So now we've got from that scumbag Kate's befriended a full description of a man who sounds, according to Kate, very like Sanderson, another sounding like his wife, and a car reg. Kate hasn't got round to putting it through the computer yet.'

Ben held out his hand. Kate transcribed the figures on to a scrap of paper, and passed it to him with a smile. She was rewarded with a wink. 'Five pence it's this bloke Sanderson's?'

'It's a nice motor for a bankrupt,' she said. 'Any news from the forensic accountants, by the way?'

'They want a meeting,' Lizzie said. 'Five-thirty.'

'Not this evening. I've got an appointment I can't break. In fact, I shall have to push off at about four.'

'Will you indeed?' Lizzie bristled.

'I'm having something done at my house and I don't want to entrust my keys to the men doing it. Oh, and I shall be in late tomorrow, too. I don't mind leaving them to it, but I don't want them to be able to copy the key or to know my burglar alarm code.'

'Haven't you ever heard of putting the job first?'

Kate flushed. OK, she should have mentioned it to Lizzie first, but she had Cope's positive encouragement and didn't relish the public criticism. On the basis of soft answers turning away wrath, she said, 'I'm sorry – I booked the time off on DI Cope's insistence. I forgot I wasn't really in his squad at the moment.'

Lizzie sniffed, but let it go. 'Colin Roper phoned, by the way. About some drugs stuff you're looking at. You don't want to overstretch yourself, Power.'

'No, Ma'am.'

'They're just playing power games, that's all. Whoops. Sorry, Kate. You must get that all the time.' Cary Grant smiled as he passed her a bag of crisps.

'Tell me about it. It's an Irish name, I gather. Originally. I guess I must have descended further than most.'

'And telling this Lizzie woman a bloke's OK'd your time off is just a red rag to a bull. You should have known better.' His smile intensified.

Kate popped the bag, and started in. She reviewed her evening so far. The floorer had arrived to the moment, giving an amiable thumbs up at the sight of her tomorrow's breakfast things sitting on a tray at the foot of the stairs.

'Only one thing – you've forgotten this.' He waved the kettle at her.

He'd finished in time for her to coach the BB football team – the first time she'd seen them for a while, and they'd been so pleased to see her back they couldn't recognise an open goal mouth even if it got up and yelled at them. And then, after the most perfunctory of showers, she'd come to this pub in deepest suburbia to meet Cary. And she was starving. Crisps weren't her favourite food, but they'd do. Perhaps they'd eat together later, perhaps they wouldn't.

It was always nice to be with the best-looking man in a place, and he seemed to be bubbling with something.

'Did you see all those photos in the papers?' she asked him.

'Every last one. I tell you, Kate, it hasn't half done me some good. They only want me to front this bloody *Grass on your Neighbour* programme when the woman doing it at the moment goes on maternity leave.'

'Hey! That's brilliant.' They exchanged a friendly five. 'Good for you.'

'Oh, don't get me wrong: I don't reckon it's my charm and good looks they want.'

'Come off it – you've got more than your fair share of both!'

He raised a cynical eyebrow and touched his cheek. 'This is what they want. My skin, Kate. Good PR, see?'

'You're sure you're not selling yourself – and the service – short?'

He shrugged. 'I don't know. It's not going to stop me, anyway. If it comes to you on a plate, your fifteen minutes of fame, grab it with both hands, that's my motto. So tomorrow night, it's big booze-up time – come along if you want.'

'So your mates will be getting pissed rather than taking the piss?'

He narrowed his eyes. 'How did yours react?'

'The odd quip about my boobs not being page-three material.'

'Bastards. Is it true, this rumour about one of your DCs? On sick leave because some stupid bastard's been touching her up, twanging her bra and that?'

'Is that what he's been doing?'

Cary leant closer. 'The rumour is that he said it was because he didn't know whether Muslim women wore bras and he wanted to find out. That's what he told her, anyway.'

'If that's true, I'm surprised she didn't clock him. Hard. She's been taking a lot of other shit from him too: she's fasting and he kept trying to press food on her. And some other stuff too,' she added lamely. It'd be nice to share everything with someone who wasn't involved, but this was one rumour best kept under wraps.

'Racism is alive and well,' he said.

She looked him in the eye. 'How do you get on?'

He gave a short laugh. 'For starters, I'm a coconut – brown outside, white inside. I don't go wearing my head covered and I don't fast. So I don't draw attention to myself. Except in nice ways, that everyone can approve of. Soccer, cricket: they're manly things, right.' He inserted quotation marks with his fingers. 'If I were a woman, and into embroidery, I guess life might be tougher. People still tend to stereotype me a bit. Assume I can run and that I've got a big cock and that I've got love-babies scattered all over the West Midlands.'

'Are the three supposed to be connected?' she asked.

'Get on with you. Tell you what, there's a good Chinese up the road. How about it?'

'Thought you'd never ask.'

'Tell you what, leave us your keys, and I'll lock up and pop them through your front door,' the floorer said. 'No need for you to hang round.'

'I will for just five minutes. I forgot to leave out any milk, didn't I? And I'm not a woman for dry cornflakes.' Nor was she a woman to hand over her keys, not even to this smiling lad. Not after what Cope had said. And come to think of it, some cons might think it really macho to rob a copper.

Teeth clean, make-up on, she flapped a hand at the floorer.

'You're not leaving the keys, then?'

'Can't. One of the locks is a Yale. I wouldn't get back in again. No spare key.'

'Oh, you want to start leaving one with a neighbour, then. In case you ever lock yourself out or want things delivered.'

She nodded. She was paranoid enough not to like leaving the place unnecessarily exposed, but had to admit that statistically she'd be unlikely – and unlucky! – to be broken into in the one day neither the Chubb nor the burglar alarm was in use.

Kate checked herself over as she presented herself at a big semi in Shirley. She looked every inch a committee woman with her skirt at a respectable, not a fashionable length, a fussier blouse than usual, and make-up abstemious to the point of invisible. The other women might be older than her – by some twenty to thirty years – but didn't know that they should observe any special dress code. She felt downright frumpy.

None of the women made any special effort to introduce themselves either, and Kate sat through a quarter of an hour of other people's gossip before the chair called the meeting to anything like order. But the minutes were actually very clear, and matters arising were concise. Then there was a lot of stuff about fund-raising which lost her.

At last a coffee break was declared. Daring to catch Kate's eye, Isobel offered to make it, and Kate quickly joined her in the kitchen. Although the women's voices rang out from the living room, Isobel still spoke in almost a whisper.

'I didn't realise you were from the police. You misled me.'

Kate shook her head. 'I was genuinely a guest: I came with Patrick, remember. It was just that no one asked what I did. But I am in the police. I work in that office you called.'

Isobel looked ready to be sick.

'I knew Alan Grafton, you see, Isobel — and when I heard his name I knew I needed to talk to you. And you to me. Now, when's a good time?'

Isobel's eyes flew open. 'You don't understand, do you? There's no good time.'

'After this meeting?'

'You know I have to be back.'

'We could meet one morning—'

'I don't have one morning.'

'But you do have information you're desperate to give someone. That's why you phoned. What we have to do is find a way for you to give it. Safely.'

Isobel had turned from her and was gripping the edge of the sink. 'I tell you there is no hour of the day when he doesn't know what I'm doing. The cameras—'

'But he can't be filming you now.'

'He'll want to see the minutes. That's why I do them. There's no point asking someone else to take them if I have to produce them anyway. And he wants accounts of every other meeting. They have to tally with the official ones. Don't you see?'

'A morning's shopping?'

'If only you knew!'

Kate laid a hand on her arm. 'Isobel, if it means my coming to every single meeting you attend, and snatching ten minutes with you to make the coffee, I promise I'll do it. Please trust me.'

Isobel shook her head violently. And then, as Kate put her arm round her, slumped. 'I'll try. I promise I'll try. There's a meeting on Monday. Green Fingers. We work with people with learning difficulties. You could come to that.' With the first proper smile Kate had seen, she added, 'Bring your gardening gloves.'

Kate managed to snatch another two minutes with her when the meeting finished.

'I will try and tell you. There's evidence. Howard and poor Nigel. I'll try.'

Kate hugged her. 'I know you will.' For a moment she toyed with a delicate threat to balance whatever Howard had threatened, to tell Isobel that it was an offence to withhold information about a crime, but she couldn't steel herself to it. 'Remember, any time you have the chance to use a phone – two minutes from a call box, perhaps—'

'I don't have money for phone calls.'

Kate stared. And then smiled, as gently as she could. 'Here's my phone card. There'll be another on Monday.'

She was in the pub with Midge and Lorraine from the Domestic Violence Unit.

'Go on, your not eating won't make life any better for her,' Lorraine said.

Kate took a sandwich from a communal plate and nodded. 'It's just I can't imagine – I can't begin to imagine – that sort of control.'

'Let's just go through what you're saying. There are cameras in all the rooms, and, of course, outside, to watch her comings and goings. I bet they're those clever jobs that have the time and date in the corner of each frame. She has to account for every minute of mornings she spends at meetings. She doesn't have money to make phone calls. Some control freak we've got there!'

'But why does she let him do it?'

Lorraine spread her hands.

Midge got up. 'Come on, Kate – you need something stronger than water. Even if we have to carry you back to work.'

'White wine, please. But why—' she turned to Lorraine – 'should she choose this moment to try to break out?'

'If you ask me, it'll be something that her conscience really can't stomach any longer. Something to do with that son of hers, perhaps. Or that Grafton topping himself. It won't be anything Sanderson's done to her.' She smiled. 'I've seen women with major injuries refusing to split until the old man's threatened the cat. It's a funny old world, isn't it, Kate?'

Chapter Twenty-One

'Long time no see,' Lizzie said, pausing in the dialling of a phone number.

'I've got an appointment to see Isobel on Monday morning,' Kate said. What did they say? Don't apologise, don't explain. 'Some charity gardening thing. Any news of the car reg?'

'That? No. Not Sanderson's.' Lizzie grinned at last. 'His wife's.'

'Not that she ever gets her hands on it. What next?'

Lizzie shrugged, amused. 'Your case. What do you suggest?' She put down the handset without beginning her call.

'She doesn't even have the money to phone me. How about we get permission to rake her in as a paid informant? That way we'd get what we need and she'd have enough independent money to be able to escape.'

'Dyson was keen on the idea, wasn't he? It won't be his say-so, of course. Them upstairs.'

'He seems to be the sort of man to carry clout.'

Lizzie nodded. 'Lots of clout. The question is, will she take up the offer, if we make it?'

Kate's turn to shrug. 'It depends how we sell it her, I suppose. The trouble is, if she's got to the stage where she accepts this total control, she probably doesn't think she deserves any better. She was provoked into calling us by

Alan Grafton's death. It's got to be something external that makes her act.'

'Stupid cow.'

'She's actually very bright, Lizzie. She held her own at that meeting this morning. They're raising funds to put together accommodation and work schemes for street kids. Like young Simon,' she added. 'Now, the word is her son's equally under Sanderson's thumb. I wonder how he got there ... Look, if you've nothing else you want me to do this afternoon, how about I find out a bit more about him?'

'Why not?'

Nigel Sanderson was not attending a state school, that was quickly established. No doubt his father had tucked money into a trust fund which couldn't be touched when his firm went under. So Kate got on to the voluntary-aided schools, which turned out to be old-fashioned boys' grammar schools. She dimly remembered hearing someone sounding off about the system before she went on holiday: yes, the Baptist minister's brother-in-law, that was it. But Nigel wasn't at one of them, either.

She moved on up the financial league, into the independent sector. Most administrators – not simple school secretaries – were even cagier than the state school secretaries had been. She couldn't blame any of them, either, much as she'd have liked to in her increasingly grumpy mood. They were, after all, dealing in young people's lives.

At last though, she pinned one down. And yes, Nigel Sanderson was on their roll.

'Good. Now I need to speak to someone authorised to give me confidential information.'

'The Chief Master won't give any information over the telephone. He will respond to written enquiries only.'

'I think he may have to respond to a face-to-face enquiry. And this afternoon, too.'

'That's not possible.'

'Would you be good enough to tell him I'm on my way. I should reach Sutton in – say – thirty minutes. I'd appreciate it if he had Nigel's file ready for me.'

Lizzie nodded without enthusiasm. 'Take Bill or Ben – whichever—'

'The word meticulous was invented for Dyson,' Bill Parsons said, pulling out of a tight parking space. He was the older half of the pair Lizzie had christened, balding and thickening and sporting, in the office, reading glasses. 'And the words good cop for Lizzie. It's a pity you two don't hit it off: I'd trust her with my life.'

'We don't not hit it off.'

'You're never going to be bosom pals, though, are you? She's had a couple of bad experiences, grooming a young man or woman – OK, usually a young man – only to find him whizzing off up the promotion ladder. Got degrees, see. Like you. And I know for a fact she'd have been DCI in another squad if this woman hadn't been shagging the ACC at the time.'

'We all have histories,' Kate agreed. 'Trouble is, when you're on this accelerated promotion scheme, that's what happens. You get stuck in and then you're pulled out. At the time I thought that was what I wanted. But the more I see of the force, the more I want to be part of a team – operational as well as administrative.'

'Fraud, then: that'd be a good place for you. Dyson has a big desk, but he's got feet too. And brains. And uses them. Or Drugs – again, the DCI would be hands-on as well as management.'

'Let me get to Inspector, first, before I start planning a career path. And let's sort out this business before I think of even that. Hey, is the traffic always this bad?'

'Friday,' he said tersely. 'I hope that bugger waits for us.'

'He better bloody had. Queen Matilda's College. Sounds posh.'

*   *   *

They were both laughing by the time Bill had driven into the school grounds and parked.

'I bet they chose the name to make you think of King Edward's – that's the top-of-the-league boys' school in Brum,' Bill said. 'But public school this isn't. Surely!'

The school occupied the sort of rambling three-storey house she'd become familiar with in Moseley: a large family home, even if this came equipped with some fine baronial touches, including a couple of turrets.

'My wife's a teacher,' Bill said. 'She's just had a week's Ofsted inspection. I taught myself for a couple of years.' His tone suggested he was asking something.

'Over to you, then.'

They were kept waiting in a square hall, heavy with stained oak and stained glass. In what had once been a huge corner fireplace, stood a glass display cabinet with a couple of trophies and a lot of brochures. Kate took one, flicking through it round-eyed. 'Hey – look at this. French: hundred per cent grade A pass-rate at A level – that's pretty good, isn't it? And History.'

'Detective Sergeant Power?' A man in his mid-thirties, sleek as a stoat, beamed at Bill.

Bill beamed back. 'Detective Constable Parsons. And you, sir, must be Mr Muirhead?'

'That's right. The Chief Master. Come through into my study.'

So who had designed this room, Ikea-bold and cheerful? It almost worked, too, until you remembered that this was the hub of this august establishment.

An electric clock announced it was four-ten.

'This is a private school, is it, Sir? Parents have to pay fees?'

'That's right. They pay for our excellent service.'

'And the fees would be?'

'They do reflect the excellence of our service.'

'And they are?'

Kate said nothing. She could see that Bill was grinding a private axe but had no problems with that.

Muirhead said nothing.

'And the teachers? Or do you call them lecturers? Are they employed on a permanent, full-time basis?'

'We have to be flexible in our response to consumer demand: we obtain staff of the highest calibre through an agency.'

Kate couldn't see where Bill was heading, so she asked, 'And the fees would be, Mr Muirhead? I don't think you answered my colleague's question.'

'Just over two thousand pounds per year per subject. Plus examination and administration fees.'

'And Nigel's taking – two? three? – A levels?'

'Three.'

'I take it Nigel hasn't been at this school—'

'College.'

'—college long, Sir?'

'It's not a college where students do stay for long periods. Essentially we take students who have as yet failed to realise their true potential and assist them in their development. If you take your examinations here, officer, you are almost guaranteed a place at university.' The words might have come well from a be-gowned middle-aged pedagogue. From this young man, who might have been selling cars – top-of-the-range cars, but nonetheless cars – they sounded pretentious.

'So you get kids who've failed their A levels and give them a little polish?' Bill said, joining in again. Kate let him take over.

Muirhead nodded. And looked wary.

'Nigel, now, what A levels grades did he come with? He had taken his A levels, had he?'

'No. Not quite.'

'Not quite? Surely he had or he hadn't.'

'He'd finished his course at his previous school. But he did not – I understand – take the examinations there.'

'So you took him on when he was sacked.' Bill wrote without waiting for a reply. 'Why was he sacked?'

'You'd have to ask his previous school that.'

'Come now, you must have asked. If everyone else has A levels and he hasn't—'

'He had exceptionally good GCSEs, of course. Exceptionally good.'

'Which were?' Kate asked.

Muirhead jumped. He flipped a thin brown file. 'According to our records, he had As in Drama, Art, Technology. Bs in English and French. Oh, Art was a starred A. C in Maths.'

'Which school did he come from?' Bill shot in swiftly. 'A local comp or one of the Headmasters' Conference ones?'

Kate nodded his question home, trying not to show she had no idea what a Headmasters' Conference school might be.

After a moment, Muirhead mentioned a name even Kate had heard of. 'Not terribly good results, then,' she said. 'OK from an inner-city comp, but not at a place like that.' It fitted in, didn't it, with what Graham had said: *they had some trouble with him, I gather. The wrong crowd. Father had to come the heavy.*

'I'm sure he'll benefit from our supportive pastoral system and small classes.'

'How many students in each class?' she asked.

'We have very small groups,' he said.

'How many?'

'Five or six.'

Bill leaned across, his finger pointing to the statistics page of the prospectus. 'But you only had two or three students at most sitting any of these exams.' Suddenly Bill looked mean. 'Are you telling me, Sir, that you don't let all your students take the exam? You take seven thousand pounds a year fees off their parents and don't let them take the exam!'

'You will see in our regulations we do not permit students

with inadequate attendance or inadequate application to enter for the examinations.'

'So you tweak the statistics and rake in the money. Nice one, Mr Muirhead. Nice little earner. Now, you're the head – the *Chief Master* – of Queen Matilda's. Who owns the college?'

Muirhead looked blank

'Someone must own the place, Sir. Some person or trust?'

'I don't see the relevance of that.'

'Just answer the question, Mr Muirhead,' Kate said, who did. 'If you're a charity, like a lot of schools, Eton, for instance, then your headed notepaper will say so. And shouldn't it also tell us – if you're a limited company – the number your company's registered under?'

The sheet of headed notepaper he pushed across to her was, apart from a florid coat-of-arms, pretty reticent.

'OK, Mr Muirhead. You've made your point. Let me put this a different way: I assume your monthly money doesn't come in a small brown envelope stuffed with greasy fivers? Who pays your salary?'

'Thank God for computers,' Kate said, clipping her seat-belt. 'Or we'd spend all our time checking these companies. Not that I'd be taking any bets on this, would you?'

'You think our friend Sanderson *père* has his fingers in educational pies, too? It's certainly odd that a school should break its own admission rules to pick up someone who doesn't look a very good bet.'

'He might have made it worth their while. Or he may have a more powerful lever. We'll find out Monday, anyway.'

'Do you want me to go back in and check now?' Bill's tone was so neutral she almost laughed.

'Didn't you say your wife was a teacher?'

'Yes.'

'Just had an Ofsted? Then I tell you what, Bill. You stop off on the way home and get her a bunch of flowers and something for tea. She'll be dead on her feet. And, come to think of it, I've got a home to go to, as well.'

It was late enough by the time she left the city centre for the traffic jams to be dissolving. But there were still red lights and clogged islands, and all she wanted to do was get to her house. At last, Kings Heath! But the traffic was solid along the High Street. OK. She'd use the middle-class back route, protected by speed-bumps. And if one took out her sump, she'd bloody sue.

By some miracle she was able to shuffle her car into a space right in front of her house – something to celebrate in itself. But she wouldn't go in yet: she'd high-tail it to Sainsbury's – if she could find a half-bottle of champagne, that would be brilliant. And if she could only find full-size, well, some of it might have to retire to the fridge overnight.

Clutching her booty, she turned her Yale key in her front door. It moved, but the door didn't. Tensing, she tried again. Had some bastard bolted the door from the inside? Was he still busy doing over her house?

She parked the bottle carefully and breathed deeply. Tears wouldn't help. And – on the off-chance – tried the Chubb lock. The door swung open and the alarm began its opening chorus. What the hell?

As she retrieved the champagne and shut the door, she found a scribbled note.

Your nice nieghbour offerred to lock up proper. We thought it was best.
Tony
Think your home looks great. Hope you do.

And it did. As he'd done upstairs with the first batch of carpets, he'd moved the furniture – what little decent stuff of Cassie's she'd kept – roughly where he thought it should be. Tomorrow she might move it. Tonight — she would celebrate. She had a home. The carpets and Tony said so. Flinging off her jacket, she gauged a line in the living room and — could she still do it? — turned a cartwheel. And back. And then — for the sheer pleasure of it under her skin — walked on her hands to the kitchen.

And found magic. Tony had put all the electrical appliances back in place, and swept up. Back on her feet, she pirouetted from one end to the other. She returned the same way, pausing long enough only to grab a glass. To hell with the fact it was a Woolie's water-tumbler.

She put it back. Could she trust herself to drink enough and no more? She'd come close to danger point in the autumn. She didn't want to spend the winter going through a repeat of her drying out. Colin? But all she got was his answerphone. She didn't mention the house in case he felt under pressure. Instead she spoke about a shopping expedition. 'Lizzie suggested she and I did it, but I'd much prefer your company. And you can tell me all about the chemists' break-ins while we shop till we drop.'

No, she couldn't be about to cry. Not again. She pulled herself straight. OK, *faute de mieux*, what about Pat the Path? They both had something to celebrate, didn't they?

'I can't wait for you to see it, Kate,' Patrick said, gazing intently into her eyes. 'Or to see you on it. Tell me, have you ever ridden a bike?'

'Student days. Pillion on an inadequate Honda.'

They were in a pleasant Indian restaurant near Sainsbury's, outside most of the champagne as an aperitif and a meal rather larger than was wise. Now — having congratulated themselves on drinking only water with the food — they were considering the possibility of something else.

'We did say, of course, that we should have coffee at your place tonight, didn't we?'

Kate nodded. Was it a euphemism? Did she want it to be a euphemism? Would the loos have a condom dispensing machine?

No. She didn't want sex with him. Not yet. It certainly wouldn't be making love. And she didn't want the first sexual encounter after Robin to be simply recreational. Did she?

'I've got some malt,' she said neutrally.

'I don't drink when I'm on my bike,' he said. His leathers hung in her hall. 'The lot we sank earlier should be metabolised by now. Actually, do you have decaffeinated?'

'Decaffeinated espresso,' she said with conviction and with more amusement than she hoped showed.

But he was decidedly more amorous in tone, if not in proposition, as he regaled her with tales of his cycles.

'But why have you never ridden one? You'd look so good in the gear for a start. The leathers. Very sexy.'

Did he mean sexy as in desirable or simply as in a fashionable good thing? Could have been either. Especially as she'd seen no reason not to have a gentle finger of Glenfiddich, and she was suddenly tired. Tired in her own home. It had walls and carpets and it would soon be – No, it was home now.

'. . . apart from the designs, which are so flattering. All those lovely colour combinations. I'd see you in – yes, scarlet and black. And imagine, the feel of it – soft, supple, under your fingers. Like silk next to your skin. Smooth as silk.'

The phone interrupted. Not an emergency, though. Only Colin saying he was on for the next morning, after football of course, provided they could look at shirts, too. But by the time she'd got back from the kitchen, where she'd taken the call, Patrick was standing up peering at one of the mirrors Cassie had left. At, rather than into. And he was ready to go home.

Chapter Twenty-Two

'Just like that?' Colin asked, as they headed down the M5. They'd come straight from the school football pitch where the BB had been playing. Considering how late it was in the year, the day was surprisingly mild, though they'd been promised heavy rain as punishment later. 'Not so much as a glance at your stairs and an amorous sigh?'

'Nope.'

'Perhaps he's a man that needs to be seduced?'

'Can I be bothered? God knows where I stand with him.'

'Must be funny having a relationship with someone who knows exactly what's in your body.'

'Not as bad as a gynaecologist.'

'Not as good. I should think one of them would know how to give a girl a good time.'

'Tell you what, you find out!'

'I'd rather have an evening with the gorgeous Cary Grant. How did your evening with him go?'

'I didn't know you knew about that! Oh, the sodding grapevine, I suppose. We had a good evening, but neither of us suggested doing it again.'

'He's a nice kid.'

'Sure. And we had a pleasant drink and talked shop, and a pleasant Chinese and talked shop.'

'But you didn't have a pleasant fuck and talk shop?'

'DC Roper: this is not a suitable time or place for this sort of conversation. We are proceeding in a southerly direction hoping to inspect Fivers in Worcester. And we shouldn't be doing eighty-five, either.'

'No, Ma'am. A good win, your team had. A couple of good players.'

They thought of someone who wouldn't ever stand on the sidelines again, and were silent.

'How did you get on at the doctor's the other day?' Colin asked eventually, as they peeled off at the junction for Worcester North.

'Doctor's? Bloody hell, Colin, I only went and forgot, didn't I?'

'So you must be feeling better.'

'No excuse for missing an appointment. I'll have to go and blandish the receptionist with a tale of being on the tracks of a serial killer. And talking of being ill, what did you want to tell me about the drug thefts?'

'I'll give you the print-outs if you pop in to us before you go on to Lloyd House on Monday. See if you can see anything odd for yourself.'

'Meanwhile, what do you see?'

'There's a lot of stuff you'd expect. Tranks and stuff. But apart from that, there's only one thing that sticks out. Vitamin tablets. And I checked, before you ask. They're not the Smarties sort. They're little diddy things, like homeopathic tablets. Maybe a little bigger.'

'The ones they're trying to put a health warning on – too many are supposed to be bad for you, or something?'

'Nope. Vitamin B1, these. Not B6. Jesus. Is this where the tail-back for Worcester starts?'

'What are you doing?'

'What does it look as if I'm doing? U-turning. We're going somewhere else!'

*　　*　　*

So there they were in Redditch, having penetrated a traffic system that would have had her abandoning the car on a double yellow and walking. Preferably home. But they were here to do a job. Even if Colin's shirts were on the agenda.

Plastic Christmas trees, real Christmas trees, plastic wreaths, real wreaths. Plenty of those. But nothing in the leather line, and no shirts Colin would even pick up and inspect.

'Come on: a bite to eat and we'll head north. I know we're nearer to Warwick, but – hell, I suppose we really ought to do Warwick.'

'Where would you prefer, Colin?'

'Lichfield. I like Lichfield. And we could take in Tamworth: there are a couple of good quality factory shops you should see. But, Kate, it'll all be like this, won't it?' He spread his hands miserably at the tat. 'And all couples with too many kids buying too many tacky presents.'

'It is nearly Christmas,' she said, mildly. 'What are your plans?'

'Clive's got family back in Wales. They think he's straight. Tough for both of us, usually, but he goes because his Dad's coughing up his lungs with pit dust. I usually put myself down for the Christmas Day rota. What about you?'

'My name's top of the list. Come on, we'll get some food and booze in and have a great Christmas evening at my place. What do you say?'

'Apart from yes? What about Pat the Path? Won't he be expecting you to join him in a leatherwear party?'

'Tough if he is. I can't quite see him and Cassie hitting it off. Oh, yes, we'll have to fit Cassie into the schedule. I can't let her down.'

'Of course not. We'll spike her gin. Great.' He gave her a quick hug. 'Now I can face Fivers ad infinitum.'

'What I want to know is what bastards reported that there was good quality stuff in these shops! They should be hanged with tinsel and stuffed with festive balls.'

'And crowned with chaplets of plastic holly. OK. OK. But you've got your shirts and refused to let me buy that lovely dress.'

'Which was designed for someone six foot tall with no hips. And – Jesus Christ, Kate. Cast your beadies on that lot.' Grabbing her firmly by the wrist, Colin pulled her towards yet another shop. 'Under a fiver they may not be, but who's arguing? Leather warehouse.'

The shop sign was so temporary Kate was afraid the next gust of wind would bring it down. They'd done no more than put piles of bags and jackets in the window. Punters could get the message – no-frill bargains.

Inside the smell of hot, sticky bodies battled it out with the scent of leather. Kate reeled.

Colin gripped her arm tightly. 'Lack of air or excess of emotion?'

'Both. Come on. Let's check those bags out. Yes: look at the label. Firenze. Leather-lined. There's the little city crest. And those shoes. Firenze. Leather-lined.' She stroked a pair. 'Hand-made, I'd say. The sort of thing Alan Grafton spoke about with such love. They'd probably fetch well over a hundred pounds in a legitimate store. And someone's flogging them for fifteen. And fifteen for that bag!'

'What next?'

'We talk to the management. Now. I don't trust this place to be here when we come back all nice and official on Monday.'

'I've never done an interview clutching Jaeger carrier bags before.' Colin flapped them.

'First time for everything, isn't there? Right. Into battle.'

The kid on the checkout was almost certainly under-age and definitely overworked. Mention of management brought tears to her eyes. 'Dunno where they are. Honest. They just told us cash only, not credit cards, and pushed off. Honest.'

'No credit cards. OK. What about cheques?' Kate asked.

'What about them?'

'If I want to pay by cheque, who would I make it out to?'

'Oh, we got a stamp. We do that.'

'OK, then. Say I want to buy these shoes. Here's my cheque and here's my card. Now, I prefer to fill it all in myself. Tell me who to put here,' Colin asked, smiling patiently.

'No. I said, we got a stamp. We fill it in.'

'When we've handed it over?'

The girl nodded. 'Look, there's ever such a queue. I got to serve people.'

Kate looked at Colin who nodded. As one they produced their ID cards. 'Like I said, we want to talk to your manager. Now. We could ask you to shut the shop until he comes back.'

'Get out the fucking way, you stupid cow.' Someone shoved Kate in the back so hard she nearly fell. 'You don't like the stuff, you don't have to fucking buy it. Just shift your fucking arse so we can.'

There was an ugly murmur in support. There must have been some thirty people backed up.

Kate smiled at the girl on the till. 'Looks like you'd better find him fast, doesn't it? Before Tamworth has its first Christmas shopping riot.' She turned to the man who'd pushed her. 'Keep it quiet, Sir, will you? We wouldn't want anyone to get hurt, would we? I'm quite sure no one would want to be buying dodgy goods, would they? Not if you have to give them up if they're needed as evidence?'

'Here – who's talking about stolen goods? You want to shut your fucking mouth!' A man was pushing his way to the front of the queue. Those at the back weren't happy.

'So long as you open yours – somewhere nice and private – that's fine,' Kate said, projecting her voice like an old-time actor-manager. 'Just lead the way and we'll follow, won't we, Constable?'

✳   ✳   ✳

The office they found themselves in would never have been spacious but was now so cramped it was difficult to sit in the chairs which the man had spirited up from somewhere. If they'd been inspecting it for a fire certificate it would have failed miserably. It would have been somewhere below zero on the general health and safety scale, too, the way his kettle, fan heater, lap-top computer and electric razor shared a socket divider.

Computer? In this mess? Kate caught Colin's eye, raising her eyebrows in the computer's direction. Colin's nod was almost as imperceptible as hers.

'So what's all this about stolen goods? I shall sue if I've lost any sales.'

'That lot down there would buy the Crown Jewels hot from the Tower provided they could get them for twenty quid,' Colin said. 'And I didn't hear the word stolen until you used it. All Detective Sergeant Power and I want is a quick look at your invoices and receipts. I mean, you're selling lovely stuff, Sir, aren't you? And no one would call it expensive.'

'It's all legit. Not even bankrupt stock.'

'Great, Mr – I don't think I caught your name, Sir?' Colin produced his pocket-book and held his ball-point ready. He might have been Dixon of Dock Green, his smile was so cosy, his posture so stereotyped.

Kate watched the man riffle through his wallet. He might almost have been selecting the card he flicked on to the desk. This was so filthy she got her fingers dirty just picking up the card, which she passed to Colin.

'Right – Mr Edmonds. Thanks.' Colin unobtrusively slipped it into his pocket book. 'Now, all we need to know is who supplies you. That's all. Who knows, we may even want to buy some items ourselves, once we know everything's OK. Real bargains, aren't they?'

Kate didn't reckon that Martyn-with-a-Y Edmonds believed

Colin's patter any more than she did, but he got up and made great show of moving slippery piles of polythene-wrapped leather so he could get to a filing cabinet so old it might have been army surplus.

And failed, of course, to find the papers he wanted.

'What I'll do is get my secretary to find everything you want and pop it in the post to you,' he said.

'I don't think we can wait quite that long. Do you, Sergeant?'

'I'm afraid not, Constable. Perhaps we'd better close the premises after all.' It wasn't often Kate employed police jargon, but once in a while she didn't object to giving it an airing.

Colin pushed the phone towards him. 'Maybe your secretary could tell you now? Or your boss? Come on, Mr Edmonds, you know as well as we do there's something strange with your suppliers. Not you. Don't think that we suspect you of any wrong-doing.'

Edmonds pushed the phone away. 'Monday. It'll have to be Monday.' He was beginning to sweat, but it could just have been the intolerable fug building up.

Kate leaned to pull out the fan-heater plug. 'You want to watch that lot. The socket's very hot,' she said. And could have bitten her tongue off. The last thing she wanted was to give him the idea of a smart bit of arson. In for a penny ... She pulled the splitter from the socket. 'Before we go we'll tape over that, Mr Edmonds. In the interests of health and safety. And suggest to our colleagues in the Fire Service they might like to talk to you.'

'But we'll only be here—' He stared. Two bitten off short tongues in the room.

'Only be here till when, Mr Edmonds?' Colin was on his feet, leaning over that filthy desk. 'Only be here until you can scarper with all the stock and all the paperwork? I think not.'

'All we need,' said Kate encouragingly, 'is names and paperwork. Then I can go and buy myself a nice pair of shoes and Detective Constable Roper can buy that briefcase he's got his eye on. In fact, we could put all the paperwork in one of those cases. Now, let me make out a cheque.' She flourished her pen.

'No, please – have one on the house, Sergeant – Sergeant Powell, is it?'

'Sergeant Power. West Midlands CID. Currently on attachment to the Fraud Squad. No, thanks, Sir. I'd rather pay in full. Wouldn't want my boss to have any thoughts about bribery and corruption, would we? All I need is a receipt, please. And, of course, the name to make this cheque out to.'

The poor man was writhing. Colin waded through leatherwear to open the door, leaning casually against the jamb. In her mind's eye Kate could see the overworked air crawling out, with a slightly cooler supply coming in at nose level. Not much cooler.

Colin shut the door. It started to get hot again.

At last, the sweat dripping off him, Edmonds reached for a briefcase of his own. He hadn't taken advantage of the stock downstairs. 'I'll call my boss.'

'Fine. So long as you tell us the number you're dialling. We need to keep our records straight, even if your company doesn't. And who, of course.' It was a long time since Kate had had the chance to use such an evil smile. If she wasn't careful she'd blow it by letting her dimples show.

He put back the phone, and grabbed a sheaf of papers. 'There, damn you. Now get out.'

Kate leafed through them. There were names and addresses all right. 'These mean nothing without an explanation.'

As he leaned towards her, she smelt Edmonds' fear. His index finger was rigid with effort not to let it shake. 'That's the main supplier. See – those are lists of what we've had. There's his receipt. These are other suppliers – the bomber jackets, not nearly so good.'

'What about future orders?' Colin asked. 'Or are they all in files on that snazzy little lap-top of yours?'

Edmonds shot him a look.

'So no future orders. You'll be closing as soon as this lot's shifted. Right?'

'Pity we'll never be able to use any of this.' Kate indicated the dustbin liners full of top-class leather goods they'd bought. 'Not even a carrier bag we could have traced back, you notice.'

Colin nodded. 'Now what?'

'Talk to our colleagues at the nick here. I don't want any of Mr Edmonds' stock coming to any harm tonight. And have a word with the Fire Service. Ditto.'

'You are taking this seriously, aren't you?'

She paused long enough to shift her grip on the heavy bags. 'I should hope so. You know the name I had to write on my cheque? Bel Canto. Them and all the other dodgy firms – they're all knitted up, Colin, like a plateful of spaghetti.'

Tamworth nick's Duty Inspector raised his hands in horror and then rubbed them with glee. If Kate and Colin were prepared to do half the cold and miserable observation, he saw no reason why his colleagues couldn't enjoy a bit of dramatic backup. It would make a change from the usual Saturday night, picking up drunken and drug-ridden yobs who'd blazed in from Brum to make a quiet copper's night miserable.

The Fire Service were also tickled, they said. Though they didn't see their way clear to checking for a fire certificate on a Saturday evening, if the premises in question were open for trade on Sunday, they wouldn't let Sabbath observance come between them and a sitting target.

Great. Except that Kate wouldn't be able to watch any Sunday fun. 'BB football coaching, of course,' she grunted, shifting in the Fiesta's passenger seat. 'You know, the first time you do obbo., you know the coffee can't ever be any worse. And yet each time you do it thereafter, it still manages to get worse. God, this is vile.'

'Serves you right for trying to play Cagney. Or is it Lacey? And the worst thing about coffee, it means you want to pee all the time. In fact, I'm going to go and have a slash right now.'

At least men could use – as Colin was doing now – the shelter of a lamp post. There was nowhere in the ill-lit delivery bay behind the leather shop for Kate to relieve herself. She never learned, did she? Opening the door, she tipped the rest of the coffee away, lest she drank it without thinking.

As Selby had wanted Fatima to do. With different consequences.

Colin got back into the car. 'He's still in there,' he said, blowing on his hands. 'Busy packing, I'd say from all the frantic activity.'

'Better than setting fire to everything. And it gives us a chance to pull him in for further questions if he tries. I only hope he moves fast. The public loos are way back down the road and I don't fancy being caught in mid-squat in the full glare of his mates' headlights.'

'Go on. Stretch your legs. We're not on our own, here.'

Considering the so-called warehouse was in a well-lit pedestrian area constantly monitored by CCTV, no one would have expected anyone in their right mind to start moving quantities of large bags through their front door. Not with some amiable local or even Birmingham youths eager to see what was inside the bags. But when Kate returned on a circuitous route from the public loos, that was exactly what she found. Before she could dance with rage, she was joined by a man and a woman.

'Don't worry: we made sure there was film in the surveillance cameras,' the woman, introducing herself as Trish Stone, told her. 'We thought it might be more fun to let Edmonds think he was getting away with it. Ah! Do we have company?'

'I want support for Colin round the back,' Kate said. 'He's on his own.'

'Your wish is our command,' Trish said. She spoke into her radio. 'There's someone on his way now to hold his hand. I bet he'll enjoy it, too.'

Her mate guffawed. 'So long as that's all he holds!'

Kate clenched her fists. How to react without over-reacting? 'Colin's my mate. And the best partner I've ever had.' Except for Robin. She bit her lip, and tasted blood.

Trish raised a hand. 'OK. Take your point. Now, let's just see what this Transit driver has in mind, shall we?'

'No, you're not under arrest, Mr Edmonds. We just want to talk to you a little more about your supplier. And we'd like to know, of course, why you suddenly decided to move all your stock after our talk this afternoon. Is that coffee all right?' Kate wrinkled her nose in sympathy.

They were in a clean, not unpleasant interview room. It didn't even smell too much – most interview rooms she'd come across had, under the stale cigarette smoke, an underlying tang of sweat and urine. A very male smell, come to think of it. Mr Edmonds was sweating, although the temperature here was nothing like as high as it had been in that little office of his. His body spray couldn't mask it.

'I told my boss about the electrics. He said not to risk it.'

Plausible. She cursed her big mouth. 'Fine. So now you'll be able to tell us who your boss is so we can talk to him.' Her pen could only be described as poised. 'Come on, Mr Edmonds. It's eleven o'clock. You've had a hard day's work and so have I. And I bet you're working again tomorrow – right? I mean, even if you close this outlet there must be another that needs a skilled pair of hands. Worcester? Warwick?'

'Hollywood,' he said, wearily.

Blast the man, still playing games at this time of night! And then her brain slowly announced that it had seen buses announcing they were heading there. Hoping he hadn't registered her preliminary snarl, she quietly wrote down the address. And — at long, long last — the name of his boss. 'It isn't Sanderson!' Kate leant against the wall outside the interview room, weak as if someone had torn a hole in her and her stuffing had slithered out.

'Your mates in Fraud'll be able to tie it up good and proper. Don't you worry.' The Duty Inspector eyed her kindly. 'What I can't understand is why you don't just barge in to this Sanderson's home and ask him straight questions.'

Colin produced an ironic grin. 'Mr Sanderson is on the Police Committee and is on first name terms with one of the ACCs. He's mega-big in the funny handshake club. Our DCI knows him quite well: pillar of the church. And I suspect if our case isn't so watertight you could sail the bloody Atlantic in it he won't even let it go to the DPP. Kate's well out of it down in Fraud — we're all tiptoeing round as if we're in a fucking minefield. So the idea is we sort out Sanderson's wife, his son and his associates, and only then do we pounce.'

The Duty Inspector nodded. 'Point taken. Look, you're both knackered, by the look of you. Come and have a bite to eat upstairs before you set off. Much safer, you know. And it's not often us lads and lasses in the sticks are honoured with a bit of city slicker company. Come on. Only don't touch the liver . . . .'

Chapter Twenty-Three

Kate could have paged from home the answerphone set aside for Isobel. But she had such a backlog of paperwork – and in these meticulous times, she was in a more than meticulous department – she decided to go in as soon as her football coaching was over.

Working her way through an overlong, underfilled baguette, she sorted and jotted; she would postpone responding to the flashing red light of the answerphone until she could give it her full attention. Three messages.

'Promising or what?'

It was Lizzie, who pointed to the machine as soon as she came in.

'Saving them up. Like Christmas presents.'

'What are you doing here, anyway? It's Sunday afternoon, for God's sake. You should have your feet up watching the footie or an old film.'

'Never heard of paperwork, Gaffer? There's quite a bit from yesterday.' She explained.

'Well done. Graham said you were a worker.'

When? 'But I'm really pissed off about this guy Edmonds' supplier not having anything to do with Sanderson. Ostensibly.'

'We'll get Bill and Ben on to it tomorrow.' Lizzie exhumed

a packet of cigarettes from her bag and pushed it towards Kate.

'No, thanks. I didn't realise—'

'My Sunday treat. Less fattening than roast beef and Yorkshire pud.'

The women exchanged a grin.

Kate wouldn't repeat an earlier mistake. 'Look, Gaffer, I've got something I ought to do back in Graham's squad first thing tomorrow. How would you feel if I came in half-nine-ish? Might be earlier. It's to do with a whole lot of pharmacy thefts. And I want to catch up on the latest news about a new woman on the squad who's gone sick.'

'No problem. Unless there's something on those tapes. Come on, Kate – the suspense is killing.'

You have three messages, the answerphone voice said. *Message one.*

And then Isobel's voice: 'Kate. I will try and help. But you'll have to be patient. All those cameras, you see. But what really worries me is what he's doing to Nigel. You've got to help me. He'll have a police record, otherwise. I won't help unless you can keep Nigel out of it.'

End of message one. Message two.

Nothing. Just the click of a phone.

End of message two. Message three.

'Kate: he knows who you are. He knows. He's furious you came to the house. Furious. And you mustn't come to Green Thumbs tomorrow in any circumstances. You mustn't even try. If I can I'll phone. But it won't be for some time.'

'Shit and fuck and all the other non-Sunday words. How did he find out who you were?'

'I had to identify myself to Edmonds at the leather ware-house place. I only used my name once, but he must have a good memory. Hell, this has blown it, hasn't it? I'm so sorry.'

'That's the way it is, Kate. The good guys have to play straight. The others don't.'

'But tomorrow—'

'Someone else can go. Will go. Any ideas? Or shall I go myself?'

Kate hesitated. Then she gestured at Lizzie's hair. 'You're very memorable, aren't you? What about Bill or Ben? Or even – yes, what about Colin? Looks like every mother's favourite son, but quietly anonymous.'

'OK by me. You and Bill had better carry on with this Nigel line. Go and see his old school. Put some pressure on. Come on, Kate – it's not the end of the world.'

Kate looked at her shaking hands. 'It's just that I'm wondering what he did to Isobel when he found out.'

Chapter Twenty-Four

Seven-forty-five on a cold, dry Monday morning. Kate was tapping on Graham's door to announce that she was spending an hour or so with the CID squad. The door was still locked. Superintendent Neville's, however, was unlocked. She went in when he called. His face was pale in the reflected light of his computer screen. He smiled at her, and quickly closed whatever he was working on.

He got up and moved to his espresso machine in one easy movement. Desk-bound officer he might be, but he still clearly found time to exercise. Not just his body, but also his charm. 'I know you'd like some coffee, Kate. Tell me what you think of this one.'

Kate raised her eyebrows as she raised her cup. 'I'm no expert, Sir.'

He flapped her into a chair. 'Never mind. Tell me.'

'Good, dark roast. Whoosh! You can feel it hitting the spot. Tell me, how much of this do you risk in a day?' Her 'Sir' was belated, but he grinned.

'Got you, Kate! It's decaffeinated. God knows what pollutants I'm taking in, and I know I may be heading for Alzheimer's, but I found I was getting twitchy. And I can't give it up altogether. So if it's fooled you, it'll do!'

She drained her cup and looked across at him. 'You'll know why I'm here, Sir.'

'To find out about Fatima. Well, for a start, she's gone down with an authentic dose of flu. Pressure here and lack of food, I'd say. So we couldn't talk much. But I made it clear — and so did Gail Walker from Welfare — that if there were any problems in her working environment we would do our level best to eradicate them. Kate: if we can't treat our colleagues right, how can we hope to treat members of the public with the care and consideration they deserve? We're in Birmingham, for God's sake. A city that celebrates its multi-culturalism. And yet—' For once he seemed lost for words, shaking his head.

'Are we any nearer in finding the perpetrator, Sir?'

His glance reminded her of the difference in their ranks. Then his face softened. 'Watch this space, Kate. We're going to bring the geeks in later today. That'll mess up everyone's work. But you needn't fret about that, since you'll still — I presume — be at Fraud.'

She grinned. 'I'm sort of semi-detached between here and Fraud, Sir. As a matter of fact, I just popped in to pick up a list of items stolen in recent pharmacy raids. I thought I'd run them past a friend of mine in the Met. The one I mentioned to you. Last time he and I spoke he dismissed our thief's activities as amateurish. I have a terrible feeling I know why they might be amateurish. But I want my facts before I talk to him again.'

'Still no contacts up here?'

She pulled a face. Not the sort of person you can bounce vague ideas off. Not yet.'

He nodded, his eyes straying to his In-tray.

She took the hint, and left.

She and Colin were standing side by side, finger to finger, working down the columns of data Rona had produced for them.

'Good morning.' It was Graham, his voice as cold as the weather.

Their heads shot up simultaneously. Whether Colin's face showed as much delight as hers, she didn't know. Graham's certainly didn't. His lips were tight, his eyes narrow. Someone had infuriated him, and Kate had a terrible feeling it was her, though how and why she had no idea.

Graham turned, apparently to stride from the room. Instead, he grabbed with both hands the monitor Selby was using and turned it so he could see what was on it.

'My room. Now. And you, Power.' He turned on his heel, leaving a shocked silence.

Selby blundered to his feet and followed. So did Kate.

'Kate!' Colin hissed.

When her eyes found his – she was already half way across the room and accelerating – he winked and unobtrusively touched the side of his nose. 'It's not you he's after,' he mouthed. 'Keep your cool.'

Selby was standing to rigid attention in front of Graham's desk. Kate, closing the door softly behind her, stood to attention too, half a pace behind Selby.

Graham flicked a glance at her. Then his gaze returned to Selby. 'You've been warned several times already about time-wasting, Selby. Three strikes and you're out is fashionable these days, isn't it? And you've had your three. And more. I'm into zero tolerance from now on.'

There was absolute silence. Graham's eyes never left Selby's face.

Kate's never left Graham's.

'Well,' Graham prompted, his voice rasping across the desk.

'*Miss* Power sees things.'

He hated using her title, didn't he?

'*Sergeant* Power saw what I saw this morning. I have written details of the occasions you were wasting police time playing computer games. I'd like you to invite the Police Federation representative to be present at a meeting where you will be issued with a formal warning. I shall notify DI Cope and Superintendent Neville of my proposed action. Get back to your desk. Sergeant!'

'Sir!'

'You will ensure DC Selby is given an appropriate workload and clears his desk each day.'

'Sir!' Now was clearly not the moment to remind him that she was currently based in Lloyd House. She turned smartly and left. Though she pulled the door quietly to, she did not shut it. There might be a conversation about to happen outside that Graham should hear.

Yes, Selby was waiting for her in the corridor, but he didn't speak. Instead he pulled on her lapel and raised a finger to within an inch of her nose.

'You brought this on yourself,' she said, in what she hoped was her normal voice. 'Caught red-handed. Get back to your desk – and stop playing the hard man, Constable.'

This time he did speak. His face a vicious mask, he hissed a stream of abuse, the sort of thing she'd heard only from men she'd brought in under arrest. She hoped her face didn't show how shocked she was.

'You heard me,' she said at last. 'Get back to your desk.'

She was trembling so much by the time she got to the loo she simply sat, her head in her hands, for several minutes. When she emerged it was to find Cope bellowing her name up and down the corridor.

'My room, Power,' he said when he saw her.

This time it was she who stood to attention, while it was Cope who let rip. 'All this bullying and harassment. You've had your knife into that lad ever since you were wished on us. And now – thanks to you – one of the best lads in the squad's gone sick.'

Gone sick? The bastard!

'Well?' Cope brought his face as close to hers as the desk would permit.

'DCI Harvey saw DC Selby playing a computer game when he'd already had a warning not to. If you wish to discuss this with anyone, Sir, it should be with him. Now, if you'll excuse me, DI King has an assignment for me this morning.'

'Oh, DI King has an assignment for you, has she?' he mimicked her. 'I've got news for you, Power: there won't be any more assignments here for you. You're out of my squad. Get it?'

'"Full of sound and fury, signifying nothing",' she told herself. '"A tale told by an idiot ..."' *Macbeth*. The play you shouldn't quote, even to yourself. Even though she knew Cope was talking out of his arse, that, thanks to Graham, she'd logged everything, it was still frightening.

'Get out. Before I forget myself and throw you out. Out!'

She turned and marched out, pausing only to close the door quietly behind her. This time there'd be nothing she wanted anyone to overhear. However much she told herself he was out of order, she shook. Any moment now she might vomit. No, that would be to let him win. Somehow she got back to her desk, but could do no more than stand there staring at the wood. There was something she ought to do. There was a card, somewhere, wasn't there? A card she'd put on everyone's desk, telling people what to do in the face of bullying. That's what she needed to do. Find that card.

How long the phone had been ringing on her desk, she didn't know. Shaking her head, she picked it up. It sounded like Neville's voice. She'd better do as he said, report to his office. She glanced at her watch. She was going to get into hot water with Lizzie, too, for being late. Cramming Rona's computer paperwork into her bag, she stumbled from the office. Where was Colin? Why hadn't Graham called her in for a kind cup of tea?

Neville looked at her appraisingly as she slipped into his room. He was obviously on his way to a meeting. But he smiled. 'Go and do your stuff with Fraud,' he said. 'Remember who runs this Squad.'

'But—'

'Kate, I'm running very late. Just do as I say.'

She would if her legs would carry her. 'Sir,' she said. And she set off down the long corridor to the stairs.

Colin wrapped her in a hug as soon as she stepped out of the building. 'Come on, sweetie. You'll be OK. With Neville and Harvey behind you, you'll be OK.'

'I've got to work with Cope. Every day I've got to work with him.'

'Cope?'

She explained briefly.

'Fucking hell. So he thinks Selby's as pure as the driven snow, does he? And you're the one leaving dirty footprints? Well, he's got a steep learning curve coming up, that's all I can say. Look, I've got to go and twirl my green thumbs. Look the part, do I?' He prinked, in a Barbour not even the Sally Army would have touched, and produced stained gardening gauntlets from one of the disreputable pockets. For good measure, he gave a cat-walk prowl and turn. 'That's better. Now off you pop and I'll report back to you over a nice cup of tea. See you lunchtime, sweetie.'

The drive down the M5 was shorter than she'd expected, largely because Bill kept up an insistent flow of conversation. He'd not asked her what was the matter, simply opened the passenger door of his Volvo for her with an old-fashioned courtesy that almost took her aback, and started talking. Family; his garden; his thoughts about Ofsted and what it had done to his wife; the possibility of a replacement car now this had clocked up eighty thousand. Good solid kindness.

At last they reached the school that had expelled Nigel: an impressive pile, no doubt the unwitting model to which Queen Matilda's aspired. She found herself responding to Bill's chuckle.

His eyes questioned her as she got out.

'Much better now, thanks, Bill. Just a bit of strife I could have done without. I'm not sure how it'll end, either.'

'You'll be all right. You only have to look at your chin to know you'll lead with it sometimes.'

'If I had, I wouldn't have minded. This was just shit dropped from a great height.'

He looked up. 'So long as they drop my share on this car, not my new one.'

'Sacked for selling grass!' Kate could contain her laughter no longer. 'Genuine grass!' She slammed the car door shut and tipped her head back.

'But the intention was there. The kids weren't to know it wasn't really cannabis. He could have been done under the Criminal Attempts Act, nineteen eighty-two,' Bill said, rolling the law round his mouth with the air of a connoisseur – or of one preparing for promotion exams.

'Absolutely. Now I'm wondering,' she said, sobering rapidly and fastening the seat-belt, 'if having escaped police notice once, young Nigel might not be pushing his luck. Or – given the general happiness and contentment of the Sanderson home – if his dad might not be pushing it for him. Find a lay-by, Bill, before we hit the motorway.'

'What do these here vitamin tablets look like?' She spread Rona's results across her lap so he could see the data too. 'Little white pills, not unlike homeopathic pills. What do E's look like?'

'Little white pills, not unlike homeopathic pills,' Bill said promptly. 'Bigger. With little pictures engraved on them.'

'And what was young Nigel's best subject at school? Art. What did the Head say? A real talent for engraving. Remember the delicate little woodcuts he'd done to illustrate that school magazine story? Nigel got into bad ways and his father brought him back home where he keeps him under a tight rein. OK, I bet he does his homework for fear of getting the push from Queen Matilda's, but how does he spend the rest of the time? Scribing doves and dollars on vitamin pills!'

Bill snorted, and pulled back on to the road. 'Better than some of the stuff they put in. Jesus, a mate of mine in Drugs said they were pushing some so-called E's full of cow anaesthetic round Coventry.'

'You couldn't get him to get some others analysed, could you? See if they're actually good for you?'

'No probs, as my kid would say. What next? Talk to the kid?'

'At Queen Matilda's, not at home. And after lunch. Depending, of course, on what Colin Roper turned up this morning. Bill — this is a complicated little case.'

He grinned. 'You wait till you've been with us a few months. We'll show you what complicated is.'

'If he hit her,' said Colin, reaching for his glass, 'it was where the bruises couldn't be seen.'

They had, on Lizzie's insistence, settled for an informal meeting in a pub some way from the usual police haunts. 'If I'm seen with him in that coat they'll know I'm not Chief Inspector material,' she'd said.

'But do you think he did hit her?' Kate asked.

'She looked cowed. But then you say she normally looks cowed. I gave her some phone cards, like you said, which sort of identified me. She didn't seem to avoid me after that. Tell you what, she's good with those kids. Well, they're not kids. Adults with learning difficulties. But she got them making Christmas wreaths like anyone's business. Never a cross word; never a raised voice. She's a nice woman.'

'Do you think she's got it in her to be party to any of her husband's activities?' Lizzie asked.

'Intellectually, no problem. Morally—' He shook his head.

'Kate wants us to recruit her as an informer. Any ideas?'

'It depends if you can put any pressure on her: she's put up with her husband all these years. Maybe if we wave her son under her nose.'

'She's already told us that her son's got to be part of the bargain, remember,' Kate put in. 'What Bill and I hope to do, Colin, is get the kid to sing this afternoon and hope he'll implicate his father. A bit of informing from him wouldn't come amiss.'

'All the same,' said Ben, who'd been too busy attacking a sandwich to speak before, 'the net's closing in. I've spent a happy morning on the computer, and I've pulled together all sorts of threads. We should be able to truss him up by the end of the week.' But his glance moved from Kate's face to a point above her head.

'That's nice,' said Graham's voice. 'We could do with some good news.'

Chapter Twenty-Five

The others, ostensibly driven back to Lloyd House by a mixture of urgent work and the bitter wind, left Kate and Graham to follow more slowly. Not that Kate had much time: she and Bill wanted to catch Nigel before he left the *soi-disant* college for whatever comforts his home might offer.

'You didn't look very well this morning,' he said. 'I thought I'd check you were OK.'

She bit back the obvious response, that he'd been quite aware of what had upset her, and had made no effort for at least four hours to do anything about it. 'I was very shaken,' she admitted at last. 'What with Selby and Cope—'

'Cope?'

'Heaving me out of the squad. Or threatening to. I don't know that he can, not without your say-so. And Neville's.'

'I think you'd better explain.'

She did.

She wasn't sure what response she expected. She'd have liked maybe a reassuring hug, at least a hand gripping her shoulder as he told her Cope was a bullying thug who wouldn't get away with it this time.

What she got was a face so grim the corners of his mouth pulled down. 'This is very serious. Have you any defence?'

'Defence? Only you, gaffer! You told me to document

everything, which I did. As you told Selby this morning, in fact.'

'That's just the computer business. What about other things?'

'Apart from him pretending to rape me? And him taking a note from my desk which might have prevented Alan Grafton's death? OK, I've asked him to do some work – including checking up on carpeting firms which might have tried to do over my house. I've had no report on that whatsoever.'

'Cope had already asked him to check up on crime reported in that phone-in programme.'

'Cope himself took him off that to check the burglary theory.'

'Are you quite sure you haven't exceeded your authority? Or handled him badly?'

Kate turned her head slightly. The wind was whipping tears into her eyes. 'Have you ever been on a course on how to question rape victims?' she asked. And walked away.

Lizzie was calling her as she turned down the corridor: 'Kate – phone for you! Kate Power! Phone!'

At least she could blame the scurry if her voice wobbled.

'Kate, light of my benighted life!'

'Hi, Dai!'

'You all right?'

'Been running.'

'And look who's run bloody marathons without even breaking into a sweat.'

'That was then. Out of training, that's all.'

'OK, well no doubt you'll tell me another time. What it is, see, is what we were talking about the other day. All those drugs thefts from that great miasma half way up the M6. And I said everything was a bit amateurish: we make our own, down here, with our own little chemistry sets. Remember?'

'I gather they've been making them with cow anaesthetic near here.'

'Oh, aye. Kettamin. What these silly kids will do to themselves. Anyway, we've got some silly bleeders down here stuffing themselves with something else. Not so nasty, like.'

'E's made from daffodil bulbs? Or leeks?'

'They'd be all right. Wouldn't like to try the daffs, though. Not after Holland in the war. No, our kids are busy taking the healthy option, see. Lite E's, you might say.'

'Don't tell me.' Colin had used almost the same words, hadn't he? In Mr Hill's burgled pharmacy. 'Don't tell me, Dai.'

But she couldn't stop him: 'Vitamin pills, my lamb. Bloody vitamin pills.'

'Hand-crafted in sunny Birmingham?'

'That's what our informant says. I'll fax through all the details, soon as I've typed my report. How's that? Now, when are you going to come back down here and let me serenade you, shepherdess of my flock?'

Nigel, a young-looking eighteen, sat the far side of the teacher's desk in a classroom that had probably once been a servant's bedroom. Kate pulled her chair to the side of the desk. Bill brought his even further round, so Nigel had to slew round to face them both.

'At this stage,' Kate said carefully and clearly, 'we just want to ask you some questions.'

He nodded, eyes huge, Adam's apple convulsing. 'Like, how long will it take? I mean – I got to—' He looked at his watch.

'Not long enough to make you late home, if that's what you're afraid of. Because you are afraid, aren't you, Nigel?' Bill's turn.

'What we want to know is what you're afraid of. Tell, us, Nigel, why did you leave your last school?'

His eyes filled. Then he got a grip. 'I don't see that's any of your business.'

Kate shook her head. 'You know it is, don't you? So let's just hear it from you.'

'Aren't you going to caution me or something?'

'You're not under arrest: we told you that.'

'And shouldn't Mum or Dad be here?'

'Only if you're a minor. But there's no reason why they shouldn't be if you want them. If you're sure you want them? Do you want me to call your dad?' She flourished her mobile. 'No. I didn't think you did. What about your mum?'

He shook his head. 'She can't . . . .'

'She's got a car. She could come over.'

'She can't.'

'What do you mean, "can't"? People with cars can dash round all over the place.' Kate winced at the hardness she put into her voice. 'If they want to. Wouldn't she want to come and help you out?'

Bill took over, as she hoped he would, kind as a favourite uncle. 'Or is there something stopping your mum coming? Is that what you're trying to say?' He smiled even more kindly. 'Something? Or someone?'

The boy's face tightened, and he chewed on a hangnail. He shifted in his chair. 'What do you want to ask me?'

'I want to know how you spend your evenings, Nigel,' Kate said. 'That's all.'

'I got work to do. For my A levels. They really check up on you. Can't miss a class. Have this pile of homework. Tests every two weeks. Talk about cramming. I feel like one of those geese. You know.' He gestured at his stomach. Then his teeth returned to the back of his thumb.

'They want to make sure your parents get their money's worth, maybe,' Bill said. He sounded as though he sympathised. Perhaps he did. He had children, an expensive luxury, didn't he?

'They sacked this kid the other day. Done nothing wrong, had he? Just failed a couple of their bleeding tests, that's all. No, not failed.' His voice changed: 'Not done quite well enough. There you are. Seven k. down the tubes.'

'So you have to work very hard, or there'll be trouble. What sort of trouble, Nigel?'

'Nigel?' Kate prompted.

He pushed to his feet and headed for the window.

'Nigel?'

'You know what happens!' He could have been in tears.

'If I did, I wouldn't be asking.'

Although it wasn't yet three the heating had been turned off long since and the shabby room was getting cold. It was a dispiriting place for a major chunk of this kid's personal tragedy to be played out.

Bill was on his feet. 'Come on, kid. It's getting late. And your mum'll be getting worried. I think it'd be a good idea if we went back to Brum and sent a car to get her, don't you?'

'She can't come. She can't come.' His voice rose to a scream. 'Christ, don't you fucking pigs understand anything?'

Kate and Bill withdrew to the corridor and left him to stew, just as if they were in fact giving him a formal interview.

'My instinct is to turn him loose and start again tomorrow morning,' Kate said, pulling her lip. 'I'm certain that woman's at risk if he comes home late. What do you think?'

'Are you sure Sanderson won't do anything to harm her this evening?'

'It's more likely if we delay Nigel. Tell you what, let's see what he says.'

'Risky.'

'It's all risky. Look, what do we want to get out of this? That Sanderson's at the heart of a nasty money-making empire. You and Ben are well on the way to doing that. That he makes his son forge E's. To do that we've got to interrogate the son and get a confession that he forges the E's. And I don't fancy doing that without a solicitor present. Which would delay things and make him late back home and put his mum at risk.' She traced a circle in the air. 'Back where we started.'

'There's one other thing Lizzie said you wanted out of this. To prove that Sanderson killed Grafton.'

She pushed her fingers through her hair. 'You know, I'd lost sight of that.'

'All this hassle – come on, we'll talk about that back in the car. Let's put this lad out of his misery.'

Nigel had bitten hangnails back far enough to draw blood. He was inspecting his efforts when they returned, as if surprised his hands belonged to him.

'What time do you need to start home to get there at the usual time?' Bill asked bluntly.

'In about ten minutes.'

'OK. And if you don't get home, your dad'll take it out on your mum?'

Nigel nodded.

'Can you tell us how, Nigel?'

'She won't talk about it. Tells me not to get upset.'

'But you do get upset. Do you get upset because he takes it out on you, too?'

Nigel found loose skin round another nail, and started on that.

'I think we take that as a yes,' Kate said quietly. 'Nigel, we're going to want to talk to you again. We think you have a lot to tell us. But I'd like it to be at a time when your mother can be present, and, preferably, a solicitor as well. In the meantime, don't say anything to your mother, because we don't want to worry her further. And obviously, you won't be telling your dad about this conversation. Just tell me one thing: why did they sack you from your last school? Just for the record.'

Nigel smiled briefly. 'Not a bad scam. Not really. I dried some grass and flogged it to these kids: said it was cannabis.'

'Neat idea. Selling them something quite legal by pretending it wasn't,' Bill said, smiling.

Nigel returned the smile.

'Except you know even that's against the law, don't you?'

The smile was replaced by a horrified stare.

'OK, son. Off you go. And remember, this conversation's just between the three of us. For now.'

'Do you think there's any hope for him?' Bill asked as they drove home, having dropped Nigel at his bus stop.

Kate thought of Simon. 'Others have had bad parents and come through as decent adults. But he's got it so damned cushy, hasn't he? And a role model who says it's OK to treat women badly and con school-kids out of their pocket-money.'

'But he loves his mum!'

'Even so, they say patterns of violence get replicated from father to son. Tell you what, Bill, the sooner that paper-work tells us we can pick up Sanderson, the happier I shall be.'

'It's not just the paper-work, Kate, is it? It's Them Upstairs. Not to mention the DPP. Can you imagine a worse scenario than shaking him up nicely and then sending him home to inflict more of the same on his wife. The only thing is, what is it that he inflicts?'

Chapter Twenty-Six

'I thought you'd died or something, it's so long since you came,' Cassie said. 'You call this stuff gin and tonic? More like weasel's pee.'

If Kate had sunk it, she'd have been reeling; but she stiffened it a good deal more and placed it in Cassie's outstretched hands. Both hands. So Cassie was losing ground. Kate bit her lip. Yes, Cassie might well think she was being neglected, even if it was only a matter of a few days since she'd made time to come. But one of the reasons for Cassie's withdrawal to this home was supposed to be readily available company. She always said she didn't expect Kate to be able to dance attendance on her. That was theory, of course. Kate couldn't blame her if it was different in practice. The old woman couldn't possibly understand Kate's work schedule, which would all too soon include those inspector's exams.

Perhaps she should risk a gin herself. Not in this heat, though. She'd already dumped her coat. Now she stripped off her jacket. What did they want to do to all these old people, bake them alive?

'This weekend,' she said, pouring a great deal of tonic on to a minute amount of gin and sitting down, 'I promise I'll take the camera all round the house so you can see how it looks. The kitchen's magic. Absolutely magic. I've got these lovely wooden cupboards, and the green of the working surface picks up the green in the flooring.'

'And aren't your walls green? It must be like living in an aquarium.'

Could you shove a gin glass down the throat of someone who needed two hands to hold it safely? Kate took a deep breath.

'And the carpets are down in the living rooms, too. One of these days I'll give that table of yours a really good polish.' *Not tactful. Try harder.* 'It suffered a bit with all the plaster dust.'

'Hmph. What about the garden? Did you get up all the leaves? You'll have very acid soil if you don't – no good for anything. I used to enjoy scraping them all up – and those from the front garden, too – and having a bit of a bonfire.'

'Not yet. I've been a bit busy.' There was no point in reminding her that there was nothing she could call a garden, yet. And that local authorities were no longer keen on people having therapeutic bonfires.

'So one of your young men said.'

Young men? Kate slopped her drink. Colin would have told her, surely, if he'd been.

'That Graham. You know his mother-in-law's moved in here. He comes to see her. When he has to. And he leaves his wife with her and sneaks in here. Can't say I blame him.' She leaned closer. 'Have you met the woman? Mrs Nelmes?'

Kate shook her head. 'I met her daughter once.'

'Once would be enough if she's like her mother. My goodness me, she's a rum one. Moan? Nothing's good enough for Lady Muck. It's fetch this, do that, every time she sees a what'sit – care assistant, whatever they're called. You'd think she was the only one with aches and pains.'

'What do you make of her daughter? Graham's wife?'

'*She* doesn't come to see me! Oh, no. Graham reckons the old woman would blow a gasket if she thought her daughter was wasting precious time seeing anyone else.'

Kate took a breath. 'Do you know what her name is?'

'Mrs Nelmes? May, I think.'

'No. Her daughter. Graham's wife's name?'

Cassie opened her mouth but shut it. At last she said slowly, 'Do you know, I don't think I've ever heard him use it. He always calls her "my wife". Always.' She took another swig, and giggled. 'Do you suppose it's like in the old books, like Mrs Bennet always calls him Mr Bennet? Do you suppose they call each other Mr and Mrs? "Come here, Mrs—" What's their name? Ah, Harvey, that's it! — "Come here, Mrs Harvey, I fancy a bit of how's your father"!'

Kate laughed. Had to. Apart from the fact that Cassie's giggles were infectious, she couldn't let the old lady get a hint of her shock. What a fool — she'd always thought of him as some poor, sex-starved man with a frigid wife. She'd never imagined them in bed with the sort of joy and gusto she and Robin had shared, the woman in the twinset and Graham with his well-cut suit.

The man who'd let her down today. Twice.

'Tell you what,' she said at last, 'you could always do a bit of detective work yourself. So long as you keep me completely out of it, mind. Next time you find your zimmers clashing, you could find out what her daughter's called. Mrs Harvey. Just as a matter of interest.'

Cassie's laugh was positively joyous. 'Oh, I shall enjoy that. Not a hint that you're interested, of course not. And I shall find out all about her for you. And him, with a bit of luck. Mind you, she'll be biased. Tell you what,' she added, holding out her glass for a top-up, gin, not tonic, 'I know he's a friend of yours — and he always speaks well of you, mind! — but he's a bit of a grumpy-boots, isn't he? Doesn't crack his face very often. Mind you, with a mother-in-law like that . . . Or perhaps he isn't persuading Mrs H to have a spot of how's your father often enough. Nice-looking man, if you like them doleful: you could always try and cheer him up.'

'Only one problem,' said Kate, economising with the truth,

'I don't think Mrs Nelmes would approve. Or Mrs Harvey. Tell me, how's Rosie these days?'

'How would you be with a split lip and a broken tooth? I've tried to talk to her myself, don't think I haven't. She said you gave her something but she lost it.'

Kate fished in her bag. Could anyone really lose a lifeline like that? A psychologist would no doubt make hay.

'Here. Give her this. And tell her to act now: see a solicitor, Citizens' Advice, even her friendly neighbourhood police. And tell her — tell her in a relationship like that, things can only get worse.'

The evening air smashed across her face as she left the cosy fug of the home. Thank goodness for an efficient car heater and the promise of central heating. She left the engine running while she scraped ice from the windscreen. That was better. The rear screen was thawing nicely, but she gave it a helping hand. There. So long as it didn't freeze while she was driving. It was cold enough: she'd lost the feeling in her hands already.

Simon! On a night like this!

Surely on a night like this Simon would have headed for a hostel. No, she couldn't risk it. No point in just turning up. She'd have to take him something practical. She zapped off home.

Cassie had left behind in her shed a little greenhouse heater. There was the arctic weight sleeping bag Robin had once used, and his silk long johns. Bundling the lot in the car, she set off for Selly Oak. At least the main road was both gritted and fairly clear of traffic. Now for his unmade road. Main beam on, she urged her car down it, dodging the worst of the hardening ruts. Leaving the engine running and the lights on, and ignoring the electronic warning whine this caused, she scuttled to Simon's squat. No padlock.

She banged on the door. There was no response but she went in anyway, opening the door with care. No light, of course, except that from her headlights. But she could sense the place wasn't deserted – the smell of underwashed young man, perhaps. And another smell. Blood. She zipped back to the car for her torch, slipping as she went. And then returned. Blood, yes. Fresh. And urine. Also fresh.

And – huddled in the far corner – Simon.

The paramedics were there before she could have believed it, and her local colleagues. And the heater and sleeping bag, not to mention her first aid training, had been useful, the woman paramedic said. 'Thing is, he's not all that badly hurt. But what with him being malnourished and tonight's big chill, well, I doubt if he'd have seen the night out. What made you come down here?'

Kate gestured at her token effort. 'I didn't realise how cold it was. And then I thought of him. Come on, let's get him moving. I'll follow you.' Leaving her name and number with the local officers, with the strongest instructions to preserve what little was left of the scene, she turned the car and prepared for a long wait in A & E.

It was only when she'd got a coffee and a couple of biscuits inside her that she thought of protocol, and how Graham regarded it. As a major issue. Well, she had Lizzie's number and Graham's, too. Bugger Cope. Standing in the bitter wind outside, she tried Lizzie first, and got a chirpy message saying there was no one at home in the Rossetti household. She left a more sober one. Then, taking a deep breath, she punched Graham's number.

The anonymous wife replied.

Formal to the point of punctilious, Kate asked for DCI Harvey, explaining they had an attempted murder on their hands. Mrs Harvey was too well bred to sniff, but Kate was left in no doubt about her feelings. It would have been nice to know what her own were. 'My husband is not in, Sergeant. I'll pass on the message when he returns.'

Was she telling the truth? Kate had to believe her. She could always phone into work and get him bleeped. Which she did.

Returning to the fug of the waiting area – five hours to see a doctor, the electronic display said – she settled down for a long wait. She wouldn't be going anywhere until she knew how Simon was. And it would be interesting to see how soon Graham responded to his bleeper.

Could she go and look in on Simon? She'd left that to the Bournville Lane nick constable who'd responded to her initial summons. Better not – they didn't need extra people milling round. But she couldn't stop herself.

The constable gave a grim smile. 'He's conscious. They've got various drains in – looks dreadful – and he'll be in theatre as soon as maybe. But he knows you're here and wants to talk to you.'

Most of all though the kid wanted his hand held. Literally.

'They say I'm bleeding inside, Kate. Does it mean I'm going to die?'

The nurse across the bed shook her head, but doubtfully.

Kate gave no sign that she'd seen her. Her smile mingled kindness and anger. 'Don't you bloody dare, young Simon. Not until your evidence at county court has had whoever did this sent down. Then you can do what you bloody well like, of course.'

He managed a smile, and his fingers tightened on hers for a moment.

'The other thing is I'm trying to get you a place to live. They're setting up this work scheme, with accommodation. I thought of you as soon as I heard.'

'Did you really?' Somewhere amidst the bruises and abrasions, he summoned up a smile.

She squeezed his hand.

'Is it right you came to look for me tonight?'

'I'd brought you a sleeping bag and some other things.'

The nurse officiously adjusted his drip.

A couple of porters erupted between the curtains. 'Coming to take you to theatre, young man. Simon, is it?'

His eyes closed as they moved him, but his grip on her fingers didn't loosen. Kate made no attempt to shift them. She caught the older porter's eye, and walked in procession with them until they reached the sterile area. She leaned down to kiss his cheek. 'See you in the morning, love,' she whispered.

'Why on earth did you have me bleeped? Why couldn't you phone me?' Graham demanded, getting to his feet as she came back into the waiting area.

'I left a message,' she said, her voice dull even to her own ears. She shoved her hands into her pockets and sat down, next but one to the seat he'd vacated.

'Got an ID on him yet?'

Kate explained. Graham didn't ask why she'd gone out there.

'Is he well enough to make a statement? Maybe tomorrow?'

'There's no guarantee he'll see tomorrow. He's a nice kid.' Her voice broke.

'I'm sorry.' He sounded it. He looked at her under his eyebrows. 'Any idea who—?'

'The scene's a mess, of course. But I'd say we might find marks of the tyres belonging to a big Merc. if we try hard enough.' She scrubbed her eyes with a tissue, and then gave up.

Graham dug in his pocket and came up with more tissues. She wouldn't be contaminating one of the white linen handkerchiefs his wife ironed so beautifully.

'He's not – important – to you, is he?'

She took the tissues, but let the tears drip off her nose. 'Of course not. But I'm important to him.' She rubbed her face. 'Bloody hell, Graham, I want to get those bastards. The poor kid's got nothing, absolutely nothing, only his life. And then someone tries to take that away from him too.'

*   *   *

The wait was interminable. She could tell Graham was impatient, but not for the same reason as her. Someone was waiting for him to go home, wasn't she? Not that Mrs Harvey was a cartoon character with rollers and a rolling pin, waiting on her front step with her sleeves round her elbows. Perhaps he even wanted to go back. For a bit of how's your father.

'I'm going to talk to the people at the scene,' he said abruptly, getting to his feet.

'You don't suppose there's any chance of a news blackout for a bit, do you?'

'Why?'

'With his well-known tact and kindliness, I'm sure Mr Sanderson would rather think Simon had simply expired, unnoticed. It'd be lovely to break it to him that we've a live witness. If we have, of course.' She tried for grim upbeat and found it. 'The thing is, Mr Sanderson may be so delighted that Simon's alive he may want to beat up his wife. Or whatever he does to her.'

Graham sat down. 'I know the man, Kate. My wife knows his wife. I really can't believe ...'

'When you hear all the other stuff we've been busily ferreting out, you'll believe it, Graham. In fact, wouldn't it be a good idea to have a conference tomorrow: all of us who are working on the case? So we can put everything on the table. Including, please God, Simon's recovery.'

'He wouldn't beat anyone up himself, Kate. He'd hire people.'

Kate nodded. Yet another thread to ravel back to its source. Then she shook her head: 'Are you sure? Perhaps he's the sort of man who'd really enjoy that sort of control over other people? He's certainly got that son of his under his thumb.'

'I told you, Nigel needs some discipline. To stay in in the evenings.'

'Does Nigel need to stay in in the evening to forge Ecstasy tablets?'

Graham turned towards her, mouth agape.

'At least that's what I strongly suspect. We're hoping to talk to him tomorrow. Well, today, more like.'

He got to his feet again. 'I'll go and talk to the Bournville Lane people about that news blackout.' His assurance deserted him. 'Are you quite sure you'll be all right? Shouldn't you leave all this to Uniform?'

She shook her head.

'You'd be better catching some sleep, so we can nail whoever did this.'

'I'm sure you're right. But he depends on my being here, Graham. If I can be. I'm the nearest he's got to family, see?'

He bent to look at her with more tenderness and compassion than she could deal with. 'Are you sure, Kate, that he's not the nearest you've got to family?'

Chapter Twenty-Seven

Lizzie looked ostentatiously at her watch as Kate arrived. 'I thought you and Bill were supposed to be doing something this morning.'

Kate nodded. Better to ride the criticism than whinge about not getting back till four, sleeping through the alarm and getting enmeshed in the rush hour. She dumped her bag on the desk. 'Has Graham been in touch with you yet?' she asked, hanging up her coat.

'Any special reason he should be?'

'To arrange a conference this afternoon. To pull everything together. Including the assault on young Simon.' She boiled the kettle. 'Coffee?'

Lizzie nodded and thrust her mug forward. 'The dosser? Tell me.'

'Some bastard beat him up and left him to die. Well, he's in a high dependency unit, so he's not out of the woods yet. But they say we can talk to him briefly late this morning. Meanwhile, Graham's asked for a news blackout.' She made coffee, passing Lizzie's mug back.

Lizzie smiled. 'Bright guy, Graham.' She wrapped her hands round the mug, and stood up to peer at the iron-grey sky. 'Very bright. University, like you. He got a very good degree. Is there such a thing as a starred first? Because if there is, he got one. Then he joined the Force. Only *he* came up the hard way.'

'He's never spoken to me about his degree.' Kate hoped she kept the hurt out of her voice. And the anger: all Lizzie's banging on about the accelerated promotion scheme wouldn't help either of them.

Lizzie gave an exaggerated shiver and turned back to the room. 'Past history, I suppose. The word is his prof. wanted him to stay on and do some research or something.'

The chance of a lifetime! 'Why didn't he?'

'Well, he'd got responsibilities, hadn't he? A wife. So he needed the security of a job.'

Kate shook her head. 'Aren't we talking about the seventies? Weren't women rather keen on equality in those days?'

'She was keen enough to support him through college. Come on, we're not all professional women striding around being career-orientated. And he doesn't seem to mind. He's got a good job, after all.'

Had anyone listened to him long enough to find out? Not that he'd complain.

'What was his subject?'

'Search me. Look, Bill's been hanging round for long enough. Not to mention the kid.'

'Nigel! He's come here?'

'Him or his twin brother. Down the corridor.' Head already bent over the next item on her desk, Lizzie pointed a finger in the general direction of the interview rooms.

She was guided to the right one by the sound of laughter. Whatever was going on was clearly not overly heavy. In fact, Bill winked at her as she came in, rather in the manner of that consumer-protection woman on TV.

'Morning, Gaffer,' he said. 'Young Nigel here's just popped in to talk to us. We've been talking football. Hey, you're into footie, aren't you?'

So he wanted to keep everything low-key.

'Well, I haven't been head-hunted by Man. United yet to replace their manager, but it's on the cards. I coach a Boys' Brigade team,' she added. 'Real big time.'

'But they're not losing any more, are they? You must be doing something right.'

'You can't be wrong all the time, Bill. How's things, Nigel?'

He took a deep breath. 'I know I should have a solicitor here. And Mum. But I want to say that I shall tell you everything as soon as I can. But not while Dad can still get at her. 'Cause I shall be in big shit with you lot. Big. After what you said about being in trouble for selling real grass. I'm not doing any harm, honest.'

'What does your dad do that scares you so much?' Hitching her trousers, she sat down astride a chair that Bill produced.

Nigel's face flushed, then returned to its usual pallor. 'I don't know. I really don't know. If I ask, she says not to worry. She says if I get to Uni she'll leave him and come and look after me. But she won't. I know she won't. Because he'd come after her and she wouldn't want to lead him to me. Fuck it, can't you just arrest him?'

'On what charge, Nigel?'

'Making me – you know, sell that grass. And – this other stuff. And he's making a lot of money. A lot.'

'Even if we had all the evidence we needed to arrest him and charge him, the chances are he'd be bailed and could go home. To you and your mum. We have to do everything step by step,' she said.

'How would you feel about giving evidence against him in court, son?' Bill asked. 'Some people wouldn't like sending their own dad to jail.'

'I'd lock him in and throw away the fucking key!' He was near to tears. 'Look, you've got to get him. Honest. And keep him in prison a long time. Look at that businessman who got let out after only six months. What if Dad came out that soon?'

'Wasn't that man in for fraud? They don't hand down life sentences for fraud, Nigel. Your dad'll be out sooner or later, anyway.'

'Even if he's killed someone?'

Kate froze. She could sense Bill freezing too. 'Killed someone?' she repeated at last. Alan Grafton swung backwards and forwards, his trousers dirtied, his jumper slashed. He lay on the slab, grimacing as Patrick Duncan pulled forward his scalp.

Perhaps gripping the back of the chair would bring her back to the present.

'As good as! You ask my mum. Only she won't tell you, will she? Because he's taken away her life, as sure as if – Hey, you thought I meant something else, didn't you?' He stood up, swallowing painfully. 'You thought I meant . . ..'

'It's OK, son. Sit yourself down.'

Nigel shook Bill's arm off. 'Has he? Has he? Oh, Christ!'

Kate touched Bill's hand, miming coffee, and left him with the lad. He was the expert, after all. A father. And she knew how kind he could be. The drinks machine responded quickly, and she was back probably before Nigel noticed she'd gone. Her pulse was racing. What she wanted to do was prod and probe the agonising spot. What she had to do was remember that the police had to obey the law.

'Look, kid,' Bill was saying. 'We're the Fraud Squad, aren't we? It's money problems we deal with. But if you've any evidence of any wrong doing, you've got to tell us. Any evidence. Any wrong doing.'

'Sit yourself down and drink this,' Kate said.

Nigel dashed the cup across the table with the side of his hand. 'You reckon my dad's a fucking killer and you give me fucking coffee! I'm out of here.'

Bill was between him and the door. 'Sit down and don't be such a bloody fool. Watch my lips. Right? We want to talk to your dad about money. The only reason we're not doing that at the moment is your mum's safety. Right? You're not under arrest so you can come and go any time you want. But if you want to have tantrums like this, you can bloody have them somewhere else.'

There was a very long moment before they detected a grudging, 'Sorry.'

'What about that college of yours?' Bill asked at last. 'Shouldn't you be there this morning?'

Nigel nodded.

'You're going to be very late. Does your dad get to hear about lateness and missing classes?'

'You know he does.'

'In that case, you'd better hop in my motor. I'll make sure no one at the college splits. OK? Come on, Kate'll sort out that mess.' At least he had the grace to wink at her as he guided Nigel out.

There was a message on her desk telling her to contact Superintendent Neville immediately – no clues why. She organised someone to mop up the interview room, and sat down to dial.

To her surprise, she got through direct to him, unintercepted by his secretary. His tone was curt, but not hostile: she sensed there was someone else in his room.

'DS Power: I gather there's to be a meeting to discuss strategy in the Sanderson case this afternoon.'

'Sir.'

'I take it you'll be there?'

'Sir.'

'I'd ask you to stay behind here afterwards. We have a squad issue to discuss. So if you have any work scheduled for then, I'd be grateful if you would delegate it.'

'Squad issue, Sir?' Cope and Selby's angry faces flew in front of her eyes.

'Correct. Till this afternoon, then, Kate.'

So despite all the formality and chill of tone, he'd ended on an informal note. Was this to offer some covert reassurance?

Dared she phone Graham to find out what the hell was going on? Not openly: he believed in the hierarchy so devoutly he'd clam up. But she could certainly get an update on Simon's condition, and phone him with that.

'Intensive therapy?' she repeated. 'But why?'

The Brummie voice at the other end said, 'There was a significant deterioration in his condition. It has to be stabilised.' All that Neville-like formal terminology from such a homely sounding woman.

'Does that mean further surgery?'

'At this stage I can't comment.'

'Is it possible to see him? I'm the police officer who found him.'

'I'll transfer you to the IT Unit.'

But whatever her nursing skills, the woman couldn't manage the phone and the line went dead.

Lizzie was beside her, her hand on her forearm. 'What's up, Kate?'

Kate stared. 'Young Simon: he's getting worse.'

'Better get round there now.'

Such unexpected kindness did what everything else had failed to do: brought tears to Kate's eyes.

'After all, you may just get something before he drops off his perch. Bill can go with you.'

'Bill's ferrying young Nigel back to college.'

'Maybe I'd better go with you. You look a bit watery. It'd be embarrassing if you wrapped a car round a lamp post.'

Lizzie? She'd be the last person Simon would want to see. If he could still see. 'I'll be OK.' She gathered her coat and started through the door.

'Kate?'

She turned.

'Check back with Welfare if he croaks. OK?'

✳   ✳   ✳

'You look rough: fancy a cup of tea?' The Bournville Lane SOCO peered at her with concern. He was a middle-aged man who looked like a TV stereotype of a police officer: sturdily built, respectably suited and tied, hair short at the back and sides.

'Love one, Bob. I've just been to the hospital. Young Simon.'

'The kid that was beaten up? How is he? He lost a lot of blood, I can tell you. Pity you lot stamped all over it.'

'Sorry. Things don't look good for him. They're talking about opening him up again.'

'Internal bleeding? Poor kid. Still all you can say is he's got a better chance than some street kids.' Bob leaned back and pointed to a calendar behind his desk. Amnesty International. Packets of cellophane-wrapped cards tottered in an uneasy pile on his bookcase.

'You mean here it's criminals that go round killing them, not the police,' Kate said, smiling grimly. 'Look: I haven't done my Christmas shopping yet. Are those for sale?'

'You choose while I make some tea. Looks as if a few biscuits wouldn't come amiss, either.' He busied himself with a kettle. 'Look, Kate, if you knew this kid—'

'He was a witness. Nice kid. Whatever the Bogota police would have made of him.' She fished out five packets at random; changed her mind and took ten. She'd have to find some Shelter ones from somewhere. Putting some money on his desk, she said, '*Is* a witness. He's still hanging on in there, isn't he?'

'That's the spirit. Now, I'll tell you what we've found so far. Tyre prints. Nice frozen ground, you see. Yours, ambulance, panda: we've eliminated those. And a set of new ones which matched some old ones. Good enough, I'd say, to match with the tyres, when we find them. Someone scuffed one of them when parking, I'd say.'

'I'm hoping for an early Christmas present here. Well, an inspired guess. Any idea what sort of vehicle?'

Bob grinned, gesturing a rabbit coming from a hat. 'Big one, not small one, that's all I'll say. Good, your colour's coming back. All tubes and machines, was he?'

She nodded.

'And deeply sedated so you can't even say anything to encourage him. Come on, Kate, they're tough, these kids. They want to live. That's half the battle.'

'I should have asked him to come and stay – it's not as if I haven't got room.' God, how had she said that to this complete stranger? She grabbed the tissues he produced.

'Inviting a witness to stay? Come on, Kate, love, you know what your boss would have had to say about that. And rightly, too. Don't you repine about something like that. Your job isn't housing waifs and strays. It's hunting down a nice flash car for me to ID. And later on I may have something else to ID. You never know.'

Kate managed a grin. And turned it into an evil one. 'You don't have to do all this stuff yourself, do you? Because young Simon was using headed, letter-quality paper as bog-roll. And the loo wasn't clearing ... You don't suppose—'

Bob rolled his eyes. 'OK. I'll get one of the young lads on that, shall I? Provided you promise not to make any jokes about it.'

She raised her eyebrows.

'No. Leave them to us. Tell you what, Kate,' he added, as he slipped the card money into an envelope, 'who would you like us to tie this to? Strictly off the record, that is.'

'A businessman with a Mercedes. Nasty piece of knitting called Sanderson. The only thing is, try as I might, I can't work out how he should have known I was in touch with Simon.'

Bob shrugged. 'That'll be a nice little job for Uniform, won't it? Come on, Kate, we shall find something. Where did you and Simon meet?'

Kate covered her mouth in dismay. 'I picked him up from

his squat, once, and took him to Sainsbury's coffee bar. About the most public place in Selly Oak. I never thought—'

'Most folk can have a coffee with a friend without getting roughed up, surely to goodness. Implies there might be a bit of guilt there, doesn't it? And wouldn't it be wonderful if we found a line in his credit card statement, to show this businessman of yours had been in Selly Oak that day, and his till receipt told us he'd bought his wife a nice bottle of wine from Sainsbury's at just the right time? Come on, Kate: we're all part of a team here, and what one of us misses another will find.'

'There is just one thing he could have done,' she said. 'Sanderson's house is alive with surveillance equipment.'

'Well, he might not have left it behind – why should he in a dump like that? – but he may have left some screw holes in a wall, a scuff in the plaster, we can match to a similar piece of equipment elsewhere. We'll do all we can. Provided you remember: leave the shit jokes to us.'

Chapter Twenty-Eight

Kate might have been so anxious she arrived for the meeting some twenty minutes early, but Graham was there to intercept her. He smiled and nodded her into his office.

'Come and sit down. You look as if you could do with a cup of tea.'

'I could really use a dose of the Super's espresso – before he went decaffeinated. But some of your real tea would be lovely.'

'On a day like this I was going to offer you hot chocolate. Tell me,' he said, busying himself with mugs, 'did you have any lunch?'

She said nothing. Surely he wasn't about to share his precious packed lunch with her?

'I thought not. Here.' He produced a paper plate flexing under an assortment of buffet goodies. 'Lunch meeting. There's a fork in here somewhere.' He burrowed in his desk. 'You must always try to eat regularly. For the job's sake as much as your own.'

Kate nodded, attacking a samosa. 'Thanks, Gaffer.'

The kettle boiled, and Graham was on his feet again. 'There. Assam, with caffeine.'

Mouth full, she smiled her thanks.

'Lizzie tells me you had to go and see young Simon again. Problems?'

'He's losing ground. How much longer will you be holding back the media?'

'As long as I can. If he – It's hard to sit on murder.' His voice was so gentle it was hard to imagine that he could often be so lacking in understanding. 'Come, I'm being previous. He's young ... he's in the best of hands.'

'I notice you didn't say, "he's fit",' she snapped. 'Sorry.'

'Sometimes a bit of anger is good for you. Point taken, anyway. Feeling any better now?'

'You're not being kind to me because of what's coming out at the discussions about the squad this afternoon?'

He raised his eyebrows. Then he laughed. 'You mean the condemned man's last meal? Surely you're not expecting any problems, Kate. You couldn't manage this as well?' With a flourish he produced another plate, this barely able to sustain two thick slices of gateau.

'I'm not looking forward to friendly conversation with Cope.'

'I heard his version. It might be useful to hear yours.'

She gave a bald account and then addressed herself to the cake. To fill the silence, she said, 'Robin used to cook wonderful cakes.'

'You don't talk about him much.'

'You don't talk about your wife much.'

He looked not at her but at his desk. And then at the big photo. 'No,' he agreed at last. Then, straightening as if before a promotion panel, he looked authoritatively at his watch and said, 'Perhaps we should make a move.'

The meeting had moved very quickly and efficiently under Neville's chairing. He was now summing up point by point.

'All the accounting evidence,' he nodded and smiled at Ben, 'points to the idea that Sanderson was deeply involved in long firm fraud. That he "bought" materials on the basis of false credit-ratings, given by companies that were mere fronts. We have evidence to suggest that he was disposing of materials thus fraudulently acquired through at least one retail outlet.'

'Remember this morning we've run to earth at least two other premises,' Lizzie put in.

While Kate was out. She'd not known of it till ten minutes ago.

Neville acknowledged his omission with a nod. 'Sanderson also seems to have a major stake in a questionable educational establishment, though despite Bill's best efforts we can't find anything downright illegal about it.' His voice changed to suggest a parenthesis. 'Somehow I don't think Bill's going to let go of this one. Ever thought of joining the Ofsted team when you retire, Bill?'

'Just let me get at them,' Bill growled.

'Now let's look at the evidence about Alan Grafton's death. Kate, are you OK about this?'

'Sir.'

He read Patrick's official report. 'In combination with the SOCO report, which finds no evidence at all of anyone else's involvement, I have to conclude that we can't put this particular case forward to the DPP as one of murder.' He smiled. 'We never know what the inquest jury will have to say, though. Sorry, Kate: I know you'd like to nail Sanderson for that.

'We have strong hints from Nigel Sanderson that his father is involved in Nigel's own drug-forging cottage industry. I'd personally like to make a connection between the vitamin tablets stolen from local pharmacies and those picked up by Kate's contact from the Met, who has kindly sent me a copy of the forensic science report.'

Kate nodded. Trust Dai to be so professional.

'I'm happy to tell you that the gilded youth of the metropolis have been forking out huge sums of money – in order to take not E's but vitamin B.' He paused for effect and for laughter, which seemed genuine enough although they'd all known what was coming. 'Meanwhile, other people, maybe on our patch, are no doubt taking all sorts of far more noxious substances as a result of the pharmacy break-ins. I want results now, ladies and gentlemen.' He paused to consult his notes: Kate could see the meticulous handwriting produced by a fountain pen. He smiled. 'The only crime we haven't been able to link in some way with Sanderson – and I don't need to tell you we need the hardest of evidence to nail a man of his standing – is Kate's carpet-layers.'

This time he didn't need to wait for the laughter.

'But we have tied that up, thanks to exceptionally hard work from Colin.' Eye-contact and an approving nod. 'No, Kate, it wasn't the young man you feared it might be. His boss. Would you like to go with Colin later this afternoon and pull him in?'

'Love to, Sir.'

'Good. Now, the only thing still to be decided is when we invite Sanderson to talk to us. Kate, you must have a view on this?'

'A view. But I wouldn't want to be the one to make a decision.'

Neville's eyebrow reminded her that that wasn't an option anyway.

'It seems to me, Sir, that Mrs Sanderson's safety must be paramount, here. Unless we can put her and her son in a place of safety, we cannot bring Sanderson in. Dare not. And that means we have to persuade Mrs Sanderson to go to a safe house. And we may have to commit resources to protecting her. I'd like a chance to work on her before we do anything. So long as we are ready to pick him up if he gets suspicious, we could continue to play a waiting game.'

Neville nodded. 'I see no difficulty with that. What do the rest—' He stared in disbelief at the phone. Clearly this time his secretary had orders to block calls. He picked up the handset.

He was not the sort of man to pull faces that would give

any hint to other people of the content of a conversation. But there was no doubt of his anger. He ended the call.

'Waiting,' he said, 'seems to be an option temporarily out of our hands. That was a call from Bournville Lane nick, Selly Oak. They've an armed siege in progress, it seems. Someone demanding to talk to Sanderson before he kills his family and torches his factory.'

'How did they get on to you, Sir?' Kate asked, fastening her seat-belt. She was in the rear of the car taking Neville to Selly Oak. So was Graham but there was a seat's width between them and as far as she knew he was keeping his eyes as steadfastly in front as she was. Not that she would avoid eye-contact should it arise: that would raise Neville's interest, benign or otherwise. Almost certainly otherwise.

'A SOCO, by name of Bob. One of those serendipitous things. He heard about the siege in the canteen, remembered the name from a conversation with you, and contacted Fraud. Who contacted me. Teamwork, Kate. Speaking of which, I trust the postponement of the meeting about the squad will not cause you any undue alarm.' Considering the drama unfolding in the suburbs, his tone was remarkably even.

'Should it, Sir?' Hers matched his.

There might have been a sharp intake of breath from Graham.

'I can see why you weren't called upon to take up a career in the Diplomatic Corps!' Neville's laugh sounded genuine enough. 'How can I possibly answer that? I see no reason, do you, Harvey, why we shouldn't tell you that all being well Fatima will be back with us tomorrow.'

'She's got over her flu at last,' Graham added helpfully.

Dared she ask about the health of Selby and Cope? Perhaps Selby did have genuine problems. Could he have some form of that gambling addiction that kept kids hooked to games in amusement arcades? Should she have referred him to Welfare, not reported him to Graham? On the whole she thought it wiser not to push her luck by asking.

The driver, who'd been seeing how much rubber he could leave on the road, braked to a dramatic halt. 'Here we are, Sir.'

As if they couldn't tell. This was one they hadn't been able to exclude the media from. Not that they could get close: the whole street was cordoned off. The negotiators were already on their way.

'Factory? Round here? This looks like any other street,' Graham said.

It did: a street of terraced houses crammed as close as those in Kate's street, with comparable parked cars. Currently, they were being used as cover by colleagues from the Rapid Response Unit.

'Family business. Just the house. All sorts of health and safety issues, of course. But it seems that's not the most pressing concern at the moment,' Neville said. 'Not that we can do much, anyway. Just be on hand to advise about Sanderson, should we be called on.'

A small Asian man was leaning from the upstairs sash window of one of the houses. From time to time he shouted something.

'I suppose you don't number Gujerati amongst your language skills, Sergeant?' Neville asked.

Was it a genuine inquiry or did she detect irony in his tone? 'A little Italian and less Spanish,' she replied. 'What about the negotiator? How will he manage?'

Neville shrugged. 'That's not my area of responsibility. In any case, perhaps the guy has enough English to cope.'

'Maybe a translator, Sir? Pity Fatima's still on sick leave, isn't it?'

Neville's smile was definitely ironic. 'Isn't it?'

Kate had never attended a siege before, and she was expecting frantic, dramatic activity. But it was all low-key and controlled. Since she wasn't going to be involved — was she? — in making immediate decisions all she could do was mill round trying to look official and useful. Why, now she came to think of it, had Neville taken her? He must have had something more in mind than a social ride. It would be nice simply to take advantage of being in Selly Oak to go off to the hospital to find out more about Simon. She stamped and blew on her hands, cold as everyone else hanging round the now brilliantly lit street, but with the strong suspicion she'd left her gloves on Graham's desk.

Graham was standing alongside her, but was so far silent. From time to time he'd flick a glance at his watch: it seemed to be with increasing irritation. Or anxiety. Lizzie was on his other side, having drifted across from Dyson's car. It occurred to Kate that this was not the best place to be: she didn't know if Lizzie was still close to Mrs Harvey, and the last thing she wanted reported back was the news that Kate and Graham had been glued together.

The best thing was to find someone else to talk to. But everyone had their appointed task. This wasn't a social gathering, was it? Gossip might appear to be the order of the day, with loud laughter billowing up from time to time, but everyone was in a predetermined spot. Except her, Graham and Lizzie. So she'd better make her own conversation. Turning her back on Graham, she dialled the hospital.

Simon was in theatre.

People didn't die, these days, not with all the expertise of the health service trying to save them! It was different for Robin: he'd been dead on arrival in A&E. But Simon: he was having transfusions and life-support and—

'Kate? Kate?'

There was a hand on her arm. Neville's.

She snapped the phone shut. 'Simon's worse, Sir.'

'I gathered.' His grip tightened sympathetically. Then he

released her. 'Now, we're going to bring Sanderson in. It seems to be the only thing to defuse the situation. The bastard seems to have played the same trick on this poor bugger as he did on Grafton. Who says fraud's a victimless crime?' He pointed. 'He's got a wife and five children and he's about to go bankrupt and the eldest girl's fiancé is breaking off the relationship because of the disgrace. All because of Sanderson. Now, I want you to go and pick up his wife. I've arranged for women from the Domestic Violence Unit to meet you there. They'll arrange medical and social services backup. I'll get someone to take you. Don't attempt to go in until Midge or Lorraine is there. Look, the negotiator's just arrived.'

So the excitement might be about to start, and she was going to miss it. On reflection, so far the proceedings had been about as exciting as watching fog thicken. And she was going to be involved in some action herself.

'What if she won't let us in, Sir? I've been before when I've been convinced that the house was occupied but no one opened the door.'

'A couple of lads with hammers and crow bars?' he asked ironically. 'What about back access? A set of ladders will be provided, Kate. I'm sure you'll enjoy scaling them.' He shed his quizzical smile for a moment. 'Your injured knee's up to it, is it?'

Her nod should have left him in no doubt. 'At least I'll get a chance to see that garden all her friends rave about,' she said. 'I'll tell Lizzie where I am and be off then, Sir.'

'Good idea.' His smile was kind, approving, and, she was afraid, amused.

Chapter Twenty-Nine

Kate had never seen a garden like this. Not an ordinary suburban garden. OK, stately homes might have close-cropped lawns, raked paths, manicured hedges and not a stray leaf to remind the onlooker of the indiscipline of nature. But they no doubt had teams of gardeners to maintain them. This had only Isobel. Unless Nigel was encouraged – or allowed or even constrained – to help her. Various aspects were spotlit: ferns and trees heavy with hoarfrost, bowers, a pond filled by a half-frozen waterfall. A wonderland. But a winter wonderland. Bitterly cold despite Lorraine's weatherproof jacket, Kate turned to Midge: 'Ready?'

They left the security of the ladder and prepared for action.

None of the back doors was unlocked: the garage, what looked like a utility room and the patio were all secure.

'I'm still convinced she's in there,' Kate said.

'OK.' Midge sounded less convinced.

'We could look at these outhouses, I suppose.' At least that kept them on the move.

There was a greenhouse at the far end of the garden, lit by two gentle glows – heaters, no doubt. To one side of the house was a spur of outhouses, stables, at one time, perhaps. Now what were they used for? The first she tried was padlocked. Just like

Simon's squat. The next too. The third had no padlock, but there was a key-hole. Almost idly, she tried it.

It swung open.

Sickened by a sense of déjà vu, Kate pushed. The door opened, absolutely silently. There, lit by one candle, in an old-fashioned deck chair, huddled Isobel. Waterproof trousers, waterproof jacket, wellies, gloves. A felt hat covered her ears and most of her face.

She was on her feet in a flash. 'You shouldn't be here. What are you doing here?'

'More to the point, Isobel,' asked Kate, 'what are you doing here? It's dark, it's freezing cold, and you've got a perfectly good house just there. Tell me, what are you doing here?'

'Let's go into the house first, though,' said Midge. 'Come on.'

'You can't — we mustn't.'

'Isobel, we can and we must. We'll all catch our deaths,' Kate said.

'No! No, please!'

'Isobel, love,' said Midge, trying not to let her teeth chatter, 'you'll have to tell us. Or show us . . ..'

It seemed that Isobel had fifteen seconds to sprint in stockinged feet — the wellies kicked off on the back step — from the kitchen door through the house into the hall to silence the burglar alarm.

She made it, Kate guessed, with a second to spare. Before Kate and Midge, who weren't wasting any time, even got into the hall.

'Why doesn't he simply have it on a longer setting?' Midge asked. 'These things can be fixed, you know.' She paused, looking at the decor which had so underwhelmed Kate when she'd come here with Patrick. 'You've got it very nice,' she said. 'Hey, what are you doing?'

Isobel was scrabbling in a cupboard under the stairs, and was on her knees before either of them could register it. Footprints, that was what she was after, with a dustpan and brush.

'Forget it, Isobel. It doesn't matter.' The poor woman continued to brush. Kate tried again. 'It's better to leave them till they're dry, surely. Now, why don't we go back into the kitchen and we'll have a cup of tea and then we'll explain what's happening.'

'The first thing to be explained,' said Midge, opening the fridge and holding up a milk bottle, 'is this.' She pointed to a blue felt-pen mark three inches down the bottle. 'And these—' figures on the biscuit packet tucked inside an old-fashioned barrel.

'I was putting on weight,' Isobel said. To cover the lie, she fussed for plates.

Kate couldn't bear to watch the frantic, anguished hands. She looked around the kitchen. Though she could see no hidden camera, she would bet her Christmas dinner there was one. With a sound-recorder, too.

'How do you switch off the system, Isobel?' she asked. 'Well, I can't believe Howard records all your dinner parties. Or all the things he says to you. This is just to check up on you, isn't it? To check on your comings and goings? And I bet it's got one of those clever features that records time as well as date. Come on, where do I switch it off?'

'In the hall. But I don't know the combination. He changes it.'

'So our little exploration of the house will be recorded for posterity? My God!' Midge, from whom Kate would have expected calm, looked appalled.

'Don't worry, Isobel. Some of our colleagues will make sure Howard never gets to see it. In fact, it may be some time before Howard comes home. Some other colleagues are currently talking to him, and they've got a lot of questions to ask. They should certainly be able to hold him long enough to get you and Nigel into a safe house and find you a solicitor able to advise you on the next course.'

'Hold Howard—'

'Here. Sit down. Head between your knees. That's it. Why don't you tell us where your things are, so we can go and pack for you? I've an idea you'd rather do all your talking somewhere other than this.'

'I have to be here when Nigel comes home. He doesn't have a key.'

She didn't mean he'd had one and lost it, did she?

'Some of my colleagues will wait for him—'

'No! I mean—'

'You said when you phoned you wanted to protect Nigel. He won't say anything till he knows you're safe.'

'He's locked in. It isn't his fault. He's locked in.'

'Locked in where, Isobel?' Surely not an icy shed? He'd need warm, steady hands to engrave such fine detail on such tiny objects.

Isobel said nothing. She drank her tea, eventually setting the cup down in its saucer with a tiny rap. And she reached, quite deliberately, for another biscuit. She stood up, suddenly, despite the layers of clothing that wouldn't disgrace a street-woman, despite even the thick army-surplus socks, a woman of character, the committee member Kate had seen and respected. 'I think it's time you saw everything.'

Her voice at first so flat she might have been a bored estate agent, she showed them all the downstairs rooms, the over-stuffed suite, the too-deep carpet. The cloakroom. Then upstairs to the bathroom, the guest bedrooms, Nigel's room. Kate hadn't had much experience of teenage boys' rooms, but she suspected this must be abnormal in its neatness, its cleanliness, its total absence of personality. Then the master bedroom, complete with en suite bathroom, and, though no one commented, a mirror on the ceiling.

Apart from Nigel's bedroom, then, the home of any affluent

suburban family. Midge caught Kate's eye. This was all so normal. Kate shook her head. There was something about the internal geography that was worrying her. Spacious though it was, this room didn't seem quite big enough.

As if she'd forgotten what she was supposed to be doing, Isobel started to reach cases from a wardrobe.

Midge heaved a couple on to the bed. 'Where are your things, love?'

'Later. Later.' Two more cases. And then Isobel stepped into the wardrobe and pushed the back panel.

Inside was a steep ladder, up which Isobel led them, into the loft. Could this be why Sanderson had picked an older house? One which would accommodate his requirements? Here was a passage, off which opened two doors.

Bluebeard's castle?

Midge was still on the steps: there was only room for Kate and Isobel. Isobel stopped short, as if making a decision. Then, again with her committee decisiveness, she stepped to the further door, opening with something of a flourish. When she flicked a switch, the room was flooded with a light so brilliant that the light in the corridor seemed dim. Midge, now behind Kate, gasped.

A cupboard, a table, a chair, an angled spot-light, and a set of tiny tools. Not quite an ordinary table: a semi-circle had been scooped from the front, the space occupied by an insert of leather.

'That's like a jeweller's bench,' Midge said. 'The idea is the leather catches all the tiny bits of gold – only in this case I'd guess it wasn't gold.'

'Not gold,' Isobel said. She reached into the cupboard. Vitamin tablets. Rank upon rank of tubs of vitamin pills.

'What did he do with the rest of the drugs he stole?'

Isobel shook her head. 'What drugs?'

'A whole lot of prescription and other drugs taken in raids on pharmacies across the city.'

'Not Nigel. That wasn't Nigel.' Her voice changed from anxious to authoritative

'Your husband?'

Isobel looked scornful. 'He might have masterminded it but he certainly wouldn't soil his hands doing anything like that.' There was a note, yes, of admiration in her voice.

'Why would Nigel do something like this?' Midge asked.

Isobel said nothing. She stepped out into the corridor, leaning back to switch off the light. Then she opened the other door.

This room was empty except for a wooden armchair. And a bucket. With a tiny movement of the head, Isobel invited them in. She shut the door. Then she placed the bucket under the chair and removed the seat. A crude commode. And she sat on the chair, arms on the arm rests. Following the line of her eyes, they could see score-marks in the wood. Whoever sat could be tethered. Kate fingered the grooves. Old, she thought. Perhaps they were from pre-surveillance camera days.

Isobel said nothing, sitting staring at the door. At the photos on the door. And then she tapped the floor with her right foot. Kate bent to pick up the board she indicated. It concealed a thick glass panel.

'The other side of a two-way mirror,' Kate said. 'You have to watch Howard and——?'

'Very respectable women, some of them. Affairs, you know, with an attractive man. Some of our friends . . . Or prostitutes. They're more versatile.' The committee woman's voice again, brisk, tinged with humour.

'And if there's no floor-show, you get to look at the photos on the door.' Kate tried to match her voice to Isobel's.

'Of course, I didn't have to watch anything. I could always stay downstairs in the loose-box if I preferred.' Isobel spoke without irony.

'Indeed,' Kate said. She was ready to do violence. She forced herself to keep her voice calm.

'Let me get this straight,' Midge said. 'If you wanted to come into the house at times other than those he'd designated, you had to come straight up here?'

'Now, ladies, if you're ready, perhaps we should go down.' Isobel opened the door. Before they could move she seized Kate's wrist. 'You're sure he's – that he won't—'

'They won't even start questioning him till we assure them that you're clear of the premises. You and Nigel.' But Kate wasn't as confident as she hoped she sounded. Surely a man like Sanderson would have a Plan B. The plan for if he were ever detained. If he could command professional burglars and move in on the London drug scene, he must have heavies at his disposal.

She nipped quickly down the ladder, making for a bathroom, she said. And tapped Neville's hotline. They had to make sure Nigel got home even if it meant stopping and searching every bus on the route. Because they might not be the only ones doing it.

Chapter Thirty

'So congratulations to DS Power on causing the biggest rush hour traffic jam Gravelly Hill has ever seen!' Neville waved his glass at her. 'No bus for half an hour and then forty-three come together.'

Kate basked in the warmth of everyone's derision. Not a bad day, after all. Isobel was stashed with Nigel in a safe house, further protected by armed officers. The siege had petered out, once the gunman had been assured by no less braided a person then an ACC that Sanderson was under arrest. Sanderson had been so shocked at being picked up they'd had to repeat the caution. Everything was hunky-dory. Nearly.

'So what excuse has young Harvey got for sloping off this time?' Ted Dyson demanded, coming back with a fresh round. 'I mean, it's a pretty neat bit of co-operation, and he ought to be here.'

Lizzie flushed so deeply it was painful to see. Kate was afraid Ben was about to comment boisterously on Lizzie, but Bill dived in. 'Tennis elbow,' he said.

'But he doesn't play tennis,' Ted objected.

'No, but he's afraid he may get it if he bends his arm too much.' Bill mimed drinking from a big glass. He took a real one. 'Cheers, Gaffer.'

'No,' Colin put in, 'It's pulling out his wallet that's the trouble. You should see the moths.' He flapped both hands.

Kate kicked herself. A woman in trouble and it was left to two men to deflect everyone's attention. 'Cope must have the same problem, then,' she said, belatedly.

'Always was a funny bugger,' Dyson said. 'Rum pair.'

So why was Colin pressing her foot, hard, and Lizzie making some fuss about fag ash on her skirt? 'It's not bleeding fair! I only smoke on Sundays and look what someone's done.'

'Ash!' Midge exclaimed. 'Ash! *We* had a bleeding Rottweiler! Well, we didn't, but we might have. And Kate was shitting herself in case we had.'

'Not as hairy as the local sheriff turning his flashlight on us and threatening to phone nine-nine-nine,' Kate said. 'Some neighbourhood watch vigilante,' she added.

'Why didn't you send Uniform over first – you had a couple of strong, silent lads in the car, didn't you?' Lizzie asked.

'Strong, but scarcely silent: the biggest gossips in Brum. If they'd thought we couldn't get over the fence and heave the ladder over, it'd have been all over town in five minutes.'

'I gather you had to borrow a jacket from one of them, Lorraine,' Neville put in.

'See what I mean? Well, we couldn't have Kate shinning over in that nice tailored affair of hers, could we, not with that razor wire to get rid of. And hers didn't quite fit me.'

'You wait till you've lost that other half stone,' Midge said. 'Then it'll fit you a treat.'

'So there weren't any dogs,' Neville pursued.

'None. Though we did borrow the Uniform lads' CS sprays, just in case,' Kate said. 'Dogs aren't really my thing, you see. I was afraid – afraid Sanderson might have trained a pair. Just the sort of thing a sadist like him would do. Like that captain in *Schindler's List*. The one who enjoyed tormenting his women prisoners.'

'Did you ever have any hint of his attitude towards women before that? I mean, you met him socially, didn't you?'

'None, Sir. He was unpleasant enough to his wife for other women to rally round her, but he wasn't a gropy, feely type. I suspect he didn't actually have all that many affairs. It wasn't sex he wanted, just to make his wife miserable. You know, she was allowed in the house only during the hours he specified. The surveillance cameras would have picked it up if she'd tried to come in earlier. Not to mention if she tried to look away from him when he was having his sex sessions, as and when he did.'

Midge pulled a face. 'I've never come across anyone so sick. Fancy having a camera in the lavatory, for God's sake!'

'So she had a choice between the outhouse – the loose-box she called it – and the use of the outside loo and so on, or that little cell upstairs, complete with plastic bucket and live sex or porno photos. Some choice. No wonder her garden was such a miracle.'

'I wish they could string the bastard up, Sir,' Midge said. 'He's destroyed her life as sure as if he'd killed her, driven that Grafton bloke to topping himself—'

'Brought disgrace on a decent Pakistani family, probably damaged his son irrevocably – and he'll get four years, if that,' Neville added.

'Justice!' someone said.

The party started to break up soon after that. Bill wanted to see his kids before they went to bed; Ben had an ailing computer to nurture. As they left the pub, their breath billowing white into the bitter air, Kate found herself falling into step with Neville. How on earth had she come to leave her gloves in Graham's room? She balled her hands deeper in to her pockets.

'Round here they call this a lazy wind,' Neville said, digging his chin deeper into his scarf. 'You know why?'

'Because it goes through you, not round you,' she said with him. It was the first time she'd seen him so informal, but she had a nasty feeling there was something everyone else knew and she didn't. Graham's absence was no doubt for the usual reason, but she couldn't understand Cope missing the chance of a booze-up.

Unless he was still so angry he wouldn't sit at the same table as her. Tough. No doubt tomorrow they'd get their heads banged together by Graham and the Super and told to get on with it.

Despite the wind, they weren't walking quickly.

'You really have had a bad time, haven't you? I was talking to Harvey. Those two dreadful accidents. Well, not so much accidents as attacks. Two deaths of people close to you.'

Despite the kindness of his voice, she stiffened. Was this going to be used as evidence that she'd come back to work too early, that she wasn't up to the staff responsibility part of her job?

'How are you coping with life on your own?' he pursued.

She breathed out slightly.

'I mean, it can be a lonely life for a cop – and then to have no one to go home to.' He spoke with more feeling than she'd have expected.

'It can, can't it?' she said. 'If you ever get to go home, that is.'

'Well, eventually I suppose we all do. Graham Harvey, for instance. What was all that about tonight?'

Friendly gossip? That was what his voice suggested. But he was Graham's boss, too, and however Graham irritated – no, hurt – her, she owed him her loyalty.

She'd settle for the truth. 'I gather his wife doesn't enjoy good health, Sir.'

'Oh, call me Rod, for goodness' sake, Kate. Come on, I'm sure we ought to find some food to mop up that booze. And that grilled BSE smells so good.'

It did. The smell of steak was streaming past them, borne on a swell of chips.

She nodded. 'Trouble is – Rod – I've got to push off. That kid in the hospital. He's had his op, and he's back in Intensive Care.'

'Poor kid. But surely they'll keep him sedated – he won't be able to talk to you for a while.'

'No. But maybe he can hear if I talk to him.'

'Where are you parked?'

She clapped her hand to her head. 'You know, I don't even remember if I came in by car this morning!'

'I'm not surprised. I gather you were up most of the night.'

'And late in this morning. Yes, I must have come by car, mustn't I?'

'So I can't offer you a lift?'

It was only after she'd bidden him goodnight that she realised his tone wasn't at all that of a superintendent talking to his sergeant, but something entirely other. She told Simon all about it. If he could hear anything, she'd rather it was her voice than all the humming instruments to which he was attached. But he gave no response, of course. His personal nurse did, smiling a little, and then, when Kate no longer felt like giggling, passing some tissues. But she made no comment either.

Kate supposed she and Colin could have picked up Tony's boss, the man who burgled the houses where he'd laid carpets, before the meeting. But another late night at the hospital had left her more drained than she cared to admit. At least Simon was beginning to show the most marginal of improvements, according to the charge nurse she got through to, but of course no one was prepared to make predictions at this stage.

So how did she feel about this meeting? The whole squad was crammed into the office, so the noise level was high. So was the excitement – yes, there was definitely a feeling of a pack. But knowing the fierce loyalty of men and women prepared to risk their lives for each other, she knew that anger was also simmering: no one would want to see official retribution strike. And what about her? How would this impact on her still fragile relationship with the rest of the group?

Yes, everyone was here. Nearly everyone. Fatima had come to perch on Kate's desk, and coughed intermittently, as if to demonstrate the genuineness of her flu. No Selby, of course. His sick note was open ended. Stress.

Neville and Harvey came in together. Everyone stood, as if for teacher, and then sat, silent, ready.

'I'm not here to debate whether racism is endemic in the police service,' Neville said. 'But I'm not having it in my squad. And there has been – as I'm sure you'll all know – an extremely ugly example of racism perpetrated against one of our colleagues.'

All eyes turned towards Fatima, who produced a harsh, rattling cough.

'I have to tell you that such offences will always be treated seriously. Two of our colleagues are at present under investigation. One of them is currently on sick leave, the other is suspended on full pay. The Police Federation representative has been informed.'

Colin raised his hand. 'Do I take it that the recent investigation into our computers is relevant to this case, Sir?'

'Off the record, you do. We needed to find out on whose computer the offending memos – I'm sure, the grapevine being what it is, you all know what was written – had been produced. We've now established beyond reasonable doubt that two officers were responsible for it. Off the record. So don't go blabbing to our friends in the media, eh?'

The only person missing apart from Selby was Cope. Bloody hell, did that mean Cope was—

Colin caught her eye, his eyebrows in his hairline. 'Cope!' he mouthed.

She responded by drawing an exclamation mark in the air. Her eyebrows must have matched his.

'The problem was,' Neville – Rod! – was explaining, 'that your computer was involved. So there was a suspicion that you had indeed forged those documents to frame someone else.' Half an hour after the meeting was over – oh, he was showing tact! – he'd called her to his room.

'But,' Graham smiled, 'you'd set it up to record the time and date each document was produced.' He looked as if someone had lifted a filing cabinet from his shoulders: he must really have feared it was Kate. So much for the trust between friends.

But she smiled. 'Oh, ages ago,' she said. 'When Cope wiped that report for me – almost my first week.'

'Well, I suspect it was Selby, not Cope, who used your machine. But poor Cope's never made it to computer literacy—'

'And he always used to right justify his text! Why didn't I think of that!' She clapped a hand to her face.

'There it all is, clear as day, on his hard disk. Right-justified.'

'What'll happen to him?'

Graham shrugged: 'Demotion, possibly. Provided the disciplinary proceedings come to the same conclusion as our internal investigation. Certainly a transfer. As for Selby – as long as he's on sick leave we can't touch him.'

All three were silent.

'Now what?' Neville asked at last. 'A squad celebration? You're all off the hook, now.'

'I think we're all too stunned, Sir. And in many people's book, Cope was a decent, old-fashioned cop. A bit of a thug, but none the worse for that. No, a quiet time for us all, I should think. And Colin and I have still got to deal with the guy who practised a spot of burglary in his spare time. The carpet man.'

'Go and bag him,' said Graham, grinning like a school-boy.

Chapter Thirty-One

'So you and this Patrick man are going to paint the town red, are you?' Cassie crowed, pulling herself more upright in her chair. 'And when am I going to meet him?'

'Soon as I can fix it.'

'I reckon you've got a few doubts about him or you'd have brought him before.'

Trust Cassie to put her finger on it. 'Well, things have been slow taking off, shall we say.' *And we've been slow taking things off, too.* 'But he's been brilliant over that lad that got beaten up. He's got a friend who specialises in that sort of internal damage and he's brought him into the case.'

'I bet that ruffled a few feathers. These doctors always like to be right, you know.' She rattled the ice round her glass before sipping.

'You're right. But Simon's at last started to make some progress.' Slow, desperately slow progress. He might yet need a kidney transplant.

'What'll you do with him when he's let out? He can't go back on the streets, can he?'

'What indeed? But it's not really my problem. Not really.'

'That won't stop you thinking it is. You should be working for the social services people, not the police. Look at that business with that lad that laid the carpets.'

Kate nodded. She'd been trying to do some last minute shopping when someone had called her name.

'Yes, you! Kate! Hey, what the fuck did I ever do to you? I did a good job on your carpets, I sort out your kitchen floor something lovely – I even lock your bloody front door! And what do you do? You lose me my bleeding job, don't you!'

Tony, her floorer.

'Lose you your job? What are you on about?'

'You fucking copped my bleeding boss, that's what.'

'So—'

'And he's going to plead guilty. Right?'

'Yes, but—'

'So his firm goes under, and I'm—' his hand threw an imaginary butt end into the gutter. And ground it in, for good measure. 'Properly fucked up. I lived over one of his shops, didn't I? So no job, no fucking flat. God, you lot don't half piss me off.' He turned from her in a movement remarkably like one of Graham's flounces. Only this wasn't hurt dignity, it was real anger. There was total silence.

She'd grabbed his arm, so he turned. 'Tony ... I may be able to help.'

'Got a bleeding carpet shop, have you?'

'No. But I know someone who's putting a work and housing plan together.' She outlined the scheme Isobel had been involved with.

He'd listened, interested at first then angry. 'I'm not a fucking street kid! I've got a girlfriend who's expecting at Christmas. And don't give me any crap about stables. I want a home, not a hostel, for my kid.'

And her rattling round on her own in her house. No. It wasn't her responsibility. She couldn't house-share with a couple she barely knew, let alone their baby. At last, she'd given him her work card. 'I'll talk to the council. Phone me late this afternoon.'

'Did you find him anywhere to live?' Cassie asked, holding out her glass for more gin. 'You and the council?'

'I pulled every string I could find, and then some. Got his councillor involved. And threatened the housing people with his MP. Nothing they could live in, not with a baby.'

'So the poor lad's on the streets. Thanks to you.'

She wished Cassie didn't sound quite so vindictive. 'Not quite. Graham Harvey – did you ever discover his wife's name? – he's involved with some church – a really out of the way sect. They found him a flat they used to save for visiting preachers.'

'I should hope so. Flavia. That's what the poor woman's blessed with. Flavia. After some saint. Apparently they all belong to this same sect. That's where he met her. And they're like the Catholics. No divorce.'

'Flavia,' Kate repeated. 'Well, that could explain a lot.' But not, she knew, everything. She tried a new subject. 'How's Rosie?'

'Still with that man of hers. He's brought her flowers and a nice shiny ring. So it's all fine and dandy till the next time he gets angry. Stupid girl. I've got no patience with people like that.' Cassie drained her glass and set it down hard on her table. 'Another please.' She set the new drink down more carefully, using a copy of *Woman's Realm* as a coaster. 'And what are you wearing for this Patrick? Not your usual trousers, I hope.'

Kate pulled a face. Surely trousers were the most appropriate gear for a celebration for a motorbike? Sitting astride, and all that? 'This.' She shed her coat and rotated.

As she'd expected, Cassie made a noise somewhere between amusement and outrage.

So why had she chosen a really slinky outfit, very short, very flattering now she was so thin? Sometime between Florence and now she'd lost nearly a stone. She looked down at her legs: how would Patrick react to seeing this much. She'd come to a decision: if something didn't tweak the chemistry between them – act as a catalyst, that was it! – she'd let the relationship go, such as it was. The champagne she was taking, her sexiest outfit – if they didn't work, finito!

Chapter Thirty-Two

So what sort of man cherished his motorcycles — some six or seven collectors' items and a modern couple he said he used regularly — not in a garage but in a living room, complete with thick, heavy curtains? She was presumably about to find out, as he steered her — both still clutching champagne flutes — to what he called his snug. It was the size of a family living room, and furnished with floor-to-ceiling bookshelves, a huge desk, and deep chairs, thickly upholstered in maroon leather. She subsided into one of these.

'Now,' he said. 'Eyes shut. Tightly shut? Good. Just keep them shut while I get your little present!'

If he was pissed enough to ask, she was pissed enough to obey.

Leather! The smell took her straight back to Florence — pre-flu Florence, when she'd located the leather market by its smell. Poor Alan. She'd have given her teeth to have been able to nail Sanderson for that. He'd certainly driven him to it, as surely as if he'd tied the rope and pushed him. Deliberately bleeding his business dry. But suicide it seemed to have been. The ultimate expression of anger. Anger at whom? Kate, whose card was in his pocket? Kate, who'd never returned his call? Yes, those long slashes in the cashmere he'd hoped would make his fortune — they were angry. The slashes that had cut into his flesh. Poor bastard. The man who'd taken the photo of her as a stranger and been kind to her on the plane. All that talk about leather and lining. He'd been right about her shoes, come to think of it, the ones she was wearing tonight. Yes, they were stretching: soon they'd need inner soles to hold them on.

'You can open your eyes now.'

She pulled herself together. She'd need a different sort of shoe to go with the outfit Patrick was holding out to her.

'Here: it's yours. Take it. Go on. For you.'

A set of leathers. Lovely soft, though presumably tough, leathers. The panels of red and white – how long would they stay white, for goodness' sake? – would highlight hips and breasts, the red give lustre to her hair. He'd chosen well.

'Go and put them on,' he said, his eyes at last showing something like interest. 'Please. And Kate, don't leave anything on underneath.' Presumably under his black set, he was naked too.

Hmm. Well, she'd never done leather before, but why not? And why this business about going to put them on. Why not strip here and don them? Still, at least if she changed in the downstairs cloakroom, she'd see what she looked like.

The answer was, very good.

God, what would an outfit like this do to Graham's blood pressure?

She gripped the washbasin. This could be a big mistake. They were already outside her bottle of champagne and were making inroads into one he'd had on ice. There was no way she would take to his pillion, no way, come to think of it, she could let him drive. Still, she'd seen no sign of helmets, and there was no harm in humouring him. And then, *then* it dawned on her: he was probably thinking not riding but – *riding*.

Better get in the mood. If that was what she still wanted.

When she emerged, he was back in his bike room. There was no doubt about the expression in his eyes. Except he hid them behind a camera.

'Just sit astride it: that's fine! Lovely. Hold it there! Love-ly.'

Alan's photo. The photo with Cary. Oh, enough of this. She dismounted.

She shook herself. It was all past tense now. Had to be, or you couldn't do your job.

She framed another photogenic smile on her face, as she leaned against the bike. But her heart wasn't in it.

Patrick wasn't smiling either. Not socially, at least. He was gathering up a length of heavy plastic coated chain – the sort people used to fasten their machines to lamp posts. And he was lying backwards on the saddle, head towards the bars.

Oh, God.

His voice thick, he said, 'Chain me to the bike. Chain me to the bike. And then—' He saw her hesitate. 'It'll be such fun. When you unzip me . . .'

She shook her head dumbly.

'Please, Kate. Please. And then sit astride me. No. Chain me first . . .' he whispered desperately.

Poor bastard: was that the only way he could manage?

It might be a bit of fun, something to giggle over. And there was no reason why she shouldn't acquiesce in his fantasies. Except—

No, fun though it might be – and he was certainly consenting – she couldn't do it. There'd been too much control in her life recently. Her life, and others'.

'Hmm,' she said. 'Tell you what, you just lie back there and close your eyes. And wait. No, no peeping.'

She blew him a kiss as she slipped out.

Leaving the leathers hanging in the bathroom, she closed Patrick's front door softly behind her and strode off into the cold of the night.